Loss

ALSO BY TONY BLACK
FROM CLIPPER LARGE PRINT

Paying for It
Gutted

Loss

Tony Black

W F HOWES LTD

This large print edition published in 2010 by
W F Howes Ltd
Unit 4, Rearsby Business Park, Gaddesby Lane,
Rearsby, Leicester LE7 4YH

1 3 5 7 9 10 8 6 4 2

First published in the United Kingdom in 2010
by Preface Publishing

A CIP catalogue record for this book is available
from the British Library

ISBN 978 1 40745 550 1

Typeset by Palimpsest Book Production Limited,
Grangemouth, Stirlingshire
Printed and bound in Great Britain
by MPG Books Ltd, Bodmin, Cornwall

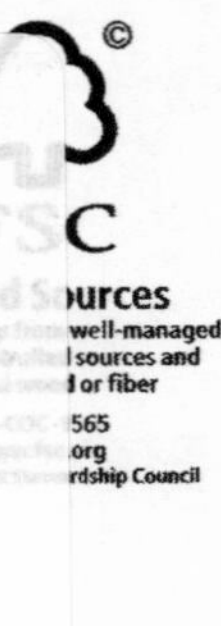

In memory of
Irving 'Macca' McCormack
1959–1992

CHAPTER 1

Calls in the middle of the night rarely bring good news. There's a drill folk go through before dialling a number at 1 a.m. – usually, if it can be avoided it will be. If it can't, expect a jolt.

The first ring woke me but I let it get to double figures before I shifted arse, reached for the receiver. The glare of the digital clock stung, nearly burned the retinas out me.

'Yeah, what?' I blurted, my voice rougher than ever on the red Marlboros, poked me into manners, 'I mean, hello.'

Formal tones. A youngish woman, but serious as the clap: 'Is that Mr Dury?'

'Yeah, it is.'

'I'm calling from Lothian and Borders Police . . . Sorry to wake you so late, but I'm afraid it's an important matter.'

The pay-off. Christ, I thought, here it comes; went with: 'It is?'

A pause. Lip-biting perhaps. 'Would you be able to come down to the station, Mr Dury?'

I sat up. A shiver passed through me as the duvet

slipped – it was another cold night. I rubbed my eyes, lifted the alarm clock. 'Do you know what time it is?'

No pause this time, a shuffle at the other end of the line, the scrape of a chair: 'Gus, Gus, is that you?'

This voice I recognised – it was Fitz. We hadn't spoken for near on a year. Even when we *were* speaking, he never used my Christian name. If Fitz the Crime was talking nicely to me, it must be bad.

'Look, Gus, I was going to call myself, I just didn't want to have ye slam the phone down at the sound of me.'

I was lost for words, couldn't fit the puzzle together: any borderline friendship I'd once shared with him, I'd well and truly blasted, with both barrels. '*You what?*'

Fitz's tone came low, calm, almost unrecognisable from his usual bluster. The Irish was still there, but this was like Wogan in his eighties heyday – tons of schmaltz: 'Gus, I think you should come down the station . . . Can ye manage it?'

I heard Debs stir behind me: 'What's going on?'

I turned, flagged her down.

'Gus, I'll send a car, okay? You can be ready in ten or fifteen, yeah?'

Debs sat up, tugged at my arm.

I reined in the confusion of being woken from deep sleep, of having the filth call me in the wee hours, and of Fitz being nice about it. 'Yeah, okay. I'll get dressed.'

Debs stared at me intently as I placed the phone back on its cradle. 'What's going on?'

'Go back to sleep.'

I felt an uneasy turn in the pit of my stomach. Was it fear? I didn't think so, didn't feel like fear, or even confusion. It was almost preternatural, a deep instinct of bad hurt to follow. Foreboding.

Debs got up, walked round to face me, a bed-head thing happening with her hair as she spoke again: 'Tell me what's going on.'

I shook myself. 'I have absolutely no idea.'

Looks askance, a neck-tilt filled with 'do I button up the back?' derision written all over her. 'Oh, come on . . .'

I looked her squarely in the eye. 'That was Fitz.' The name was enough to wipe away any doubts that I was keeping something from her.

'*Fitz* . . . What the hell did he want?'

I placed my hands on her shoulders; she felt cold. 'Get back to sleep. I have to go out.'

'No way, I'm coming too.' She spun past me, went to open the wardrobe.

I got up and slammed my palm on the door, held it shut. 'Go back to bed, Deborah . . . I mean it.'

She sensed the tone in my voice wasn't there for show, folded her arms and cricked her jaw to one side. 'I don't like this, Gus . . . Police ringing in the night. It might be—'

'Yeah, well, I'll find out, won't I?'

I got a finger pointed at me. 'Gus . . .'

I said, 'Look, as soon as I know, I'll call . . . okay?'

She thinned her eyes, returned to bed. I took my 501s off the chair; the white T-shirt and the black trackie top on the floor would have to do too. I dressed quickly.

'Do you want me to make you a coffee?' said Debs.

'No thanks, they're sending a car.'

I pulled on my Docs and stepped out of the bedroom. The dog had been woken and was prowling about. He clocked me but seemed to doubt his eyes, gave a sniff at my leg.

'Back to bed, boy.'

Eyes widened, an almost insulted expression, then a slow return to the living room.

My Crombie hung in the hall. I sparked up a tab on my way out the front door. Some jakey had taken a Pat Cash in the tenement's stairs. The rank smell of pish made me hold my breath on the way down. Let me catch the bastard next time.

Outside I exhaled – my breath came white against the freezing air. It was sub-zero. The city was in the grip of the worst winter for twenty years. I certainly couldn't remember a colder one, and I had a bit more than twenty years on the clock. I turned up my collar, chugged deep on the Marlboro. There seemed to be a hollowness in my chest – the apprehension? The unknown? I kissed the tip of my cigarette, cupped in my hand prison-yard style, hoping the burn in my lungs would dislodge the feeling. It didn't.

I saw the white Audi, flashing blue lights in the grille, long before I heard it coming down Easter Road. I moved out to the kerb, dropped my tab in the gutter. It landed in a tinfoil container half full of boiled rice and frozen curry sauce. The car pulled up. A uniform got out, said, 'I could do you for that.'

I stretched out my arms, wrists together. 'Wanna cuff me?'

He said nothing, pushed past me and opened up the back door, pointed inside.

We drove up to the lights – they burned red. The driver halted short of the hill-crest, next to the Italian tailor. I sat reading the one-hour alterations promise, then the lights changed and we pulled onto London Road, some movement of the back tyres confirming the iciness of the road.

'Which station are we going to?' I said.

Uniform turned round, spat, 'Fettes.'

It wasn't the closest, but it somehow tied in with the scenarios I had playing in my head. I'd never been on the Chrimbo card list at Lothian and Borders plod. There were more than a few down there who'd like to see me banged up. Christ, they'd went for it enough times already: trying to hang a murder rap on me was their last effort. I'd narrowly wriggled out of that thanks to Debs's evidence; I'd promised to chuck poking about into other people's problems, just for her. I wondered if she'd still be there when I got home. *If* I got home.

'Any idea what this is about?' I said.

Uniform again: 'Haven't a scooby.'

I picked up the Maccy D's coffee cups littering the floor at my feet, tried to play it chatty: 'Busy night?'

'Same old shite – cold keeps the jakeys quiet.'

'Behaving themselves for a bed at the doss.'

'Nah . . . drink themselves paralytic then cark it up some close.' He spoke of people dying in the cold of the street like it was something to be thankful for. I shook my head; driver caught me in the rear-view. Like I cared. I slumped back and vowed no more chit-chat with the filth. It was too soul-destroying.

'Oh, there was a wee incident out at the Meadows, though,' said Uniform. He turned round to make sure I was listening, that he had my full attention. 'Some bloke got plugged. They found him about ten bells, got to be a radge walking there at that time. Looks like he was mugged . . . Be some wee schemie with his first shooter – all got them now.'

The uniform guffawed, set his mate off; he slapped the dash then the pair of them high-fived. They laughed me up, but I wasn't in on the joke. Hoped, by the kip of them, I never would be.

My heart thumped as we reached the station. I saw Fitz standing at the glass-fronted doors, his hands stuck deep in his coat pockets. He looked more like a university lecturer than a copper. It had been a while since I'd seen him and he'd collected some grey streaks at the sides of his hairline. More than a few pounds had been added to the waistline as well.

The flatfoot changed his tone before Fitz: 'This way, Mr Dury, please.'

'*Please* . . . You found the charm manual on the way in, then,' I said to him. Fair bust his little act.

Fitz removed a hand, held it before the lad. 'Jaysus, has this little tool been giving ye a hard time, Dury?'

I shook my head, said, 'As if.' I was delighted to hear Fitz revert to my surname. Things couldn't be so bad then, could they?

He flicked back his head. 'Don't think about getting yerself down the cannie, Wallace. The city won't patrol itself.'

The uniform slunk off, his driver coming in at his back and removing his hat at the sight of Fitz, who sparked up again: 'Go on, the pair of ye . . . Won't ye be tucked up in your wanking chariots soon enough.'

I watched them retreat, prodded: 'You been jumping the ranks again, Fitz?'

He smiled; a roll of meat spilled beneath his chin. 'Holy Mother of God, 'tis a sight for sore eyes ye are, Dury.' He thrust out a hand, I took it and his other tapped my elbow. It was all a bit of a show. I felt the hollowness in my chest return, shoot up my throat and freeze my jaw. 'Get away in, Dury.' He turned. 'Come on, follow me.'

We moved towards the back staircase. I read signs indicating routes to the morgue and various offices. Fitz yakked away about this and that. Mainly that. It was all avoidance chat, the kind of clatter that I usually switch off to. None of it bore any relation to my current predicament. None of it raised even the slightest amount of interest, except for his uncharacteristic gratitude for my handing him yet another collar from my last case, allowing him to put one over on his number one rival on the force.

'But still, Dury, that was some name ye made for yerself there, was it not . . . You must have had a power of offers come yer way since grabbing that killer.'

That case had nearly been the end of me. 'Fitz, I'm out the game.'

'You're what?' His lip curled up – his teeth seemed whiter than I remembered; he'd either had them bleached or been fitted with veneers.

'I'm out that racket for good. Look, I'm back with Debs and . . . we're happy.'

Fitz blinked, pushed through swing doors to a small office, sat on the corner of a desk. He took a pewter hip flask from his pocket and unscrewed the cap. 'I don't believe it.'

'Believe it.'

He slugged deep, flashed his teeth again, offered the flask.

'No thanks.'

'You what? 'Tis Talisker, Dury.'

I shook my head.

'Fuck me, you're not off the sauce as well!'

I nodded. 'Six months without a drop.' I still carried a quarter-bottle of Grouse in my pocket, but that was to test my mettle, not for emergencies.

I fired up: 'Look, Fitz, what the fuck is this about? I've been hoicked out my pit in the middle of the night. If I'm on a charge, or there's something else, it's time to shit or get off the pot.'

He rose. 'Okay, okay.' Fumbling about, fidgeting, hands in and out of his pockets, until he found a packet of smokes, B&H Superkings. He lit up and offered me one. I waved it away. 'You're not off those too.'

I took out my Marlboros. 'I'll smoke my own.'

'Suit yerself.' He paced over to the other side of the desk and removed a black folder, looked inside and then turned back to me. He sighed, closed the folder, then picked it up, tucking it under his arm. 'Shall we?' He indicated a doorway marked 'Morgue'.

Fitz started chattering again, some bullshit about the bigger picture and most of the force's young hotshots wanting to walk before they could run. ''Tis the world we live in, everyone wants something for nothing. They see those feckin' bankers with their bonuses and the celebrities and footballers and the idea of graft goes out the window . . . *Graft*, feckin' no clue of it.'

He had a key for the morgue. Inside there was a strip light that took what seemed like for ever to flicker into life, then the grey sterility of the place dominated.

'We're heading for the feckin' abyss this recession, 'tis only the starter – we haven't brushed the cuff of this feckin' credit crunch bollocks.' Fitz fiddled with the black folder again, turning over pages. I saw fag ash falling on the floor; it seemed like sacrilege.

I felt my heart quicken again. My spine grew rigid and a cold line of sweat formed on my brow. I was getting twitchy, then I spotted the stainless-steel table, holes punched in the metal, heavy legs supporting a long drip-tray underneath. On top was a blue-grey cloth: it was clearly draped over a corpse.

Fitz caught me staring, stopped talking.

'What's that?' I said.

Silence.

I dragged my gaze away from the mortuary slab, said, 'Fitz, what is this? Why am I here?'

He fumbled – for the first time since I'd known Fitz the Crime he fumbled his words. I had a moment of clarity. Suddenly everything became clear. The call. The uniform jokers. Fitz's fucking stupid avuncular manner.

I walked over to the slab, my hand trembling for a moment. I watched my fingers hover over the blue-grey cloth that hid the face of a corpse. My thoughts danced. I jerked my hand away, wiped at my mouth. I was shocked to feel my lips so cold, so dry. I felt the cigarette fall from my other hand and I looked to the floor to see the head of ash collapse in a million pieces, followed instantly by a shower of orange sparks.

Fitz came over. 'Gus, I-I . . .'

I turned to look at his face. His brows made an apse above his eyes. He was the image of inscrutability; a shrill scream for answers. I looked back to the corpse and removed the cloth.

My mind filled with mist.

Nothing could have prepared me for this. Nothing in the world.

I drew the cloth further.

The body was white, clean. Not a mark. Except a small grey hole beneath the heart, barely half an inch wide, where the bullet had entered, and taken a life away.

I felt Fitz's hand on my shoulder: 'Is it?'

I realised my breathing had stilled. I felt dizzy, drew a gasp of air. 'This is Michael . . . This is my brother.'

CHAPTER 2

There's a phrase, *I was a million miles away.* Were it possible, I was two million miles away. My head felt as if it had been used as a battering ram. Thoughts raced in and out, questions, assumptions. And anger. Fitz spoke at my side, words, all words. I couldn't access the part of my being that processed communication, it was all sensation to me now. Feelings. The predominant one, hurt.

I saw Fitz out the corner of my eye gesturing to a chair. I didn't move and he wheeled it over to me, tried to cajole me to sit. I lowered myself into the stiff, hard-backed, office-issue plastic and tried to regain composure. I looked up towards the ceiling; the strip lights hurt my eyes. Fitz offered me some water. I shook my head, tried to say 'No', but it felt as though someone else was in charge of me, my somatic nervous system in the hands of a puppet master.

There was a moment, a memory sparking:

I'm about seven or eight, in the school playground and someone has ran up behind me and slapped my ears like a clash of cymbals. My hearing's distorted, like being underwater but I'm not, I know where I am. There's kids everywhere laughing. I've seen this happen before, it's been a craze around the school, slapping ears and watching. I strike out, there's a face to hand and I feel my knuckle hit bone. We fight, roll about on the ground. I can feel my knees tearing on the tarmac. There's blood in my mouth from a cut lip. My ears hurt. Everything feels strange to me. Like the world is cruel . . .

'Gus, is there anything . . .?' I heard Fitz again.

I found some words: 'I was just . . .'

Fitz stared at me but I couldn't comprehend the expression. He turned to the side, walked out to the water cooler in the hall and filled a cup. He held it out. I watched him but couldn't take it. He crouched, left it on the floor beside me.

'Gus, I don't know what to say, it must be an awful shock for ye. I know, I know that.'

I looked up at him. I hardly recognised the face, my mind was still in the schoolyard. 'I can see it clear as day, y'know . . . I can actually remember it, where I was, how it felt,' I said.

'What's that, son?'

'I could only have been eight at most, I was only young. I'd ripped the knees out my school trousers in a scrap but nobody said a word. Nobody said a thing.'

I felt Fitz place a hand on my shoulder, 'I'll get ye home, Gus. I'll get a car.'

'It's the day he was born – Michael – I can remember it as clear as if I was there. I tore the knees out my trousers, but nobody even noticed.' I started to laugh uncontrollably. The laughter shook me on the chair, I moved up and down with it.

Fitz left me. 'I'll go call a car. Sit tight.'

I laughed harder. I rocked in the chair, to and fro, the high of a great craic upon me. I was in such mirth I hardly noticed the tears begin to roll down my cheeks. Slowly at first, then faster. I cried for my dead brother, laid before me on a mortuary table. I jumped up. The chair skated behind me on the hard floor as I ran to Michael's side.

I clawed back the cloth again. He looked so cold and pale, his lips blue. He wore no expression I'd ever seen on his face before. It hardly seemed like him at all. I touched his hair. It hadn't changed, sitting high and wavy as he always wore it. I felt my throat convulse, my Adam's apple rise and fall in quick succession.

'God, Michael, what happened?' I said. I touched his still, dead face and recoiled at the waxy texture. 'Why?'

I saw my tears fall on his face and I wiped them away, straightened myself and felt a breeze of composure blow in. As I looked down at my brother I wanted to lift him up and hold him in my arms, but I knew at once it was futile. This wasn't Michael. This wasn't the brother I had grown up with, had fought and argued with, had watched soar far in excess of any pitiful achievement I had attained on this sorry earth. Below me now was merely the vessel that had once held my brother's spirit. He was gone.

I pulled the blue-grey cloth over the corpse and stepped back. Leaning onto the table, I felt my breathing return to normal. I wiped at my eyes as I heard the door opening behind me.

Fitz brought in a cup of coffee. 'You okay, mate?' I noticed he avoided eye contact, sparing me the embarrassment of admitting to that crime against manliness – crying.

'I'm fine.' I took the coffee. 'Can we get out of here?'

'Sure, I mean, of course.'

We went through to the adjoining office and I sparked up another Marlboro, offered one to Fitz. The coffee tasted like the standard watered-down office fare, the styrofoam cup giving it the tick of authentic vending machine.

Fitz spoke: 'I called in a car. Laurel and Hardy are out at Balerno, a break-in, some bastard's Christmas ruined.'

I shot him a glower. 'I can sympathise.'

'Ah, now, I'm sorry . . . I wasn't thinking. Look, I've called you first, Gus . . . thought you might want to break it to his wife. I'm being a bit fast and loose with the procedure but, well, rules are made to be bent at times like this.'

I nodded my head. 'I'll do it.'

'Okay, as ye say . . . we'll need to, likes as not, talk to her, 'tis Jayne I believe . . . But we can do that later.'

I clawed an ashtray from him, flicked the cigarette filter with my thumbnail. 'What the fuck happened, Fitz?'

He sipped his coffee, swallowed. 'Don't ye be worrying about that now. Get home to Debs and get yerself a bit rest.'

I shook my head. The very thought set a bomb off in my gut. 'No chance.'

Fitz gave a nervous cough into his fist. 'I'm just suggesting you take it a bit easy for now, till you get over the shock. It's a terrible, terrible shock you've just had, Gus.'

I stubbed my tab. It was barely smoked past the halfway mark and it snapped in two before I could get the tip extinguished. I left it smouldering, said, 'Now listen up, Fitz, my brother is lying on a fucking slab because some bastard put a bullet in him – do you think I'm going to go home and make a nice mug of Horlicks, try to get some kip? Fuck that! I'll be tearing down this shithole of a city till I find who put him there and then . . . then God save them.'

Fitz showed me his palms, waved me calm. I turned away from him, paced the room. I felt like a caged beast. I was ready to run into the street and start interrogating the first person I put eyes on. My anger was off the dial.

'You have to leave this to the force,' said Fitz.

I almost laughed at the suggestion. 'You can't be serious.'

A sigh, followed by a sharp intake of breath:

'I'm only saying, you can't go taking matters into your own hands, Dury. That would be . . . counterproductive.'

'You what?'

'We want to find his killer . . . Let the investigation run its course.'

'Spare me the corporate speak, eh.'

Fitz moved behind the desk, picked up the phone to enquire about the car, blasted someone on the switchboard, told them to get their finger out their arse. I watched him put out his tab, extinguish mine too, then take another sip from his hip flask. He looked on edge, nervy. Didn't want to be asked for any more favours.

'What can you tell me?' I said.

He snapped, 'Nothing.'

'Come on, this is me you're talking to.'

'You're a fucking hack, Dury . . . I can't tell you a bloody thing.'

I leaned on the desk, hovered over him. 'Fitz, that's my brother through there. I know you don't need reminding of that.'

He looked away, gnawed on his lower lip.

I went on, pushed his buttons – ones I knew worked: 'Fitz, you have family.'

He drew back his gaze, drumming his fingers on the black folder in front of him. 'Just what do you want to know?'

I lowered my tone, kept it businesslike. 'What have you got?'

Fitz opened the folder. His face was impassive

as he scanned the contents. 'We have very little to go on; it's early days.'

'Well, let me know what you have.'

He spoke slowly: 'We found him on the Meadows. A single bullet wound. His wallet was empty . . . Looks like a mugging gone wrong.'

'That's it?'

'Pretty much.'

'Who alerted you?'

He went back to the folder, 'Anonymous caller.'

'Male or female?'

Another sigh. 'Male.'

'Age?'

'I don't know . . . We haven't even interviewed anyone yet.'

I wasn't for easing up any. 'Do you have the shooter?'

'No, no weapon.'

'Any witness statements, forensics, clues?'

Fitz slammed the file shut, said, 'Look, Dury, I know it's your brother lying there, but I can't magic up a case-solved stamp out of thin air. We want the killer as much as you.'

'No you don't.'

'*What*?'

'No one wants this fucker as much as me, Fitz.' I started to fasten my Crombie.

'Now where are you going?'

'Home.'

'Wait for the car, man . . . It's four-below outside.'

'I need to cool down anyway.'

'You'll feckin' freeze, man – are ye mental?'

There was only one answer to that. I pulled up my collar. Fitz stood as I opened the door. I said, 'Don't want you to think I'd try pulling any favours on this, Fitz.'

'Dury . . .'

'No, I gave you your get-out. We're quits.'

'Dury, would ye ever just listen? Please, man, leave it to us.'

I put a serious eye on him. 'My brother's been murdered, Fitz . . . I'm not letting anyone else settle that score.'

CHAPTER 3

I set off for home. The snow had started to settle and the streets felt slippy underfoot. I toyed with the idea of a night bus, but I didn't want to be around anyone else; I wondered how I would react to seeing Debs.

My brother had a family, a wife and daughter. Just how do you tell a teenage girl her father has been murdered? It would wreck her. They would both want for nothing: Michael had his own business, was set up as they say, but that was little consolation. I looked up the street. Flats above the shops were kitted out with Christmas trees and little fairy lights. A glowing sleigh, waving Santa inside, shone down from a window. I couldn't look at it.

The snow grew heavier, great mounds of it gathering on the street. I started to shiver. Felt the quarter-bottle of Grouse in my pocket. It hung there like an invitation to an alternative Christmas. *Go on, down it! Block out the whole lot, wake up some other time. Sometime when the hurt has passed.*

I held the bottleneck tight, knew I had more reason than ever to stay sober.

Memories of my brother flashed into my mind, but I tried to drown them. There would be a time to remember him, but now wasn't it. Now was the time to stay focused, to keep my thoughts straight. A roar was building in the pit of my gut that would see me through, but as I reached my own doorstep my heartbeat ramped.

I got inside the flat and kicked the snow off my Docs, brushing the sleeves of my jacket. My hands felt numb with cold as I fitted the key on its hook. The dog jumped up, clawed at me.

'Get down, boy . . . come on, calm down.'

Debs spoke: 'He's been sitting at that door like Greyfriars Bobby since you left.' She was in her dressing gown; I guessed she had been since I left.

'You stayed up.'

She came towards me, leaned on the wall. 'I didn't know if I was going to have to come down and bail you out or what.'

'No danger of that.' I brushed past her, went to hang up my Crombie.

'Gus . . . what's up?'

'Go back to bed . . . You'll be wrecked in the morning.'

She followed me through to the living room. 'I won't get any sleep after that call. What's going on?'

I moved to the kitchenette, opened the fridge, took out a can of Coke. 'You better go and sit down.'

I kept my voice calm, laid it all out. Debs took the news as I expected; I put my arms round her as she started to sob. 'Gus, I'm sorry, I'm sorry . . . I was thinking the worst, but not this.'

I knew what she meant. She'd thought I was in trouble with the police again – we were still at a fragile stage in our reconciliation. I said, 'It's okay.'

'I only saw Jayne and Alice last week . . . Gus, they'll be in bits.'

'I know.'

She pushed away. 'Your mother, Gus . . . Oh my God, what about her?'

I felt a kick to my heart at the thought of more pain for my mother, after all she'd been through; it didn't seem so long since my father's death. I tried to calm Debs down, stroked her hair, made her take a seat; she only started to sob harder. I went into the bedroom to grab some tissues. She said, 'I just can't believe this. I mean, why? It just doesn't make sense. What did the police say?'

I tutted. 'Mugging . . . it's the default solution. And utter shite.'

Debs scrunched up the tissue, I went to get her another. When I returned she looked puzzled. 'What the hell was he doing in the Meadows at night?'

I stood up, turned away from her. I didn't want Debs to see the anger I felt rising on my face.

'Gus . . .'

'There's a lot of unanswered questions.' I turned round, caught her look of utter stupefaction, her mouth twisted on the verge of tears once more. I knelt down before her, said, 'Someone must've had a reason to put that bullet into Michael.'

I wanted her to throw her arms around me, show me support, but she didn't. Debs jumped out of the chair and let out a wail: 'No. No. That's not what I want to hear. No, Gus . . .' I watched her eyes light up, their whites huge above the redness caused by her tears. 'You promised me there'd be no more of this.'

'Debs . . .'

She was hysterical, ranting, screaming at me, 'I'm not going to watch you get yourself killed too!'

'Debs . . .'

'No . . . you promised!' She lowered her head and held her face in her hands.

I touched the back of her neck. She cut my hand away.

The intensity of Debs's reaction wasn't unexpected. I knew where she was coming from, sympathised even. The last thing I wanted was for this to come between us, but then I didn't want any of this.

In recent months I had found a route back to normality, something Michael always managed to locate with little or no effort. I didn't want to lose it, though I felt my new-found happiness starting to buckle now. Debs had got up early and locked herself in the bathroom. I heard her snivelling inside, but left her be. I wanted her to understand I couldn't just let my brother's murder go, but now wasn't the time to tell her.

I tweaked the dog's ear, then put on my Crombie. The car keys hung by the door. The rank smell in the stair had got worse – I held my breath again on the way down. Outside the street looked whitewashed by snow. It was too early for footprints, or to see the roads turned to slush. Everywhere lay silent and still beneath the pure-white blanket. I felt the cold seize me, go for my chest. I fastened my coat and raised the collar.

As I trudged down towards the car the grey sky suddenly turned to a black mass. A vast group of starlings swirled into view, cutting treacherous angles as they darted in first one, then another direction. I watched the darkness form and dissemble then reform again. Nature amazed me; I felt sure I was of its lowest order.

The windscreen of Debs's Punto was frozen over. I cleared it with the scraper, but then the engine refused to turn over. Automatic choke chugged a bit; when it bit, the tyres spun on the road. I dropped into second to give more traction to the hill start. Got a break at the lights and took a steady pace on the quiet roads all the way to the Grange.

My brother and his family stayed in Edinburgh's millionaires' row. A house round here was said to have set you back the best part of three mill until recently. After the banks crashed and demand plummeted, it wiped a third off the valuation. As I reached their home, I checked for any signs of movement. I rolled down the car window and sparked up a Marlboro. Got about two drags in when I saw a bloke appear from round the side of the house, dragging a wheelie bin behind him. He looked about six-two, early twenties, with a shaved head and broad shoulders. He clocked me sitting in the motor and frowned. I got out.

'I can help you?' He had an Eastern European accent. We had so many in the city now that it was hardly worth noting.

'Who the fuck are you?' I said.

'*What*?'

I nodded to the house. 'That's my brother's place . . . What are you doing there?'

He scrunched his brow at me and turned away. I followed him up the path, saw he had a bit of a limp. He turned back to look at me twice in quick succession before he speeded to a hop, got to the gate and slammed it behind him.

I tried the handle – it held fast. 'Hey, open up.' I banged on the gate, yelled at him, 'Get back here.'

As I stared through the slats, Jayne appeared in her dressing gown. She hovered on the back step for a moment, then bawled: 'Who's there?'

I set her right: 'Jayne . . . Jayne. It's me – Gus.'

She dipped her head, ran down the path and opened the gate. 'Gus, what are you doing here?'

Now I wondered if I should have left this to Fitz, fought the urge to hug her, smiled. 'I think we should go inside.'

The kitchen was vast. A huge oak table in the corner overflowed with plates and cups. The stranger was emptying the dishwasher. I squinted, nodded in his direction.

Jayne said, 'That's Vilem . . . He's our lodger.'

The bloke barely acknowledged me, save a slight once-over in my direction. His manner noised me up. 'You've got a lodger . . . Since when?'

Jayne sat down at the table, took a cigarette from a pack of Consulate menthols, lit it. She hadn't smoked for years, since Alice was born. 'In case you haven't noticed, these are straitened times, Gus.'

Sitting in this house, in this area, it was the last thing I expected to hear. Vilem clattered the dishwasher closed, flicked a switch and gave me one more long stare before limping out the door. I kept my tone low. 'A lodger, Jayne. Are you in that much strife?'

She peered over a cloud of grey smoke, didn't look like answering the question. 'We're just helping Vilem out – he works at the factory . . . Nice as it is to see you, Gus, I don't think you've come over here to talk about the state of our finances.'

My mind hazed over. I knew why I was there, but had I dreamt it all? I felt my heart slump with the thought of Michael. I tried to lock down my emotions. I took out a chair, sat opposite Jayne. 'Where's Alice?'

'Bed – a late night.'

'Doesn't she have school to go to?'

Jayne laughed; sharp radial lines creased the sides of her eyes. I hadn't seen them before. Age was catching up with all of us. 'School and Alice are not, shall we say, getting along right now.' She went to the sink to flick off her ash, checked the cupboard, said, 'Bugger it, he's washed all the ashtrays.'

She returned with a saucer in her hand. I looked at her with my mouth open, desperately trying to summon words, any words. How did I break this to her? She seemed to be on edge as it was. I felt my neck seize with tension. The Grouse bottle in my pocket pressed on my hip. 'Jayne, I have some news for you and, well, I think you might want to wake Alice.'

'What *news*?'

My mouth dried over. I touched the back of my teeth with my tongue – it made an embarrassing clacking noise. 'I, eh . . .'

'Well, come on then.'

I opened the top button on my Crombie, then the others. 'God, it's so hot in here.'

'What is it you have to tell me, Gus?'

I felt my brow lifting, my jaw clench. I didn't want to utter the words. But there was nothing I could do to lessen the blow: she had to know.

'Last night I got a call from the police . . .'

'*Police.*'

I nodded. 'They took me down to the station. Michael had been in some kind of a confrontation.'

Jayne stalled with the cigarette midway to her mouth. 'Confrontation? Oh, my God, he didn't come home . . . I thought he'd stayed at the office.'

I started up again; my lips trembled over the words. 'The police thought it might be better you hearing it from me. I'm sorry, Jayne, but . . . There was a gun fired and Michael was shot.'

She remained perfectly still. 'Shot . . .' She stood up – she actually smiled, like this was all a joke. 'Where is he?'

I went round to her side of the table and put my hands on her shoulders. 'Come on, Jayne . . . sit down.' I placed her in the seat. Her face was immobile. 'I'm sorry, I wish I didn't have to tell you this but . . . he's gone.'

All blood drained from her features. She jerked away from me. 'Gone?'

'Jayne, I'm sorry . . . Michael's been murdered.'

Her eyes remained fixed on the middle distance,

somewhere behind me, beyond the oak table. I tried to read her, then came a clatter of noise from behind us; her eyes sprang to life.

I turned to see Alice running out the back door.

'Alice! Alice!' wailed Jayne. She jumped up to see out the window, then squeezed her face in her hands. 'Oh, God, she heard every word . . .'

I watched as Jayne took off after Alice. She didn't get far, but wouldn't have made any kind of escape anyway, thanks to the footprints she was leaving in the snow. Jayne chased her to the edge of the street, where they both fell to the ground. They wrestled for a brief moment before Alice grabbed out to her mother and they held each other. As they started to sob, I looked away.

When they returned to the house I saw their eyes damp with tears, the edges of their noses red with cold.

'Alice, you okay?' I said. It was a lame remark. She ignored me, held her mother.

I rubbed her back with my hand. 'I'm sorry, Alice.'

She sobbed deeply, cries that came from a part of her that was too remote to reach with any words.

I looked out to the snow-covered street, tried to imagine myself somewhere far beyond the rooftops. Nothing felt real any more. *Christ*, what had happened here? How did everything go from being so normal to so fucked up?

Jayne stroked Alice's hair. They were both bubbling with tears as they sat down on the sofa in the living room. In the open doorway, the lodger appeared. Something inside me wanted to give him a slap and say, 'This is family business.' But I let it slide, closed the door on him.

Jayne took a blanket from the shelf in the bay window, wrapped it around her daughter. She watched her shiver for a moment then started to stroke her hair again. She turned to me, put pleading eyes on me. I nodded, said, 'She'll be fine.'

Jayne said, 'Come on, let's get those Uggs off . . . Look, they're soaked.' She pulled at her boots and then the pair fell into each other again and hugged.

As the full realisation of the news I'd brought them hit in, I saw the misery they felt. I couldn't watch. I eased out of the room, went through to the hall. I wandered over to a table by the window. A pile of letters beside the phone drew my eye. I picked them up, bills mostly. Gas, leccy, council tax. It took just a glance inside to see they were all printed in red. I looked up to the ceiling, sighed. Michael's house was just as I remembered it: if he'd been feeling the pinch, it didn't show. There was even a new plasma through in the living room. But then, maybe that was the problem: maintaining a lifestyle without the income to back it up.

As I put the letters back music started playing

upstairs – bloody Lily Allen, same track that had been on heavy rotation all over. I followed the tune to what I presumed must be the new lodger's room. I wondered about knocking, then thought, Fuck that. I pushed open the door; Lily pitched up a notch or two on the speakers. I walked in and the lad immediately bridled, turned on me, palms out: 'Hey, you cannot come in here.'

I laughed in his face. 'Calm down, bonnie lad. Just a little room inspection, shall we say.'

'No. I don't think—'

I cut him off, put a finger up to my mouth, went, 'Shhhh.'

He looked at me like I was some wido off the street. He was almost right. I paced around, picked up a book here, a CD there, opened a drawer.

'Why are you doing this?' he said.

'I'll ask the fucking questions.'

He looked at the door. Was he contemplating a bolt? A wee bleat to Jayne about me? Think again. I kicked it shut. 'Now, you tell me . . . what are you doing here?' I don't know what I expected, I was merely testing him. I prodded him in the chest with my forefinger. 'Well? Let's have it.'

He retreated into the wall, said, 'Leave me alone.'

I used the flat of my hand to press him up against the plaster, tried to keep the threat low, but make my point. 'Come on, now it's a simple question. How did *you* come to be kipping in my brother's home?'

He snapped, 'Keep your hands off me!' He cuffed my arm away, puffed his chest. I smiled in his face. Had seen Clint do this in the *Dirty Harry* movies – someone wearing a grin before a pagger says *I enjoy this shit, try me on for size*.

He didn't flinch: there was more to this guy than he let on.

I was ready to pound him into the bricks when, 'Gus, Gus . . . Are you up there?' It was Jayne.

Lodger man took a step to the side. He winced as he put weight on his bad leg, said, 'Go please, you have no right to come into my room.'

'Oh, no . . .'

His eyes blinked a spasm. 'I can expect some privacy.' He limped away from me, went to smooth over the duvet on the bed. He tugged out the edges, stood up and put his hands on his hips. Sweat glistened on his upper lip.

Jayne called again, 'Gus?'

The lodger lifted a hand from his hip, indicated the door with his palm. I put one foot in front of the other, but kept a bead on him as I went. For a second I wondered if I had him all wrong, but I still had my suspicions. At the door I turned, said, 'Pray I don't take an interest in you.'

Jayne had climbed the stair, was waiting for me in the hall.

'She's quietened down.'

'That's good. Look, I know this must be a shock and you must have questions and . . .'

She looked back at the door I'd just walked through. 'Were you talking to Vilem?'

I tried the name on. '*Vilem* . . .' I looked back to the room – the door was closed now, 'Yeah . . . Where was he last night?'

Jayne tugged nervously at her earlobe, playing with the little gold hoop in there. 'He was here with us . . . He watched a movie downstairs with Alice.'

'He was here all night?'

'Yes, all night . . . Well, he was here when I was. I went out to my book group.' Her eyes misted over as she remembered. She turned away from me and sucked in her lower lip. I could tell that she was replaying the last time she saw Michael.

'I'm sorry . . . I don't mean to . . .'

Jayne snapped, 'Are you checking our alibis or something, Gus?'

'I'm just . . . checking.'

I watched her closely for a change of tone, a tell; nothing came. 'Vilem is a nice boy, he's one of Michael's new workers. He's just here till he finds a flat. Michael was helping him out.'

I took her back a few steps. 'New workers?'

'After the lay-offs . . . Michael was . . .' Her face drained of blood; she flattened her hair back with her hand. I watched her eyes follow the ghost of another memory.

I hadn't heard about any lay-offs at my brother's

firm. He always prided himself on looking after folk, last of the great cradle-to-grave employers. I wanted to know more but couldn't face the tears; knew this was the wrong time to press her. I said, 'I'll let you be, Jayne.'

She jerked back to me, rubbed at the outside of my arm, then hugged me. 'Thanks for everything . . . I know you mean well. For Alice and me.'

I didn't want to hear the words, they put ice in my belly – the thought of them on their own, without my brother, wounded me. I stood silently – nothing seemed the right thing to say, then some stored response began to play: 'Jayne, if there's anything you both need, or I can do . . .'

I didn't have the words to make her feel any better. I was stood in my brother's home, talking to his wife about his death when he had been with us less than twenty-four hours ago. It seemed like I'd started to inhabit someone else's life.

'Thank you,' Jayne said. She looked wrecked, black circles forming beneath her eyes. 'Oh God . . . Davie.'

Michael's business partner Davie Prentice was a golf-club bore, what we refer to in Edinburgh as a cheese merchant. 'I'll go and see him: you need to know the lay of the land with the business.'

I walked to the stairs. I'd reached the bottom

step before Jayne hollered to me, ‘Gus, please don’t give Davie a hard time.’

Her words sliced me like a rotor blade; was I carrying that much threat? I lied: ‘I’ll be on my best behaviour.’

CHAPTER 4

I felt punchy. Numb. I palmed off the job of telling Mam about Michael to my sister. Catherine would handle the task better, but it stung. I consoled myself that I wasn't up to the job – it would have ended me and I needed to keep it together. Was struggling though, even drove home with Debs's Katy Perry CD playing and didn't bother to switch it off. The dog greeted me like a Ritalin-deprived six-year-old, jumping and clawing, diving all over the furniture to land a paw on me. He was a dog that I'd rescued, took the name 'Usual' from the regulars in a pub I ran for a while. Another failure of mine; something else to forget.

I shut Usual in the living room and hit the hay. I'd been up all night without any sleep. As my head hit the pillow the dog clawed at the door. I realised I didn't actually want to be alone and got up to let him in. As I climbed back into bed Usual chanced his luck and jumped up. I allowed him to curl silently at my feet.

I felt tired. Damn-near exhausted. But sleep didn't come. I pulled the pillow over my head and tried to block out the light streaming in through the curtains.

Wasn't happening.

I knew whatever I did next, none of it would sit well with Debs. After our divorce we'd went our separate ways but we'd patched things up now; there was something that pulled us back together. A bond? Shared history? We'd been through so much misery that maybe we just knew where to stack the ballast to keep each other afloat. My jaw tensed at the prospect of her reaction to me raking into my brother's death.

A child in the flat upstairs started laughing. Sounded like it was trapped in the floorboards. It was all I could take.

Grabbed my mobi, dialled: 'Y'right?'

'Gus, lad, how's it hanging?'

I didn't need to soft-soap Mac the Knife. 'My brother's dead.'

He rasped, 'Michael . . . dead?'

'Killed. Plugged.'

'What the fuck?' His voice dropped. 'Where are you?'

'Home. I need some gear. Can you get me some speed or something?'

A pause.

'Erm . . . is that a good idea?'

I sat up in bed, took a bit of a flier: 'Don't gimme good or bad idea here, mate, can you get me fixed up?'

Mac took the blast well. 'Aye, sure. I'll be round.'

'Fine.'

I hung up.

There was a stack of folk I needed to see and Davie Prentice topped the list. If there was some trouble at my brother's business, I needed to know. *Shit*, I needed to start somewhere. The factory seemed like the best place to turn up a motive. Fat Davie needed to face some harsh questioning.

I got out of bed and put on the shower. Got it burning hot; pushing up the steam, I crouched down and let the hot water burn into me for the best part of an hour.

When I came out, the dog was sat at the bathroom door, lying on the rug with his chops between his front paws. He looked up when I appeared.

'You're a smart animal,' I said. He sensed the change in me; I felt it myself.

I hunted for some music, but nothing seemed right. The nearest I approached was Johnny Cash, toyed with it, put it in the player and cranked up the track I wanted to hear: 'Hurt', his Nine Inch Nails cover, but I couldn't bring myself to press 'play'.

Got dressed in a new pair of Gap jeans and a top from River Island that Debs had bought for me. They didn't feel quite comfortable enough, like I was trying too hard for trendy. Still, she hadn't quite succeeded in weaning me off my Docs yet.

I had the kettle brewing for coffee when Usual let rip with a burst of loud barking. Someone was on the stairs. The door went.

It was Mac.

He strolled in, eyes down, never raised his gaze once, said, 'That's some bad shit about Michael . . . I'm sorry for your loss.'

I thanked him, but I really didn't want to hear it again. I didn't want to hear it the first time. I shouldn't have been hearing it at all. That was the truth of the matter and nothing was going to change it.

I steered him off course: 'Did you get my gear?'

He fished in his jacket pocket, exposed a 'Vote for Pedro' T-shirt. 'Some fast powder.'

I snatched the wraps off him, got fired in.

'Go canny with that stuff.'

I rubbed my nose, backed him off with my eyes. '*Why*?'

'Just, y'know . . .'

'Just what? . . . Think it'll turn me back to the drink? Get a taste for one drug, it'll whet my appetite for another?'

'Gus, cool the beans, eh . . . I'm just saying, watch yourself.'

I gave him a nod – his concern was genuine.

'Mac, I need a clear head. I also need to get moving, that's all this is about.'

I bagged up the wraps of speed and started to comb my damp hair. Needed a shave but wanted to maintain the roughneck vibe for Davie's visit.

I put down the comb, turned to face him. 'Someone plugged Michael for a reason.'

Mac looked deep in concentration, probably on a number of fronts. He had tried to get me on the straight and narrow many times, preaching to me about his own rehabilitation after a stint in Barlinnie's Nutcracker Suite. He and Debs had been in cahoots to get me to see a head-shrinker but that plan was turfed when I showed them I could handle the sauce on my own. I didn't want to let them turn my brother's death into another cause for concern but I saw Mac was wondering, were we wading into choppy waters?

'Gus, y'know, the filth aren't going to be best pleased with you poking about in this . . . after the last time.'

I volleyed that one back at him: 'Well, don't think for a second I'm going to leave the investigation of my own brother's murder to plod. Don't even contemplate that.'

Mac took the hint. He knew he was onto a loser, he'd tried that lark before. 'Okay, count me in.'

'What do you mean?'

He squared his shoulders. 'I'm on the team, on the case.'

'Not minding . . . I don't need minding on this, Mac.'

'No way. I want to help.'

'I'm serious, man, I don't need looking after.'

'I know that, Gus.' He zipped up his black leather jacket. He looked like a door lump; I had to admit it was the kind of help I could do with.

'Okay, then. Let's go pay fat Davie a visit.'

'Who?'

'My brother's former business partner . . . See what he has to say for himself. Though I warn you, I never liked the cunt.'

'Can we expect trouble?'

'Expect it? . . . We're taking it to him.'

Mac the Knife smiled, lifted his jacket and exposed his heavy gut, a claw hammer tucked in his waistband. 'Good job I got tooled up, then.'

As soon as the front door opened the dog bolted off down the stairs. Mac scowled. 'Smells of pish in here.'

'Is there a stair in Edinburgh that doesn't?'

'You want to catch them at it . . . It'll be the same bastard, y'know.'

I put on my 'shut the fuck up' look.

'Serious,' said Mac.

'How many jakeys are there in this city, not to mention assorted pish-heads?'

He ferreted in his jeans, produced a Jimmy Denner. 'Ten-spot says I'm right.'

I took his money – was way too easy.

Outside the snow was falling heavily again. Usual raised his nose to it, sneezed a bit, then wagged his tail as he shovelled his snout along the pavement. The road had been turned to slush; a bus on the way to Ocean Terminal chucked up a black spray as it went. Never ceased to amaze me how quickly the whiteness turned to blackness.

We got in the Punto. 'So, this Davie character, what's the SP?' said Mac.

'Wide as a gate, real man on the make. You'll suss the type.'

I turned over the engine. Katy Perry was still going on about kissing a girl and liking it. Mac jumped for the dial: 'Jesus on a fucking rubber cross, Dury! What are you listening to?' He was about to throw the disc on the back seat next to the dog but I snatched it.

'It's hers.'

'Debs . . . she's not sleeping head to toe now, is she? Sounds like lesbo music to me.'

I gave him a wry grin, closest I'd got to a smile in the last twenty-four hours; I was grateful for it. I put on the radio – it seemed to suit him.

'So you were saying, Davie . . . what's his full handle?'

'Davie Prentice. Used to be a big wheel in the computer business, ran some number for an American outfit when we were their best buddies, height of the boom.'

'Silicon Glen . . .'

'Don't know her – she one of yer porno stars?'

A laugh. Snort on the end of it. I managed a laugh myself too, maybe trying a little too hard. The car's wheels spun on the slush.

'Keep yer eyes on the road, Gus, gritters haven't been out.'

The speed was making me jumpy, my eyes began to itch. 'Okay. Okay.'

'So, Davie was a what, manager or something?'

'Plant manager, like I say, a big wheel. The Yank firm pulled out, though, or as good as. Downsized in a major way. They still needed to keep a presence here, though, keep the supply chains open for the European plants and fat Davie went it alone.'

'Michael tell you this?'

I nodded. 'Davie was manufacturing bits and pieces – soldering circuit boards and popping in memory SIMMS for the PCs. Stuff a trained monkey could do, but it needed doing and he had the contracts, big poppy behind him. That's how Michael got hooked up: fat Davie needed a haulier and Michael's firm fitted the bill.'

'Sounds like a cushy set-up.'

I dropped a gear as we came off Leith Walk and onto Pilrig Street, gunned the engine to put the tram works behind us, said, 'Well, it *was* . . .'

'Joint in trouble now?'

'That I don't know. His wife was a bit vague.'

Mac pointed out the window. 'Seen the nick of this place?' Boarded-up shopfronts and 'closed' signs. 'Everyone's feeling it, mate.'

I started sweating and yabbering as the amphetamine worked its magic. 'Well, I know this much, if Davie Prentice is feeling it, we're all fucked. He's the type makes money from muck. Then there's my brother's lodger—'

Mac cut me off: 'A fucking lodger in the Grange?'

I turned, rapid nods. 'Aye, that's what I thought. Jayne said it was temporary, that Michael was helping this Vilem guy out.'

'You think yer brother's missus is busy with the lodger?'

I shut him down: 'No way. Never. That's not Jayne's style. She was devoted to Michael.'

'Okay . . . if you say so.'

A teeny skank in skinny jeans that hung below his arse stepped in front of the car. I hit the anchors; Mac hit the horn, yelled, 'Ye twat!' The kid couldn't hear a word – headphones that wouldn't look out of place on a road-drill worker – and kept walking, oblivious. As the car slid to a halt on the slippy road Mac shook his head. 'No sense of danger.'

I agreed: 'Walking in front of a car, in this weather – lunacy.'

'I'm not talking about that.' He whipped out the claw hammer, put it on the dash. 'I could've brained the cunt. That thing nearly cut me in two.'

I was glad to have Mac beside me. There had been times in the past when I thought the friendship was at an end.

'How you faring this weather, Mac?'

He scratched the corner of his mouth, inflated his chest, said, 'Och, you know me.'

I knew better than to press him. 'What about Hod? He putting any work your way?'

'Bit . . . you know how it is.'

I didn't like the sound of that. Hod, our mutual friend, had taken over the Holy Wall pub, once a going concern but truly junked after my efforts. 'How's the Wall looking?'

'You not been in yet?'

'Uh-uh.' I couldn't face it.

'It's a bit plush, but fur coat and nae knickers if you ask me.'

True Scots wisdom, defies logic.

'Sounds . . . *different*.'

'Well, he's taken down your pictures of the dogs playing snooker, if that's what you mean.'

'The heathen.'

'You'll have to pay a visit.'

'Yeah well, when I'm a bit more flush.'

'You still looking for work?'

I gave him a look that said *Isn't everyone*? 'There's nothing out there. My racket's finished: they write newspapers with work experience and student interns these days.'

Mac followed a loose train of thought: 'Still, you have *this* to be going on with.'

This wasn't any kind of work either, deffo not anything I wanted to pursue, even if I had Debs's approval for it – which I certainly didn't.

As we reached the factory gates, the conversation shifted immediately – we weren't alone.

'What's the filth doing here?' said Mac.

I pulled up the car, yanked the handbrake on. 'Mugging my hole.'

CHAPTER 5

The dog got excited, prowled the length of the back seat, jumped up to the window and scratched at the glass. I pointed him down. He sat, then lay on his stomach watching Mac and me as we readied ourselves.

'Get that hammer under the front seat,' I told him.

He grabbed it off the dash, stashed it away. 'The powder – get it over.' He opened the glovebox, made space among the petrol receipts and empty Smints boxes Debs stored in there. I passed over the speed and gave him a nod of recognition.

We opened doors, got out and started to cross the road.

A cold haar blew off the sea – felt like we'd be encased in ice in seconds. I remembered Shir Shean's advice from *The Untouchables* and stamped my feet: made no difference, but set Mac off.

'What you doing?'

'Stamping out the cold. It's the haar.'

'Hardy-haar . . . Don't be daft, you look mental. Want us lifted?'

The smell of frying onions came wafting our

way from a burger van. Bloke inside looked out and nodded. He was after the goss on the police visit, or maybe a quick sale. I fired him back a friendly wave: 'Something smells good.' A bloody lie, but thought he might be useful to me at some point.

I felt the speed racing through my veins now. I had a slight twitch on my upper lip but I was primed, ready for action. Fitz the Crime had let me think my brother's murder was an open-and-shut case: coming down to Newhaven to turn over his business didn't square with that.

As I reached the front doors I caught sight of two uniforms coming our way down the corridor: they were getting gloved up. At their backs was Fitz, kitted out in a chalk-stripe three-piece and a red tie. It was an outfit designed to make those he met feel underdressed. Well, he was mixing with the seriously wedged-up – can't expect him to turn up in his baffies.

The doors eased open and the two uniforms passed by us without a nod. Mac eyed them up and down and got some stares, reminded the pair of shitheads to strut, shoulders back. Funny the effect Mac has on some people, I thought.

When Fitz reached us, Davie Prentice came into view behind him. He copped an eyeful of me and lunged for Fitz's hand, a great sweeping shake that near raised him off the ground. 'Well, if there's anything else I can do, please don't hesitate to get back in touch,' said Davie.

I watched this scene, my gut fighting to keep its contents in.

As fat Davie dropped Fitz's hand, I said, 'I'd count those fingers now, if I were you.'

Silence.

Davie was first to gasp into action, a histrionic luvvie air shining from him. 'Gus, I'm so sorry for your loss . . . Michael will be missed.'

I raised a hand, said, 'Really?'

The tension jumped a notch. Fitz broke it, turned to Davie and thanked him for his help, then, 'Dury, if I may . . .?' He indicated the car park; a quiet confab was called for. A warning, perhaps?

Davie went inside and Fitz quickly turned me by the elbow, led me away. As he passed Mac he stopped, rocked on his shiny brogues and said, 'I might have feckin' known you'd be putting in an appearance. Slightest whiff of trouble, yer like a feckin' dog with two dicks.'

Mac huffed, shoved his hands in his trouser pockets, rattled his change. It was a practised 'bollocks to you' look. Served him well.

[illegible]owed Fitz for a few steps then spun him. 'What the fuck are you playing at, man?'

He was indignant, eyebrows shot up. 'What am I playing at? Jaysus, Holy Mother of God . . . I told ye, Dury, to leave this investigation to the force.'

I squared my shoulders. 'You told me it was a fucking mugging.'

'Yes, yes . . . and all evidence points to that. This is procedure, Dury, procedure.'

He had no right to be so rattled. He hadn't lost a brother. Where was this coming from?

I jutted my head forward. 'What's your angle here, Fitz?'

'Y'what?'

'You're not coming down here' – I flicked his lapels – 'in the good bag of fruit to talk procedure with Davie Prentice.'

Fitz's mouth drooped, a thin line of saliva stretched between upper and lower lips. He looked scoobied. 'I don't believe what I'm hearing.'

'You want me to put it in writing?' The drugs had me racing through the gears; I needed Fitz more than he needed me but I was too rattled. 'Draw you a picture? . . . I dunno, interpretation through the medium of fucking dance?'

Fitz closed his jacket, fastened the buttons. 'Go home, Dury.'

'Fuck off . . . *mate*.'

His voice was low, flat. 'I mean it, go home. Get some rest. We'll talk another time.'

'We will that.' I pointed at him. '*Mugging* my arsehole.'

I watched him get in the car, drive away.

As I turned to the building I saw fat Davie at a window. He clocked me and ducked inside.

'What d'ye make of that?' I said to Mac.

Mac shrugged his shoulders, removed his hands

from his pockets. 'I never trust the filth, me. Asking the wrong bloke.'

'But did you see the way he was with fat Davie . . . all pally?'

'Aye, I got that impression – the auld pals act.'

I turned for the door, the speed ramping in me, stormed past Mac. 'I'm gonna burst him.'

I got about two steps before I was grabbed. 'Calm it, eh.'

'Y'what?'

'Gus, just turn it down a bit. You don't want to be going in there guns blazing, you'll get fuck all that way.'

I knew he was right, I needed to watch my mouth. I was getting agitated; the anger I felt was hard to control, though. 'Okay. Okay. You lead the way.'

Davie had disappeared from the window. As we went through the front doors I was overcome by the shoddiness of the set-up. Cheap carpet tiles on the floor, budget emulsion on the walls, institutional magnolia at that. I'd always imagined the place my brother earned such a good living from to be a classier affair altogether. I was wrong. It was designed with a purpose in mind, and the purpose wasn't comfort, it was graft.

A pretty blonde girl on the reception desk piped up. Polish or something, a definite Eastern European – there were still stacks in the city despite the papers insisting they were all headed home since the economy nosedived. I imagined the ones that were left got a pretty hard time from the native troglodytes – in the seventies they all shaved their heads and chanted jingoistic slogans; now they were harder to spot, but I'd bet no fewer in number.

Mac nudged me, whispered, 'Wouldn't mind going a few rounds wi' that!'

I shoved him away, went for warmth: 'Hello there, can you tell your boss I'd like a word, please?'

'That would be Mr Prentice. Do you have an appointment?'

'No. I've no appointment . . . I think he'll see me, though. I'm Michael Dury's brother. We just, er, spoke.'

'One moment.'

She picked up the phone – one of the old BT jobs, must have been a few years old. I didn't think I'd see one of those again; this place was in a time warp.

'Yes, if you follow the red tape.'

'Follow the what?'

'The tape, Gus,' said Mac. He pointed to the floor. Where the carpet ended there was a lino-covered floor, two thick strips of tape running side by side along the edge, one yellow, one red. 'You never worked in a factory? It's how they get about.'

I looked over. 'It's like *The Wizard of Oz*.'

'Come on, we're still a long way from Kansas.'

The tape led us through the shop floor. It wasn't what you'd call heavy industry. Couple of assembly lines, lots of people in starched white dustcoats packing boxes. Occasional forklift. Radio playing 'Eye of the Tiger'.

Mac tapped my arm. 'You remember this? . . . *Rocky*, innit?'

'Got that right.'

He curled his lower lip. 'Ain't gonna be no rematch.'

As we walked I caught sight of a familiar face: it was Vilem, the one Jayne had described as 'the lodger'. He was on the line, but didn't look to be grafting. There was a group of dustcoats around him but Vilem was in full flow, barking orders. He caught me staring and stopped, mid-blast, then crept away with that limp of his. I saw him remove a mobi from his pocket and press it to his ear.

'Watch out,' said Mac. A forklift forced us into the wall. We got pelters in a foreign tongue from the driver, who pointed to the floor.

Mac was none too pleased, looked set to lamp him. This time I hosed him down: 'Think he wants us to stay behind the line,' I said.

'He should have fucking said that then.'

'He did . . . in Russian or something.' As I spoke I saw Vilem disappear from the line; I turned head.

'There any Scottish folk in here?'

'Oh, aye,' I nodded up the corridor, 'here's one now.'

Davie stood outside his office, waiting for us. For a man in his mid-to-late forties, he wasn't wearing well. Pot belly, ruddy lardass complexion and the classic sloping shoulders of the desk-jockey. He did himself no favours in the style stakes either: an unruly side-sweep like Bobby De Niro in *The King of Comedy* and thick square-framed glasses that I hadn't seen since Frank Carson was last on the telly. He wore a striped shirt, frayed at the collar, and a too-wide-to-be-trendy tie that looked as if it had been cut from the tablecloth in a greasy-spoon caff.

'Yes, gentlemen, what can I do for you?' he said, smiling – fucking optimistically, I thought.

I walked past him through the doorway.

Mac said, 'Get inside.'

Davie stepped back into his office, Mac shut the door behind him. A large window faced out onto the shop floor. Venetian blinds were tied up: Mac lowered them, blocking out the view.

'Is that really necessary?' said Davie. He smiled, tried to appear relaxed. He was convincing, I'll give him that.

Mac said nothing, stood with his hands behind his back, played pug.

I answered for him: 'Now, you tell me, Davie, is it necessary? Suppose that depends on whether you have something to hide.'

He creased his nose and I noticed something about fat Davie I hadn't until now: he had a tache. It was a completely different colour from his barnet, much lighter, and it sat above his mouth like an anaemic slug. I'd never seen a mouth more inviting of a punch. He said, 'I've nothing to hide, why would I have anything to hide?'

I took out my Marlboros, sparked up. A chair sat beside the wall. I nodded to Mac and he dragged it into the middle of the floor, manhandled fat Davie into it. 'Is there any need for this?' he barked.

'Need for what, Davie?'

'This . . . this rough stuff.'

Mac laughed, shot him a sideways glance.

'Rough stuff, Davie? We haven't even got started yet.'

'Look, I'm not about to stand for this.'

'You're sitting, Davie. We gave you a seat, remember.'

He started to get up. Mac pushed his shoulders, forced him back down. Now Davie sat quiet. I expected him to finger his collar, take out a handkerchief and dab at his brow but he was ice. Fair shook me.

'Okay, Davie, let's take it from the beginning . . . When did you last see my brother?'

Now he flared up: 'You surely don't think I have anything to do with *that.*'

Mac crossed the floor again. 'Answer the fucking question.'

Davie didn't know who to address. He started to speak to Mac: 'I don't know anything about that . . .'

Mac put a mitt on Davie's jaw, spun his face towards me, said, 'Tell *him*, you prick.' He bared his bottom row of teeth, looked tempted to panel Davie into his soft slip-on shoes.

'I-I, come on, you can't seriously . . .'

'Davie, this is a simple enough situation we have here. Now, you're an intelligent man, are you not?'

Silence.

Mac kicked the back of his chair. 'Answer him.'

Rapid-style: 'Yes. Yes.'

'Good. That's very good, Davie. Now, as an intelligent man you must know I'm not playing with you here . . . You know that, don't you?'

He turned around swiftly to watch Mac. 'Yes. Yes, of course.'

'Excellent. Then, purely in the interests of clarity, let me confirm: you will answer every fucking question I ask of you, fully, truthfully and without hesitation, Davie, or Mac there is going to punch you a new hole. Got it?'

Head in spasm: 'Yes. I understand. Yes. Yes.'

I took a drag on my tab, said, 'When did you last see my brother?'

'Erm . . . it was, er, last, er, yesterday afternoon.'

'Where?'

'Here . . . it was here in the office. Erm, in his office. Next door.'

'What time exactly?'

'It was lunchtime.'

'What fucking time exactly?'

'One . . . it was one-ish . . . one-thirty.'

'Who else was there?'

'No one. We were going over the returns for the

accountant. They have to be in by the new year and . . .'

'And what?'

'Nothing . . . That's it. Look, it was just another day at the factory. I never thought—'

I leaned into his face, blew out smoke. 'You never thought he was going to get plugged out on the Meadows?'

Davie turned away, wiped at his soft moustache. 'No, I never . . . You don't think he was murdered? The police, I mean, they don't think he was . . .'

I walked around the chair where he sat. I flicked ash from my tab as I went. 'Maybe the police don't have all the facts, Davie.'

'What . . . what do you mean?'

I nodded to Mac. He tipped back Davie's chair – his slip-ons went in the air. 'I mean, do the police know how things are here? About the lay-offs? Sounds like cost-cutting – you must be feeling it.'

Mac let Davie's chair go. He fell backwards onto the floor. His glasses came off, he flapped about like a recently landed cod. When he found his specs he jumped up and ran to his desk, picked up the phone.

Mac was on him: 'You fucking cheeky wee [illegible].' He grabbed the line and yanked it out of the wall. The thin cable snaked up and whipped a polystyrene ceiling tile, showered a little dust. Davie put his hands to his head like the sky was coming down.

I said, 'You never answered the question, Davie.'

'What question?'

I moved over to face him, sat on the edge of his desk and brushed the white dust from his shoulder. 'Do the police know about your financial troubles?'

Davie shifted his gaze, left to right, 'I don't have any financial troubles.'

'You *don't*?' I turned to Mac. 'How about that? I'm all right Jack, he says. Funny your business partner was finding things so tough, was it not?'

Davie straightened his tie. 'I don't know anything about that.'

'You don't?'

'No. I don't.'

I felt my pulse pounding. There was an angle being worked here. What was this shithead saying, that my brother was in some kind of trouble of his own making? Michael was the canniest man I'd ever known: he wouldn't get into any difficulties if his own firm was still paying its way.

'You're telling me this place is sound?'

'Of course it is . . . There's no trouble here at all.'

I flicked his tie. 'Very well, Davie, I'm impressed. You seem to be the only businessman in Edinburgh riding out the economic storm, with no ill effects.'

He tipped his head, smirked. 'Well, I don't know about that.'

'No, Davie . . . and neither do I. You see, I might

not be a businessman myself, but I do know when someone is trying to sell me a crock of shit.'

I nodded Mac to the door. He opened it up and waited for me to step through. I didn't give fat Davie the benefit of a backward glance.

Mac said, 'We'll be seeing you.'

I felt the menace of his words.

CHAPTER 6

On the way out of the factory, the young girl on reception was taking dog's abuse from what sounded like an irate former employee. He was what the Scots call *ropeable*, had the sweaty brow, bulging eyes, the lot. Every now and again he'd fling back his head, put on a glower then regain his rant, slapping the desk for emphasis.

'I'm owed money, wages, not the peanuts they pay you cunts!' He leaned over her, his face lit red as he showered the hate. 'What you gonna do about it? I want fucking paying . . .'

He caught sight of us as we appeared in the foyer, started to wave his hands about. He had a wage slip that he slammed on the desk. 'This place went to shit the moment they started hiring your lot. No understanding of the workplace – just cheap fucking trash!'

I shot a sideways glance at Mac: he had a swagger on, the kind bouncers wear before throwing folk down the stairs. I'd been on the end of a few like it. I thought about hauling him up, putting in a word to the wise, but this bloke was arcing up big time. I thought there might be an interesting response coming if I let it go.

The girl got out of her chair, cowered behind the phone and dialled for assistance. Mac strolled over, put a hand on the bloke's shoulder. 'What's your problem?'

'*Eh*?' The guy's face turned to a grimace; his lower lip drooped to reveal two prominent teeth poking up like a bust wicket.

Mac moved his hand from the bloke's shoulder to his chest, edged forward. Mr Angry took a few steps back, said, 'It's got nowt to do with you, pal.'

'Maybe I'm making it something to do with me.'

I had to laugh, couldn't get enough of Mac in badass mode. I checked the girl was okay: 'You all right there?'

She nodded. Seemed a bit shaken.

'Have you called for some back-up?'

She didn't catch my meaning, words falling behind the language barrier.

'Is there someone coming out?'

'Yes. Yes.' Her speech came staccato. 'The foreman from the shop floor, he is on his way.'

As she spoke the doors behind us were flung open. Two big biffers in overalls ran through, trailed by a little baldy bloke in a white dustcoat. The big lads took over from Mac, who had the furious worker pinned on the wall by a forearm. 'All yours, lads,' he said.

'I just want my fucking wages . . . I just want

what's fucking owing to me.' Soft lad got carted off, raised on his elbows. He didn't know what was good for him, wouldn't shut up. 'You're a bunch of wankers . . . I'm owed wages. Think I don't know what's going on here? I know the fucking score!' I reckoned he'd be getting paid in a currency he hadn't bargained on, probably out the back. I was interested to see how they did business around here – was nothing like I expected. I caught Mac staring at me. We were on the same wavelength: he leaned over and pocketed the wage slip the bloke had put on the desk.

Dustcoat sat the young lass down, patted her on the head as though she was a spaniel. 'You sit yerself down, hen. I'll get you a nice cup of tea, eh.'

'She going to be okay?' I asked.

'Anna, oh aye – they're hardy, these Czechs. Isn't that right, hen?'

She looked up, put heartmelter eyes on the old fella. He smiled at her, in a fatherly way.

Mac checked out her rack, said, 'I think you'll live, love.'

I shook my head, got a *wha'? wha'?* stare in return. I turned to the young lass, crouched on my haunches at her side. 'So you're a Czech?' I said. 'How long have you been in Scotland?'

She crossed her legs away from me, shifting her weight uneasily. 'Not very long.'

The old boy hovered, turned attention to me. 'I don't know you, do I?'

I looked up at him. 'You tell me.'

'Are you after something?' He wasn't used to front-of-house duties, checked himself. 'I mean, is there something I can help you with?'

The place seemed strangely quiet without the shouting and roaring. Even the air seemed stilled, calmer. I played a long ball: 'You've got a lot of Czechs working here . . .'

'Yes.' He was abrupt, brusque even.

'That causing trouble with the locals?'

Now he bit, nostrils flared: 'No. Look, I don't think this is a discussion I should be having with you, Mr . . .'

'Dury. The name's Gus Dury. My brother used to be a partner here.'

The girl got up, patted down her skirt front, seemed to mumble breathlessly in Czech, then ran off down the hallway.

Dustcoat calmed, watched the girl stumble a bit on the carpet tiles, then, 'We, eh, all heard. I mean there was an announcement, before the police came . . . I'm sorry for your loss.'

I breathed deep. Looked away.

'He was a good man, always very . . . fair, with everyone.'

I drew back my gaze. I still had the speed firing and my thoughts ran from one end of my mind to the other. I knew this wasn't the place for a beat-down; hadn't worked with fat Davie. I said, 'If you think of anything that might be worth my looking into, maybe you could give me a bell.'

I picked a Post-it note off the desk, scribbled down my number.

Dustcoat snatched the piece of paper from me, buried it in his pocket. 'Yes, of course.' He quickly turned, went off in the same direction as the girl.

I hollered after him, 'Wait a minute. What's your name?'

He stopped still, cricked his thin neck to face me, said, 'Andy.' It was almost said too quietly for me to hear.

'Andy what?'

'. . . Just Andy.'

He'd disappeared round the corner before I had a chance to weigh up what I'd just seen.

'What you make of that?' I said to Mac.

He shrugged, thinned his eyes. As we went for the door, he said, 'That Anna, though . . . Think I'm in there?'

'Mac, I don't think she'd give the likes of you a date on a calendar.'

He clutched at his heart. 'So cruel.'

I gave him a wee reminder: 'You're married.'

'What she doesn't know can't harm her.' He actually smiled as he said it.

I gave him another dose of reality: 'You're deluded too.'

'Well, there is that. But still, I can dream.'

He had me there. 'We can all dream, mate. Though I'd say our Anna's dreams are turning into nightmares.'

Mac trudged through the slush of the car park

to the car. The dog jumped about on sight of us. 'How do you mean, nightmares?' he said.

'Couldn't you tell?'

'What, being dug out by . . .' He produced the wage slip belonging to the mentaller. '. . . Ian Kerr of, where's that? . . . Pilton.'

'Yeah, but there was more than that. I got the impression that was a regular occurrence. See the way yer man Andy fired through those doors with a couple of lumps? He had a routine. That was all a little too practised for my liking.'

I turned the key in the car door; the central locking was slow in the cold but got there in the end. Usual was sitting in my seat. As I got in he jumped first into the passenger's side then over to the back again.

Mac got in and frowned at me. 'Those boys were hardy, deffo. I think they're just off the shop floor, though. Andy probably just grabbed the biggest going.'

I reached for the seatbelt. The inertia-reel stuck a bit, gave it a good tug, said, 'Well, maybe our man Ian fae Pilton will fill us in.'

Mac grunted, 'If he can still speak after he's been filled in!'

I punched the engine, spun tyres. Gave a last glance to the factory: thought I might rumble Davie at a window but he was nowhere to be seen. The place looked so ordinary it unnerved me.

On Newhaven Road I sparked up a Marlboro, chucked the pack in Mac's lap. He still looked deep in thought, cogs turning like Windy Miller's gaff. 'Are Czechs legal here?' he said.

'Oh yeah. Don't get so many of them as the Poles, that's all.'

'Still, legal or no', times are hard and nobody likes to see their job being taken by a foreigner. See all those protests on the telly, barricading in those Italian workers? . . . Mental.'

I nodded, wound down the top of the window to let some smoke out. 'They'll be undercutting the wages. By how much, though – that's the question. I don't deny anyone a job, but if they're getting below the going rate then everyone's getting ass-fucked.'

'Except the boss man.'

I wound up the window again. It was too cold to let any air in. 'Michael wouldn't go for that.'

Mac swivelled on the seat, 'I wasn't trying to say—'

'No. I know . . . I wasn't having a go either. What I'm saying is, Michael wouldn't go for that kind of racket, I know it.'

Mac's mind ground out an answer: 'But fat Davie might.'

'Bang on.'

CHAPTER 7

I drove Mac back to the Wall.

'It really as bad as you say in there?' I asked.

'Pretty much.' It was a bad scene. I wondered what Hod had been up to with my old pub. 'You should come and take a swatch at the place.'

I hadn't ventured into the Wall since I sold up. Sounded like Hod'd turned it into – the worst of things – a style bar. Just the thought of trendies in Jimmy Choos laying waste to my memories of the place had me about chucking up, said, 'Maybe later.'

Mac got out the car, bent over the door. 'Move on, Gus. Stop living in the past.'

Felt content where I was, didn't see anything so fucking great about the present, or any future to come for that matter. Went Judge Judy, said, '*Whatever.*'

'I'm serious, mate . . . Come down later, Hod'll be rapt to see you.'

I knew he was right. Hod was my oldest mate and I'd good as blanked him because of this pub. I still felt sore that I'd lost it – Col had left it to me in his will. I said, 'Aye, okay. Soon, promise.'

Mac thinned his lips. Wasn't buying any of it. He closed the car door. Usual jumped into the vacated seat.

The drive home was slow, the traffic ponderous as the endless Edinburgh buses struggled with the elements. Snow and freezing temperatures did not go with double-deckers, hills, and lazy lard-ass drivers, all looking for an excuse to piss off anyone that crossed their route. They were an almost perfect symbol for the modern Scottish workforce: why devote your time to making the customer happy when it's far more satisfying to make them miserable?

I got parked across from the shop where they sold the aquariums and exotic fish. The drains reeked round here, real bad. I'd caught a bloke tipping a bucketful of dead little fish down there once. My powers of deduction told me that it wasn't a first.

Usual chanked it up the street, sat at the door to the stairwell. I tugged his ears as I reached the step, put the key in the door. Some jakey had taken another slash on the wall. I held my nose and waved the dog on. As I took the stairs I saw the old woman from across the way. I'd seen her a few times before. Never knew her name – Debs and I referred to her as the auld wifey at number three.

'Hello there,' I said. She was struggling with a couple of Iceland carrier bags. 'Want me to get those for you?'

She beamed. 'Oh, would you, son?'

My heart went up a gear; I pressed out a smile. 'Surely.' She had a great hand-knitted scarf wrapped around her neck, I think the term is Fair Isle. 'That's a fine knit there. You do that yourself?'

She was still a bit breathless after the few steps she'd taken. 'Oh no, my late sister did this for me, many a long moon ago.'

I immediately felt the tragedy of her life; it seared into me. I felt my own age too – I'd now lost a brother. I carried up the bags and listened to the old woman tell me about her sister's great talent for knitting. 'I've a flat full of her jumpers and scarves. Each one is a memory, and you can't have too many of those.'

I had no words for her. She took the bags from me and disappeared into her flat and her reverie. I felt my hurt rising, but I fought it. I wouldn't let myself weaken. I turned and went into my flat. Took off my Crombie and removed the quarter-bottle of Grouse. I placed it on the coffee table and sat before it, staring.

I knew it would be so easy for me to open the whisky, neck the lot. I tasted the fire of it, running over my throat. I sensed the burn in the pit of my stomach as it landed. I felt the hum in my head that would come soon after, the hum that made it all worthwhile. I knew I was a trouble drinker because of that hum. Other people – normal people – drink for the taste, for the pleasure of it.

I drank for the sensation, the effect. I drank to attain the hum in my head that said the louder noise outside had been deadened. The sound of reality, the world of living and breathing was drowned out by drinking.

I stared at the bottle, the little Grouse on the front, the *low-flying burdie* that we call it in jest. *Would you like a low-flying burdie, Gus?*

God, yes, would I ever.

Just to whet my thrapple.

Just one or two.

Just the ten.

Just a bucket, then.

I knew there was no safe number, not after one.

But I was tempted.

I picked up the bottle, held the cap between my thumb and forefinger; all it would take was one quick twist.

I fought it.

That's what I'd done for so long now. One drink was too many, and after that, a thousand wouldn't be enough.

When Debs had taken me back in, when we'd set up home together again, I'd vowed not to drink.

'I don't want you to do it for me,' she said. 'It's got to be for *you*.'

I understood. I saw where she was coming from. The change had to come from within. I'd done the one thing I had thought I never would. Went to the one place I had previously laughed off all suggestions I go: Alcoholics Anonymous.

Was I an alcoholic?

Did I know what it meant?

That's what they'd asked me.

I read every description I could find. None of them seemed to fit me, but in every one of them there was *something* that fitted me. I admitted defeat.

'My name's Gus Dury and I'm an alcoholic.' I said the words, but it was all meaningless to me. It was all ritual. I sat through their meeting, listened to their plaintive, whining tales of woe. *Poor me, poor me, poor me a drink!*

It churned my stomach.

I wasn't like them.

They were weak. They were the societal chaff. The dregs. The limp-willed. Losers. All with a sob story of how they got into such a mess. How they just couldn't stop themselves. How they needed AA to keep them on the straight and narrow.

My relationship with the sauce wasn't about support. Or substitution. Or lassitude born of a hard life. I drank because I wanted to. And now I stopped because I wanted to, I told myself.

It was a simple pay-off. I could stop when I wanted and I could start again when I wanted. I controlled it; it didn't control me. To admit the opposite was to give up on the game of life.

I put the bottle back in my coat pocket. I was exhausted. I thought to grab a wrap of speed, but I'd left the lot in the car. I knew I was too hyped for sleep. My mind was awash with thoughts of Michael and of the police investigation, of fat Davie Prentice and of a dose of Czech workers, and one Czech lodger.

I needed to unwind.

I ran a bath. Climbed in.

I was soon far enough gone to feel my mind pull up to its new preoccupations. Nothing was fitting into place. If this was a jigsaw, I wouldn't have more than a couple of pieces stuck together. Sure, there was something going on at the factory – Davie's denials, and the sight of Vilem lording it about, only confirmed my suspicions. That angry worker, Kerr fella, might turn up some answers when we gave him a knock but I wasn't hopeful; had my suspicions he'd be given a good few reasons to keep schtum.

I leaned out of the bath, grabbed over my tabs that I'd sat by the sink. I lit a red-top, caught the familiar Marlboro stench.

Davie Prentice was, for sure, as wide as a gate. But I didn't have him down as a killer. Taking up that kind of damage took bottle and fat Davie had none of that. The suggestion that he might even be mixed up with someone who had the cobblers required to put a bullet in a man didn't square with the devout coward I knew him to be. If Davie Prentice was mixed up in my brother's murder, he was being fucked over too, worse than any Calton Hill rent boy.

I turned the sum of my thoughts over to my

subconscious, zoned out in the warm water. In no time I was comatose, dead to the world.

Had been crashed out for God knows how long when I got jerked back to reality. The bathroom was in darkness, the water freezing as Debs stormed in and pulled on the light.

'What the fuck is this?' she yelled.

She held something in her hand, but my eyes wouldn't adjust to the sudden brightness. 'What, what is it?'

She slapped the item into the bathwater; the little wraps of speed fell out of the baggie. I tried desperately to pick them up.

'Gus, how could you?' She started to sob. 'I trusted you.'

She couldn't look at me, turned and fled.

The wraps were a bust. No way back for them. Let the lot go down the plughole with the bath-water. When I dressed, Debs was sitting in the living room, there's a phrase, *stony-faced.*

In the time I'd known her, I'd seen every expression there is to see on Debs's face. I'd say there were some I would never want to see again, and prayed I never would, but this one was perhaps the expression I knew least how to deal with.

Said, 'Sorry.'

Her look went up a notch in intensity, almost a wince – an 'Are we here again so soon?' God, it wounded me.

Added, 'I am, truly.'

She stood up, raised her hands, dropped them again. 'Gus, I can't take this any more.'

This shithole flat of ours was too small to hold the tension. You couldn't have a barney when there was nowhere to run off to, slam doors behind you. I went for the mainline: 'Well, what do you want me to say or do? Tell me, I'll do it.'

She walked to the kitchenette, filled a glass with water from the tap. The dog watched her as she moved. I did too. A bellicose look burned in her eyes, kind that kept the whites permanently on display. I admired her ability to keep her anger in check; I never could. She slammed down the glass. It wobbled on the counter, some water spilled over the brim. 'I don't know what you can say or do, Gus . . . you've said and done it all before. But bringing wraps of charlie into our home.'

'It was speed.' I knew I should have kept my mouth shut.

'I don't care what it is – it's drugs!'

Fuck. Hoped she wasn't gonna go Nancy Reagan on me, start the *just say no* spiel. I sighed, knew I was onto a loser. I dropped myself in the chair. Truth told, I didn't have the heart, or the passion, for another row. I wanted to make her see I was contrite, but I wanted her to know I was hurting inside for reasons I could do nothing about. I wondered if she'd forgotten about Michael for a second, but I knew Debs better than that: this was all about my brother. She was wondering where it was leading me, and us, to.

Debs raised the glass again, sipped. I watched her put her hand through her hair. 'Look, Gus. I'm *sorry* too.'

I turned to face her. 'You are?'

She came round the edge of the counter, crouched before me. 'I know you're hurting.' She took my hands in hers. I didn't want her, or anybody's, sympathy. My pain was my problem. I removed my gaze. She said, 'I just don't want you going back on the drink. You said you'd stay clean.'

'I am clean . . . more or less.' I pushed my luck: 'I think you're making a bit of a fuss over nothing.'

She sparked at that. 'Well, I don't!'

I got up, went to the other side of the room. We'd drawn our battle lines; I didn't like where this conversation was going. When she shouted and threw things, I could handle it. When she locked me out, no trouble. But the close control freaked me out. My father had tried to control me with beatings and harsh words and it never worked. I didn't do control.

I picked up my tabs.

'Where are you going?'

'For a smoke.'

Outside on the stair I fired up, got about a third of the way down the smoke when a gadgie with a mop and bucket showed. He wore a black and red Adidas coat like the footy managers have. 'All right, mate.'

I gave a non-committal nod.

He had a beanie on and it stretched the corners of his eyes. I saw some tats on the back of his neck when he lowered the bucket. 'There's, eh, cash due for the stair cleaning.'

I drew on my smoke. 'What's this?'

'Been a stair meeting and that . . . Three pounds, chief.'

'Three pounds . . . this weather. I don't think so.'

He started to get twitchy, kept rubbing the tip of his nose. 'It's three pounds.'

I knocked the tip off my tab, crushed the embers under my boot-heel. 'You're getting bugger all out me.'

He looked scoobied, not sure what had happened.

Inside the flat I watched him through the spyhole as he tapped up the auld wifey at number three. She handed over the cash without complaint. I shook my head.

Debs had prepared for my return. She put her hands in the back pockets of her jeans. She'd been at the lip gloss in my absence, said, 'Look, Gus, I know you're not equipped to cope with, y'know, the news about Michael.'

There was a whole other row waiting to go up once she heard of my moves to root out his killer. Swearing off the drink was only one of her ultimatums that I'd signed up to. Not looking for trouble was another; and of the two I'd say the latter was the one she placed most store by. If I wanted to keep hold of Debs this time, I had to play by her rules. Only, since Michael's death, I just didn't know how that was going to be possible.

'He was my brother, Debs.'

'I know.'

'I can't just forget he existed.'

'I'm not asking you to.'

My neck tensed. 'What *are* you asking for?'

Debs took her hands out of her pockets, came towards me. 'I know it can't be easy, and I know you've done really well up until now, but I'm frightened.'

I knew what she was frightened of. She thought I was slipping back to my old ways. She didn't want to be around me when I was arrested, beaten up, or worse. I didn't want to confirm her fears, said, 'Oh, yeah.'

'Gus, you need help to get over this.'

I saw where this was going, felt my breathing stall. 'Uh-huh . . .'

She had a card in her hand. She held it out.

'A psychiatrist . . .'

Debs nodded.

'You want me to see a psychiatrist?'

She handed me the card.

'I don't know, Debs.'

Her brows shot up. I saw I wasn't getting a choice. She put her hands back in her pockets and left me holding the card.

CHAPTER 8

Ian Kerr's address was dangerously close to Muirhouse.

'Fuckin' Apache country round here, man,' said Mac.

We turned off Ferry Road, headed east. I said, 'Yeah well, keep those windows shut. Don't want any stray arrows coming in.'

He grinned. 'All they fire round here's fucking needles.'

I took the corner into the street that was listed on Kerr's wage slip. Two skanky-arsed kids ran alongside the car, sliding about on the icy path and shouting abuse. One of them, a rough wee ginge, carried a butterfly knife and spun it through his fingers with a fair bit of skill – must've been playing with it since he put down his rattle. I booted it away from the neds and they hauled up on the kerb, giving us the Vs and dropping trackies to flash arse cheeks.

'Ah, the youth of today,' said Mac, 'another beautiful crop of schemie fodder in bloom . . . Fair gladdens the heart.'

I'd read recently that the cost of a home round

here was less than one-tenth of what it was in the New Town. Of all the property-obsessed ramblings I'd read since our real estate tanked, this one caused me the most surprise: I was completely stunned that property round here was worth fuck all.

I parked on the street. Usual jumped into Mac's lap. 'Chrissake, beast . . . Trying to end me there?' The dog planted a wet nose on Mac's face, followed by a wet tongue. I laughed it up.

'Better take him in, don't want to give the local young crew any ideas about snafflin' him for a pit.'

Mac let out a growl. The dog pinned down his ears: he got them ruffled. 'Och, I'm only messing with you,' said Mac.

As we got out the cold bit. I buttoned my coat and made for the front door of the weather-beaten concrete block. Who would call this a home? The windows were rotting away on the ground floor and yellowed net curtains, blackening with damp at their corners, flapped behind cracked panes. There was a light burning inside but apart from that there was no sign of life.

Mac picked a torn bin liner from the lawn. The empty Cally Special tins inside were frozen solid – never made it to the tip. He dropped the lot on a beat-up old fridge that sat by the house, shook his head. 'Joint's more than a wee bit neglected, eh.'

I scanned the street. 'Take a look about – not exactly fucking Peyton Place.'

'Aye, but this one's the pick o' the lot.' He kicked the fridge door shut.

A bloke from the next garden, face wrapped in a Rangers scarf, leaned over the fence. His donkey jacket was about three sizes too big for him; he looked like he was fighting it for survival. 'You after Big Ian?' As he spoke he tugged his scarf down, revealed a mouth twisted to one side, a nose spewing grey hair.

I turned. 'Yeah . . . seen him about?'

A tut, splutter. 'You from the bookies or the buroo?' I didn't answer; gave him the once-over look his type are used to. He went on: 'Nah, haven't seen him the day. He was makin' a fair clatter last night but haven't seen hide nor hair all day.'

Mac cut in: 'Clatter?'

The old gadgie tugged back his sleeve, brought a scrawny wrist out, scratched his hairline with a dirty fingernail. 'Probably had a bucket in him. Came in rattling about after a night at the howf . . . He's lost it since he got punted from the work.'

We'd seen that for ourselves at the factory. I scanned the house; there was no movement now. 'What happened? I mean, do you know why he lost his job?'

The bloke's eyes lit. He ran a manky mitt over his mouth: thought he might get a few sheets for his trouble. 'He was on the wagons, had a big rig out there every night,' he pointed to the street, 'used to wash it and polish it when he wasn't on a run . . . Fair buggered up his heid when that got taken off him.'

He was at it – nothing to offer. 'I'll take that as a no, then,' I said.

Mac was growing impatient. He edged towards the building, pointed at the door. I gave the neighbour a wide berth as I went. He called out, 'Eh, got a smoke there, pal?'

I dug in my pocket and gave him a Marlboro.

He looked at it with derision. 'That all you got?'

'Do I look like a fucking mobile tobacconist?'

He took the tab, sparked up. He coughed away, hacked a gob of phlegm in the garden. I thought, Was I expecting too much looking for a thank-you?

At the door Mac leaned over and knocked hard. The crumbling paintwork lost a few flakes – like it mattered. There was no answer. Mac knocked again, a rusting bell by the door got a hit, then he looked through the letter box. He seemed to dwell there, breathed deep a few times then stood back.

'Anything?' I said.

His face looked pained. He pointed. 'Take a look for yourself.'

The place was a shambles, arse over tit. A picture on the wall – looked like the classic Green Lady – was squint. A folding table, couple of chairs, had also been upended. One of the table legs had been snapped. The phone had been pulled out the wall and what looked like a collection of souvenir tat – cheap figurines and plastic snow-domes – had been spilled on the floor. I couldn't see any further than the living room door because a coat stand had been rammed into the plasterboard wall – a blue anorak and a bust brolly were blocking my view.

'Duly turned over, I'd say.'

Mac agreed, tugged the dog's lead and headed round the back. The driveway skirting the edge of the property was blackened with oil and heavy tracks. A rainbow of spills covered the path and burst, worn tyres sat against the gable end of the house. On the back wall, patches of pebbledash had fallen out, exposing brickwork beneath. One of the gutters hung loose, rattling in the wind and threatening to fall.

Mac kicked at a couple of fallen tiles on the path. 'I'm thinking this geezer's no' been keeping up appearances that well.'

'You think?'

The back door had a large frosted-glass window that had been put in. The nicotine-stained blinds on the inside crashed against the frame with every belt of cold wind that came along. The door frame had been booted; wood splinters littered the step. Mac and I looked at each other, but said nothing. I pushed the door and stepped through. As I walked in, the broken glass crunched under the soles of my Docs. I turned to Mac. 'Pick up the dog or he'll cut his paws.'

We walked in slowly, cautiously. It was freezing

inside; the wind and rain and snow had got in through the smashed window and soaked the linoleum, made it slippy underfoot. The first room we came to was the kitchen. A newish-looking fridge door hung on one hinge and two large shelves had been pulled off the wall. A stack of pots and plates, obviously once resident on the shelves, had been thrown on the ground. A mop handle had been snapped off; I couldn't see the missing portion but wondered about that.

It was all eerily quiet. Far too quiet. Was beginning to wonder what we'd come to. 'I don't like the look of this,' I said.

As I spoke, Mac returned fire: 'And I don't like the look of *this* . . .' He pointed to the hallway leading from the kitchen: along the magnolia woodchip was a streak of blood. It ran almost the full length of the hallway and sat three inches thick at its widest point.

'Fucking hell. Lead on.'

As we walked into the hall Usual started to sniff at the air, he struggled in Mac's arms. 'Settle, boy.'

The door to the living room sat open about half a foot but as I tried to push it something was blocking it on the other side. 'It's stuck,' I said. I could see into the room: the television screen had been smashed and lay in shards on the carpet. Time-warped teak chipboard units had been pulled over, their contents scattered everywhere. A carriage clock had been bounced off the wall, its face smashed. What caught my attention the most, though, was the splatter marks. They covered everything. Red to black. I knew at once it was more blood. Lots more.

'Give it a push,' said Mac.

'I *am* fucking pushing it . . . Something's blocking it on the other side.'

Mac weighed in, between us we heaved enough of a gap to get through. Behind the door was an armchair. Sat in it, his back to us, was a man. Stood behind him, we could only see the top of his head – black hair, some male-pattern baldness, a streak of blood. He wasn't moving.

'Oh, fuck,' said Mac, 'what have we got ourselves into?'

We looked further into the room, copped an eyeful. It was clear what had went on: there had been a serious working-over in here. The dirty-beige carpet was thick with blood; the castors on the armchair squelched in it as we pressed our way past.

As we walked into the middle of the room, the dog struggled in Mac's arms again. He held him tight. Patted him quiet. Usual was anxious, unsettled. He wasn't alone.

As we turned to face the bloke in the chair my guts turned. It was Ian Kerr – could make that out, but only just. He'd been beaten, and badly marked with some kind of chib. I'd say there'd been an attempt at gouging at his eyes as well. His lids were black and torn and his cheeks distended. If there was a tooth left in his head, I couldn't see it. A flap of skin had been torn clear of his forehead, so severely that the white of his skull showed beneath. For a second I hoped his throat had been cut, that they'd shown some mercy, but they were savages.

I felt my breath faltering; my mind raced. This was a man I'd seen only a short time ago, in rude health. Kerr had been kicking off, but nothing to deserve this. The pit of my stomach cramped; I couldn't take it all in. My eyes adjusted to the scene, but my mental processes stalled. It seemed unreal.

'Do you see this?' said Mac. He pointed to Kerr's hands: not a mark on them, save two matching bruised and bloodied holes in the centre of each, just below the knuckle where he gripped the arms of the chair.

'Holy fuck.'

He'd been nailed through the hands.

'Didn't want him running away . . . Probably used a nail gun for that.'

'This is fucking medieval,' I said. My thoughts raced, darted on to Michael and how he'd met his end. I wondered who and what the hell we were dealing with here. Kerr's sound-off at the factory played before me again.

'It doesn't make sense . . .' I said.

Mac had a tight hold of the dog as he spoke: 'Some folk get off on this shit, get a taste for blood . . . Maybe they got carried away.'

'But in his own fucking house. And to just

leave him here . . . This is a warning, Mac. Someone wants this to get out; there's no point to it otherwise.'

Mac nodded. The dog struggled again. 'We better fucking nash. Plod won't be chuffed to find us here.'

I was all set to agree when the door we'd walked through a few moments ago was suddenly edged open again. In the living room stood the old gadgie from next door. 'Och, no,' he said, 'what in the name of God . . .'

I looked at Mac, could tell he was contemplating lamping the bloke, making a run for it. It was an idea. Had I less to lose, I might have went for it, said, 'We better call the police . . .' The thought didn't exactly tickle me, but we were up to our nuts in it. I took out my mobi, called Fitz. As I did so, I caught sight of Mac edging the neighbour out the door. I kept the call businesslike – could tell Fitz was raging. An arse-caning was coming my way. I'd take that standing, just hoped there wasn't worse to follow; had known the filth to hang worse on me.

When I rang off, I joined the other pair on the back step. The old giffer was shaking; I offered him a tab.

'Thanks, son . . .'

I sparked up myself. 'You all right?'

'The blood . . . Fuck tae fuck. I never saw blood like that.' I thought I was going to have to take hold of his hands to help him get the cigarette in his grid. He managed it, just. 'I never imagined . . . The noise, last night, y'know.'

I pressed him: 'You said there was a bit of a barney . . .'

He coughed over his palm. 'Aye, aye . . . a bit ay shouting and that. I thought he just had a good bevvy in him . . . I didn't, I mean, if I thought . . .'

'I know. I understand.' What I understood was that he was obviously blootered drunk himself; I could see he was gantin' for another bash at the bottle now. He wasn't alone. 'Did you see anyone?'

He shook his head. 'I didnae get up . . . sometimes I take a deck oot the window, but I didnae even get up to batter the wall last night. You know how it is, you just get used to it . . . Big Ian was a right washoot lately, he was getting tanked up every night after the job went and the missus left and all that.'

I took a pelt on the Marlboro, caught Mac sighing. He took the dog to the corner of the garden. I said, 'Did he say anything about his job?'

Head shakes, still trembling. 'Naw, we never spoke much.'

I knew I was onto a loser, but tried anyway: 'Look, you must have saw some coming and going at the house . . . any, y'know, funny business?'

He laughed. 'Oh, aye . . . every fucking night. All Big Ian's, mind – he was a radge.'

I could hear sirens, the police were on the way. Moving fast too – not a good sign. I left the waste of space to himself. He tried to tap me for some folding; I ignored him.

'Last laugh!' shouted the gadgie.

I turned, looked at him.

He was tucking his hands into his jacket pockets, thin shoulders trembling in the cold. 'That's what he said to me . . . He was gonna have the last laugh.' Tyres screeched, the filth were just about on us. 'He was pished, said something about being fucked over but he was gonna have the last laugh . . . Said he had nothing left to lose.'

I had my mouth open, words waiting as the divvy van suddenly shot into view. A pack of uniforms made a rush for the house. There was no sign of Fitz. The first of the woodentops into the yard grabbed the gadgie round the neck; two came straight for me. The cuffs were on before I could draw another breath.

CHAPTER 9

At the counter sat the standard-issue Lothian and Borders battleaxe: peroxide-blonde hair and kebab-meat complexion, topped off with a hefty dose of attitude. Your perfectly balanced Scottish woodentop – a chip on both shoulders.

'Hello, there,' I said.

Eyes rolled, a twist of the gob. 'Oh, please.' She shuffled over to the phone, gave me an eyeful of an arse you could turn an artic on. A few moments later and she shuffled back; I wondered why she wore her bat belt, one with the cuffs and the spray and mini-nightstick. 'Empty your pockets, gimme your belt and shoelaces.'

I could see my last run-in with Fitz had got his goat. This wasn't so much going to be a matter of swallowing pride, but of burying it altogether.

'If you could just tell Fitzsimmons I'm here.'

She had a Bic biro in her mouth, took it out to point at me. 'Shut up, eh.' She scribbled some more. Thought: Can be few so content in their job; she was really getting off on this. I wanted to leap the counter, run past her and through to Fitz's office, but I didn't rate my chances of getting that far without a few pairs of size tens bouncing on my napper.

'Look, I think there's been a mistake . . . I actually called you in, I'm not a suspect.'

The biro got slammed down. 'Are you telling me how to do my job?'

A bulb went on above my head – filth do not like that – said, 'No, I'm not.' Fitz's warning about leaving things to the force flooded back.

I got a cell to myself. Knew Mac would have one too. He wouldn't be chuffed – with his record, plod goes in hard. Still, there was no way they could hang anything on us. I knew this was all for show. For Fitz to make a point, the point being that it was his case, not mine.

I paced about a bit, rubbed my wrists where the uniform had tightened the cuffs. The thought of being back in the nick really boiled my piss; the filth could make it difficult for me to get to the bottom of things if they wanted. If I was looking at being tore up every step of the way, things were going to get messy. I was only just beginning to draw some conclusions, but I was still a long way off the point where I'd like to be.

My lungs were calling out for nicotine; a few other cravings chased them. I tried to figure in my mind what it was that Ian Kerr might have known, might have been able to put a threat on someone with, but nothing sparked. All I could see was his gouged eyes and battered face;

figured the image was staying with me for a while. I'd seen blood and gore before, but there was something about the brazenness of this that unsettled me; these bastards didn't care who they noised up.

After an hour or two I was taken from the cell. I walked holding up my beltless jeans to an interview room. A dippit-looking uniform, drooping lower lip, pushed me into a plastic chair. As he closed the door behind him he stared at me through the crack, glowered, said, 'Don't get out that fucking chair.' I had a wee laugh to myself – fucksake, I'd had worse warnings.

When he finally showed, Fitz the Crime wore the same suit that he had on the time I saw him with Davie, but his expression had changed completely. He shone red, forehead and cheeks. The tie was loosened and the shirtsleeves rolled up. He barked orders at a pug who scurried to the wall and stood silently.

Fitz ignored me, slammed down an envelope and a note file. He cursed and scratched at the edge of his temple; a heavy vein beat on the opposite side of his brow. When he'd read the closely typed note, his head jerked back, he tapped his shirt pocket, seemed to have forgotten something. 'Oh, Jaysus feck . . . my smokes.'

I knew this was theatre. He took a quick sketch at the pug on the door. 'Nip up for my tabs, boyo.'

The pug was sold, rushed out.

'Hold it . . . and get this c[illegible] a coffee.'

Nods, bowing and scraping.

Fitz rose, walked to the edge of the desk. His fat thigh seemed ready to burst from his trouser leg as he raised himself to sit on the desk. He rested there, silently, for only a moment, then he punched a fist into the air before me.

'I ought to crack yer feckin' nut, Dury,' he yelled.

Did that require an answer from me? I doubted it, went, 'Cut the shit.'

He riled up: 'A man's been clubbed to death on my feckin' watch, Dury. I'm answerable for this case, you know. Just what the feck are ye playing at?'

I played it cool. Slowly, I turned my head towards the wall, spoke: 'Funny, I don't remember you being this worked up about my brother's death.' I turned to face him.

He touched the tip of his nose. 'I don't like having you in here, Gus . . . after your loss.'

I tutted.

Fitz removed himself from the desk, walked round to the other side and sat down before me. 'Look, Gus . . . you have no idea how bad this looks.'

'What the fuck . . .? Do you think I give a shit about appearances, Fitz? My brother's been killed, and now there's another body to add to the count.'

Fitz ran a large hand through his greying hair. He exhaled slowly, said, 'What the feck were you playing at with Kerr?'

I knew where he was going with this. 'You know

what I was doing there: Ian Kerr worked for my brother.'

Fitz's eyes went Ren and Stimpy on me. 'Are you telling me you're working this feckin' case?'

I shot back, 'Of course I fucking am. My brother's been murdered, man.'

He squeezed the edge of the table in his hands, let it go. 'Well, that's where we have an issue . . . Don't think for a second, a millisecond even, that I won't haul your arse in if I catch you bollixin' about.'

I wasn't listening to any more of this. He knew I wasn't about to back off. He could have my help, or he could fumble about on his own. Fitz knew I was more use to him onside. 'Look, this Ian Kerr boy, he was at the factory five minutes after you left the other day . . . He was kicking off big time.'

He played coy: 'And, so?'

'Well, if you've done your checks you'll know he was on the wagons, but got punted. He thought he was due wages and he was none too chuffed about losing his job. When I saw him he was going scripto . . . And the bloke living next door to him says he was set to take matters into his own hands.'

Fitz sighed, pulled out a chair, dropped himself. 'That feckin pisshead. I wouldn't rate what he says too highly.'

I raised my tone: 'He was going to have the last laugh, so he said . . . I saw how they dealt with him at the factory, a couple of pugs hard-armed him out the back. Now, you're not gonna tell me he invited them round to his gaff to redecorate the place in his own claret, are you?'

'Dury, for fecksake, you're reaching.'

'No, Fitz, something's not right. Who works over a bloke in his fucking own front room? It's insane . . . unless they want to send a strong message.'

Fitz played with the knot on his tie. 'Dury, it doesn't stack up.'

I became agitated, stood up, leaned over him. 'Look, I know Kerr wasn't killed because he got lippy; he got killed because someone's got a lot to hide, a lot to lose.'

Fitz ran fingers over his sweaty brow; he looked suddenly tired. He had a fresh murder on his hands and was clearly wondering how much grief that was going to create for him, without my adding to it. I knew he was under no obligation to help me out, especially after I cracked it with him at the factory.

I said, 'Fitz, we go back.'

'Ah, go way outta that . . .'

I winced inwardly – it was a weak play. 'I know you don't owe me shit, Fitz. But that's my brother you have on a slab.'

He looked at me. I saw the flecks of red at the edges of his eyes; something told me he knew the territory, if not personally then he'd seen the effects of it enough times to sympathise. Now I saw a side to Fitz I wouldn't have believed existed. He looked away, exhaled heavily.

I sat down, said, 'What did you get from your visit to Davie Prentice?'

He shifted his weight, a large gut pressed on the table. 'He's a queer fish.'

'Got that right. Tell me what you found out.'

He shot me a glower. 'I can't give you anything, Gus.'

It freaked me out when he used my first name. '*Why*?'

'Let the force do its work . . . We're on the case.'

'Fitz, this is me you're speaking to. Just fucking spill, eh.'

He tapped his fingertips together, looked to the door. Clearly wondering where his lackey had got to with the tabs and coffee. Said, 'There's some . . . irregularities.'

I felt my mind ping. 'What do you mean?'

Fitz laced his fingers, then quickly pulled them apart. 'You'll have to trust me, Dury, I can't tell ye anything. How the fuck would that look to the folk paying my wages?'

I could tell he was coming around; I pressed him: 'Give me a hint.'

'I have no hints for ye, man. Jaysus, wouldn't ye only go off on one, getting into feck knows what. Let me spell it out for you: this is a police investigation, a very serious one and you are not exactly mascot material round here. Do ye really want to feck the force off again, Dury? . . . Well, do ye? Think about it, man – you know what it'll lead to.'

I was beyond threats or intimidation. I'd made all the calculations, knew I was onto a loser, but when was I never? I had one card to gamble on. I lowered my tone, tapped on a nerve: 'This is to do with the Czechs.'

Fitz's head jerked. 'Czechs?'

'Oh, come on, fuck off . . . The whole workforce has been laid off and replaced by cheap labour. Lot of ill feeling floating about.'

I was feeding him a line – I had nothing solid on the Czechs – but he was feeding me a line too. 'I don't know about any Czechs. All I will say to you is this . . .' He shifted forward, spoke softly: 'Be very careful who you tussle with, Dury. Our man Davie Prentice is connected . . . to some very serious people.'

I'd got Fitz's attention, maybe even got him back onside, said, 'When you say connected, do you mean the type of connections that might get me into trouble if I was to, say, stamp on fat Davie a bit?'

Fitz watched me as I spoke, then leaned back in his chair. 'I'd say that was a fair bet. In fact, I'd give you better than evens.'

I felt my voice drop low in my chest. 'Well, it's already too late for that. I'd place your bets, Fitz.'

CHAPTER 10

She looked the sort that I didn't run into a whole lot. Going by those I did run into, maybe this meant we'd get along just fine.

'So should I call you Dr Naughton?'

'Would you like to call me Dr Naughton?'

I figured pretty quick that this was the way it was gonna play out: she'd be big on questions, short on answers. 'Well, I suppose.'

Somewhere in my mind, I'd formed an impression of what a psychiatrist should look like. I blame television. She fitted none of the clichés, was too relaxed in a black linen shirt, grey-to-black cords and Kicker boots. Looked like she'd walked out of a Gap advert. Only the candy-stripe neckerchief bust the image, brought her back into the professions.

Dr Naughton sat to the side of her desk, explained she didn't want the object to be a barrier. I saw a young child's drawing in a picture frame hanging behind her, wondered: One of hers, or a client's maybe?

She eyed me over a clipboard. 'I usually ask new patients to tell me what they'd like to achieve with their first session.'

I laughed. 'Sorry . . . until recently I was going for a whole other type of session.'

She didn't say anything, gave me that over-the-glasses stare as a prompt.

'A *session* . . . y'know, a few bevvies.'

She smiled, an indulgent one, wrote something down on her clipboard. There was a cycling helmet and a Karrimor rucksack in the corner of the room; figured an outdoorsy type wouldn't approve. 'Is that me down there as a drinker now?'

'Is that what you want me to put down?'

Sighed, 'Wouldn't be wrong.'

She placed the clipboard to one side, took off her glasses altogether. She had very grey eyes. They unsettled me, reminded me of a caged wolf I'd once seen; but I was prepared to admit I was imagining things, making life difficult for myself. That was my usual modus operandi.

I scanned the pine bookshelves behind her. They looked pretty light on books.

Another question: 'Can you tell me a little about yourself?'

'Not much to tell.' I sounded defensive. Maybe it was just nerves but I didn't want a bad report to go back to Debs; tried to play along. 'Well, can you give me some pointers? *Yourself* covers a multitude of things.'

She returned to the clipboard and glasses, read from a list, 'Patient. Ambitious. Sensitive . . .' She stopped, looked at me again, continued, 'Temperamental. Pedantic. Domineering.' She put aside the notes once more. Removed her specs again and folded them in her hands. I noticed a wedding band and a very large rock sat above it.

Said, 'Yeah, that sounds like me.'

'You identify quite a few aspects of yourself in there?'

I nodded. 'At one time or another I think we all have the potential to be sensitive or patient or . . . temperamental.'

'When have you been temperamental, Angus?'

'Gus, please.'

'I'm sorry . . . Gus.'

She waited for my answer.

I sighed. 'Temperamental . . . I'm pretty temperamental now, have been for a few days . . . Look, my brother just died, you must know that.'

'Yes. It's in your file. How many siblings do you . . . did you have?'

The answer bit me: 'One. I've one left.'

The doctor looked to be weighing possibilities; something formed behind those grey eyes. 'What position were you in the birth order?'

The question seemed ridiculously formal. 'What does that matter?'

She shrugged. 'It doesn't really, I only ask to find out a little bit about you.'

She'd laid a guilt trip on me. This line of questioning had me rattled. I didn't want to talk about my brother. I didn't want to talk about our childhood, didn't she get it? 'I was the eldest . . . Michael was the youngest.'

She fidgeted in her seat, then pressed on. 'Was there a big age difference between you?'

'Eight years,' I snapped.

A lengthy silence drew out between us; she caught me checking my watch. She knew she'd unsettled me, made me feel uncomfortable with her questions. I wasn't ready to talk about my brother. I stood up. 'Can I smoke?'

She shook her head. 'I'm afraid not. We can take a quick break if you like.'

I nodded, took my tabs out my coat pocket and went to the door.

I walked straight out of the building in a white rage. I didn't know where it had come from. *Temperamental.* That was one of her words; yes, I was temperamental. I sparked up and took the smoke deep into my lungs. A ferocious chill filled the air; I'd left my Crombie inside and the shock of leaving the centrally heated rooms near knocked me out. I felt my shoulders start to tremble. *Debs, what the fuck have you signed me up to?* God, there wasn't much I wouldn't do for that woman but this was edging close to the limit. I felt like I'd just stepped out of a *Far Side* cartoon. The therapist was nice enough, but her professional sangfroid set my nerves jangling. Get a grip, Gus, I told myself. I knew I needed to open my mind to new experiences; like Mac said, I had been too closed-minded for too long. Christ, this might even help me. And I needed all the help I could get.

I dowped the tab, crushed it under my boot and went back inside. The waft of warmth gave me a smack. I felt myself automatically rub at the outside of my arms.

'Chilly out there,' I said.

Dr Naughton smiled. 'Yes, it is. You feel it when you leave these overheated buildings.'

I sat down, had grown more relaxed; she had a way of setting you at ease. Did they teach them that?

'Would you like to take off where we left?' she said.

'Where were we?'

'You were telling me about your brother . . . but if it's too painful to talk about him so soon after . . .'

I wanted to say 'he was murdered' but went with, 'No, it's fine.'

'What kind of upbringing did you have?'

I crossed my legs, fiddled with the seam of my jeans. 'Not your average.'

'Oh, no? In what way?'

'Aren't you supposed to say, what's average?'

She stayed silent, waited for me to continue.

'My father was a sportsman, a footballer . . . He had aggressive tendencies and, well, a violent streak.'

'Was your father violent towards you?'

'Shit yeah!' I uncrossed my legs, leaned forward. 'I'm sorry . . . I mean, yes . . . He was a drinker.'

She looked concerned – they taught her *that*,

surely. 'Did his violence extend to other members of the family?'

I nodded.

'To Michael?'

I nodded again.

I felt the middle part of my chest hardening, a stiffness spreading up my neck and into my jaw. My throat grew paralysed.

The doctor spoke: 'Perhaps that's enough for one day.'

I felt enormous relief. 'You sure?'

She stood up, extended her hand. 'Quite sure. You've been very strong. Thank you for that, Gus.'

It seemed a strange thing to be thanking me for. I felt utterly confused by this whole experience. Didn't know where to file it away in my head. I took my coat down from the stand. 'Do I make another appointment?'

'Yes, I'll see you again in a couple of days.'

I was surprised. 'So soon.'

'Yes, is that all right?'

I put on my coat. 'Fine.'

I walked to the door. Neither of us said goodbye. I turned, 'A couple of days – I must be a special case . . . or a nutcase.'

She said nothing.

CHAPTER 11

Felt relieved to be away from the doctor's questions. As I walked back to the car I rolled the quarter-bottle of Grouse in my hand. My heart was pumping hard. I didn't know whether I felt exhilarated to have got the session over with, or relieved it hadn't ended with my being carted away by the men in white coats.

In the car Usual was sitting in the front seat. I moved him aside – wanted to check the glovebox to see if Debs had missed any wraps. No joy; it was empty. I always kept a Shakin' Stevens 'Best of' on the dash – to deter thieves. It had found its way in here so I put it back. Debs had dropped off a couple of new CDs too. I picked them up, turned them over. 'Leona fucking Lewis . . . Holy crap, Debs, sure it's not *you* that needs to see a shrink!' The other CD looked more promising, an eighties compilation: 'Town Called Malice', 'Ghost Town', 'Golden Brown'. I knew she'd bought this for me. And what had I done? Ruined her surprise.

I felt low.

Put on the CD, tried to listen.

The first track was Bowie's 'Let's Dance'. I remembered I hadn't liked it at first, seemed too slick for the Thin White Duke. By the time it had gone to number one, though, I had the thing playing in the house all day long. As I listened to it now I saw the old video of the child finding the red shoes in the desert and dancing. I was taken to a different place:

There's a baby crying. I'm only eight or so, and I've never experienced a child in my home; my new brother cries constantly. I have to turn up Bowie just to drown him out. 'Let's Dance' gets louder. The neighbours bang on the wall. My father shouts. The baby screams on and on. My mother walks the floor patting his back. And then my father, roaring angry, rises and puts his foot through my record player.

I ejected the CD.

I couldn't listen to it. Dredged up too many memories. Wondered: Is this what a trip to a shrink does for you?

I pointed Usual into the back, pulled on my seatbelt. As I drove to Newhaven I tuned in the radio. The newsreader said there were riots in France at the government's handling of the country's economic collapse. I figured we were a ways off riots here: if the Scots had put up with being governed from England for three hundred years, it might take more than a shove.

The dog sniffed on the back seat, tried to lick up some leftover Bonio crumbs. I had forgotten to feed him. I'd been a bit remiss on the walking front too, but he would have to put up with that. I had more pressing matters to attend to.

At the gates of the factory I kept shoatie for Davie Prentice but he didn't show himself. The place looked to be in full swing, a few snout-casts out front hanging off tabs but they didn't stick about like the ones outside pubs. It was a quick drag, then back to work. I saw no sign of Andy the foreman either – he'd need shaking down later. Maybe Ian Kerr's death would give me some leverage, get him talking. He knew what the set-up in there was, and that was something I was going to have to take a closer look at.

I parked up, told the dog to sit. He watched me as I locked the car door. The sky threatened more snow, but the wind carried only the stench of onions from the burger van. I took a deck at the van. It said 'Chuck Truck' on the side in big yellow letters. Thought: More like make-you-fucking-chuck truck.

As I crossed, my Docs slipped on the icy road; wasn't about to land on my arse, so I calmed it. Steam rose from an aluminium chute at the side of the burger van. As I got closer the bloke inside leaned forward.

'All right, mate,' I yelled.

He seemed glad to see me, wide smile and a wave. His jet-black hair looked beyond Bryl-creemed, it sat so flat on his head it could have been ironed. 'Hello, hello,' he said.

'Christ, this is some weather.'

The bloke had his sleeves rolled up; a thistle tat on his forearm moved as he rubbed his hands together. 'Worst winter in twenty years, they say!'

'I bet they're right.' Cupped my hands, blew into them. 'You gimme a coffee?' He looked pissed off at that; I figured it was going to take a bigger parting with the readies. I scanned the menu for anything other than a heart attack. 'What's that there . . . *Wurst*?'

'Aye . . . sausage. Got it for the Czechs in there.' He motioned to the factory. 'They won't bloody touch it though.'

'They won't?'

'Nah, bloody bags of them I've got. Bought them off a Polish bloke, told me the Czechs would be gantin' for them.'

'But no takers, eh? . . . Sounds like your *wurst* nightmare.'

He laughed at that. 'Aye, very good. Very good.' He dropped off my coffee and I ordered a wurst, just to seal the deal.

'So, what's the go with the Czechs?'

He scooped out the long, grey sausage, put it in a styrofoam box, said, 'You want sauce on that?' I shook my head. He returned to leaning on the counter, continued, 'They're all Czechs in there now . . . punted the rest.'

'That sounds rough.'

He mock-laughed. 'That's about right – *rough*.'

I removed the lid from my coffee; a rainbow of

oil sat on the surface. 'I saw a pair of them the other day, looked hardy lads.'

A snort: 'Fucking crooks.'

'*You wha'*?'

He looked down the road, called me closer. 'I hear they're all living down in Leith, in the one big hoose . . . forty or fifty of them, fucking crammed in like rats.'

I played up: 'Get away.'

'I shit you not. There's a bloke runs squads of them about in a big Pajero' – he raised his thumb to the roof – 'kind of thing I could use to tow this . . . No' cheap. Nice black one it is too, all chromed up and that.'

'So what's his game?' I sipped the coffee; it was shithouse.

'You tell me, pal. He doesn't do a day's work in there, though, I'll tell you that for nothing.'

This all sounded dodge to me. 'This bloke, where's his house?' The burger man started to clam up, thought I'd went a question too far. Had to distract him again. 'Chuck us over a Mars as well, eh.'

He turned to the rack. I counted out the cash.

'Somewhere in Leith's all I've heard,' he said.

He thinned his eyes, waited for my reaction. I didn't want to press him. I might need to tap him again and I had the black Pajero to go on anyway. I took the Mars and the wurst, said, 'Grand coffee, chief. I'll catch you anon.'

He nodded and grumbled, slunk back in the van and picked up a copy of the *Star*.

In the car I opened up the box with the wurst; the smell of it made my eyes smart. I pushed it over the back for Usual. He sniffed at it and went to the other side of the seat. 'What? Not good enough for you?'

He put eyes on me, curled up and pretended to go to sleep.

'Stick, then.'

Mac stood outside the Wall: he was doing the door. This surprised me. He'd been manager when I had the place.

'Hod's got you at the coalface?'

He motioned me in. 'Aye well, it's a living and work's tight.'

I shrugged, said, 'You got that right.' I hadn't seen him since the filth had lifted us at Ian Kerr's gaff. 'You get any grief down the nick?'

Mac laughed it up: 'Fucksake, my record . . . what you think? Nothing I couldn't handle, though.' He led the way indoors. As we went, I felt my Docs sink in the heavy carpet – Hod had gone for the expensive stuff. It didn't seem to fit with the old Holy Wall I remembered. Our mate Col had run this pub for years: we'd added the 'Holy' prefix as a nod to him being deep in his religion. I hoped his beliefs served him where he was now.

'Well, what do you think?' said Mac.

I tried to hold back, but couldn't: 'It's a fucking eyesore . . . like *Pimp My Pub*.'

Where my picture of dogs playing snooker had once hung, mirror tiles and a matte-black handrail-cum-shelf had went up. New uplighters in the floor gave off – that worst of things – mood lighting. The entire place was bathed in an unnatural glow. There was a time when the only glow in here came from the tip of a Woodbine. I felt ready to chuck.

'Come on, man, it's Manhattan-style. Move with the times.'

I couldn't believe this was Mac talking. 'Aye right . . . it's tits. And you know it.'

Hod spied us, made his way over. He wore a tight white shirt, open at the collar, and there was a new bandido-style tache above his lip. The whole lot seemed to have been dyed, several shades darker than his natural colour. He looked like a man galloping towards a midlife crisis. Experimentation with facial hair – never a good idea for our age group.

'Fuck me, it's Quigley! What's it like Down Under, mate?' I said.

He dipped his head, patted his crotch. 'I got no complaints!'

Mac shuffled off to the bar. Hod grabbed me by the shoulders, put a bear hug on me. 'Come here, buddy.' He slapped my back, let me go, then stared in my eyes. 'Sorry about Michael.'

I had no words for him. We turned for the bar, watched Mac pour out a pint of Guinness. He took his time. I stared at the creamy head as it settled and felt every fibre of me twitch at the memory of that taste of dark.

'Still on the dry bus?' he said.

'Big time,' I snapped back to reality, '. . . gimme a Coke.'

Mac supped the head off his pint as Hod ducked under the bar and grabbed a bottle of Stella Artois. We moved towards the windows. They'd been widened, but the view outside still sucked. People bent double into the wind, clutching at Aldi carriers.

'How's trade?' I said.

He laughed, pointed to a couple of young lads in the corner drinking cans of Lech. 'If it wasn't for the Poles we'd be shut already. Fucking hope they don't nash back home anytime soon.' I got the impression business wasn't Hod's favourite subject at the moment. I knew he'd shut up his building firm a few weeks back. He was probably living off savings. 'Anyway, what's the Hampden Roar with your brother's joint? Mac told me about the Kerr bloke . . . Fucking rough.'

'You're not kidding. I was back round today.'

'And?'

I slugged on the Coke. The ice made my teeth twinge as I told them what the gadgie with the burger van had said.

'Labour scam,' said Hod. 'Saw it a few times in the building game.'

'What's that?'

He took a pull on the Stella, put down the bottle and started to chop the tabletop with his hands. 'It's like this: those fuckers round them up in some poor shithole abroad, take a wad off them for transport and papers, accommodation and the like. Most of them don't have the knackers so they get into debt, before they even get over here.'

'So, what, some boss man shifts them, puts them up . . . Then what?'

'Gets them set up with the social . . . all totally above board so far. They get them signing on, then they get hold of their books.'

'The Nat King Cole?' said Mac.

'Aye, aye. Take their dole books and their giros. The poor bastards can't go anywhere because the gang boss – and that's what they are, gangsters – has their passports and their papers, the lot.'

Mac piped in, 'Probably putting a threat on them back home too: you do this for us or such-and-such happens to yer maw or yer kids.'

It added up. I just didn't see where my brother's business came into all of this. It wasn't something Michael would entertain as a bad joke. 'Hang about. If they're signing on, how can they be working for Davie Prentice?'

Hod and Mac laughed together. Mac raised his bevvy to his mouth.

Hod said, 'They're crooks, Gus . . . heavyweight fucking crim-jobs. Think they're giving an Aylesbury duck for the law? They've got this house, probably several houses, full of totally desperate migrants and, what, they just let them sit about all day waiting for their giros?'

Mac put down his pint. 'Dream on.'

'They had them on the sites,' said Hod. 'All cash in hand, mind. Some bloke in a fancy motor would turn up at the end of the week and take the wages for twenty or thirty workers. And nobody, but nobody, batted an eyelid. These guys are hard core, this is a big racket and there's big money in it.'

I picked up a beer mat, folded it down the middle, sat it on the table. 'It's slavery,' I said.

Hod agreed, 'Aye, it is that.'

'One thing I don't get is, what I mean is, I can't see Michael having been involved in anything like that. He wouldn't have stood for it.'

Mac butted in: 'I can see that fat Davie cunt going for it. Man's a parasite – fucking reeks out of him.'

I agreed. 'Yeah, I can see him being in, if the numbers added up . . . but not under Michael's nose, and this set-up's been on the go long enough for my brother to have rumbled it.'

Hod lowered his voice, leaned back and tucked a thumb in a belt loop. 'Maybe he didn't like it, Gus. But maybe he *did* know.'

I knew what he was trying to say, and why he didn't say it. I spoke for him: 'You think my brother got offed because he was making a fuss about some Czech labour scam?'

Hod shrugged. 'Bears thinking about.' He stood up, looked out the window, confirmed the snow was back on. 'You want to go pay another visit to this fat Davie?'

I rose; Mac did too. I faced the pair of them, said, 'Let's leave him for now.'

Mac was ready to bust heads, ready to let swing with that hammer. 'Oh, come on, man, he's clearly up to his nuts in it!'

I took his point, but there was nothing to be gained from giving Davie another belt; yet, anyway. I started to fasten my Crombie. 'You'll get your chance with him soon enough. I can't risk putting the *big* frightener on him too soon.'

Hod spoke, 'He's right: if the guy's as piss-weak as you say he is, Mac, he'll only bolt.'

I said cheers for the drink, that I'd be in touch, headed for the door.

Hod slurped the dregs of his Stella, turned for the bar. 'Look, seriously, Gus, if there's anything I can do.'

'Well, there is one thing . . . Can you do some sniffing with your builder boyos, suss out who this Czech is?'

'I'll do my best.'

'He's got a houseful in Leith, drives a Pajero . . . if that's any help.'

He raised his bottle, tipped it to me. 'I'll get on it.'

As Hod went behind the bar, Mac grabbed me, said, 'Hold up a sec.'

I stopped at the doorjamb and he slipped something in my hand. As I looked down I saw he'd come good on some more speed.

'Nice one,' I said. 'I'll be in touch soon, real soon. Keep your hammer handy.'

CHAPTER 12

On the street my thoughts were gnashing in my head. There was more to the killing of my brother than I had first thought. I knew from the off it was no mugging gone wrong, but I couldn't grasp the idea that there was so much serious shit attached. There was a war going on inside me: demons wanted me to burst fat Davie's head for answers, and they were teamed up with the crew who wanted to get me back on the drink. At the moment the only force waged against them was the need to find justice for Michael, but that lot were being held back by my desire to do right by Debs. The way things were stacking, with Czech crims in the picture, it didn't augur well for our reformed relationship.

I battled with the snow. It was coming down hard. A bloke with a Christmas tree in polythene wrapping T-boned me at the junction. I slipped into the road but got held up by a big biffer in a parka. I thanked him; he had the hood up, couldn't speak, but nodded. I read the North Face badge on his chest, said, 'Be warmer there, likely.'

I carried on back to the car, got the notion I

was being followed and turned round to see North Face trailing me. He had the parka hood zipped up to the hilt. I saw two eyes, there's a phrase, *like pissholes in the snow*. I upped my pace – wasn't easy, the soles of my Docs had worn thin. I cursed Debs for refusing me a new pair. Still, the toecaps were hard enough; might be grateful for those soon, I thought.

The parka guy stayed on me as I reached the car. He'd upped his work rate but was obviously feeling it, took down the hood to expose a shaved head and bright red cheeks, puffed with the exertion.

As I got to the car, Usual sprang up at the window. He saw me and lobbed himself into the driver's seat. I looked up the street and saw North Face get into a run. A few yards off he reached out a hand for me as I got the keys from my pocket. Usual sensed my anxiety, started to bark. I had the key in the lock, turned it as the biffer appeared, put a grip on my shoulder – sent the dog ballistic.

'You got a fucking problem, mate?' I said.

He held tight. 'Trying to do you a favour.' He was Leith, I knew the accent. Saw him at Easter Road on a Saturday; not for the footy, for the post-match pagger.

I pushed him away. 'I'm very careful about who I take favours from. Never know what they might want in return.'

He turned his head towards the car, saw the dog snarl, teeth bared. I had a grip on the handle – if he moved he could go a few rounds with those jaws. He got wind of his predicament. I watched him look back up, caught sight of a spider's web tattooed on his neck. It looked amateurish, probably prison-issue. He spoke: 'Man up there wants a wee word.'

I glanced into the road. There was a line of cars. 'And who might that be?'

He brought his hand up to his nose: a sovereign ring on every finger, more tats. 'Come and see.'

I didn't like where this conversation was going; I saw that collection of Elizabeth Duke's finest coming the way of my mush soon. 'How 'bout I don't.'

The dog went Radio Rental, sprayed white froth at the window. The pug weighed his options; snow collected on his eyelashes. Any second now that one lonely brain cell was going to overheat. 'The big man won't be pleased if I tell him that.'

'Your trouble, not mine.'

'I could fucking drag you.'

I pressed out a grin, indicated the car. 'You could *fucking* try.'

Bastard did. Went for a low headbutt. He was too tall to disguise the move and I ducked it in time, pulled open the car door as he nutted the air and landed on the ground. Usual went right for his throat. The pug screamed like a loose fan belt as the dog tore into his parka. I let Usual take a few chunks out of the fabric, some orange lining spilled out. People in the street turned around; I didn't give them enough time to grab any details for a witness statement.

'Usual, drop it.' He stopped, stared up at me. 'Come away.'

The pug's feet slipped out before him as he pushed up the street on the bones of his arse. The dog watched him cautiously, growling. When North Face got far enough away to feel safe he leaped up, pointed to me and said, 'You're done, pal.' He drew a finger down his cheek. I'd seen this before: it meant I was to be marked with a razor. No one had ever come good on any ripping threat made to me. I put the dog on him again; Usual went for his heels as he ran. He attached jaws as the pug reached a dark Daimler.

I whistled and the dog let go, ran back down the street and jumped in the car. He sat on the passenger seat, panting. I swore he was smiling.

I got in the car and spun the wheels. Chucked a U-turn, palm in the windscreen like the taxi drivers do. I got blasted by the oncoming traffic, but I made my manoeuvre with only one front wheel clipping the kerb.

As I drew alongside the Daimler I checked out the pug. He had his Timberland boots up and was rubbing his ankle, grimacing. Beside him, sat between us, was a face I recognised instantly. Long and dour, pasty white. It was Ronnie McMilne. The man they called the Undertaker. I didn't know him, I only knew of him. I knew about lots of people I wished I didn't.

McMilne caught me staring at him. His face looked hollowed out, the cheekbones poking beneath the skin like meat hooks. I wondered if my own face registered what I was thinking: *Holy fucking shit*.

An electric window went down. I heard the pug cursing; rolled down my own window. The Undertaker put a bony hand on the edge of the car. I could make out the veins and liver spots from where I sat. He said, 'You're Gus Dury.' His voice unsettled me, a low rasp that sounded like sandpaper on glass.

I spat a quick reply: 'Yeah, that's me.'

'We need tae have a wee chat, Gus Dury.' I knew what one of his wee chats might amount to. I felt my chest tighten, like a belt was being pulled around it.

'Why would that be?'

The pug sussed me, couldn't believe what he was hearing and started to roar, 'I'll fucking do him here!'

He got out the door before McMilne calmed him, 'Sit doon, Sammy.' It only took three words: the big mug stood in the street, glowering over the car's roof towards me like he'd been tied to a post.

McMilne turned slowly around. He had the movements of a man much older than he was, or perhaps a heavily medicated one. He wore a double-breasted grey jacket, a black T-shirt underneath with a heavy gold chain sitting below the neck. It wasn't a good look, like a jakey trying to dress as Tony Bennett. His lips looked blue; little flecks of spittle dislodged as he spoke. 'I'll no' ask you again, laddie.'

I saw a break in the traffic. I got edgy now, creeped out by him to tell the truth, said, 'Glad to hear it.'

I didn't give him any time to reply, floored it.

The pug slapped the roof of the Daimler as I gunned the engine. I left the Undertaker, and whatever the fuck he wanted with me, behind. Vowed I'd worry about him another day.

CHAPTER 13

I'd never met Ronnie McMilne before. But I'd heard all about him. You live in Edinburgh, you move in my circles, it's impossible not to have heard of the Undertaker. It was a name that got put up when there was some serious threat called for. The story of how he landed the tag has been a city legend for the best part of two decades, and still the source of fevered pub talk. For years the rumour merchants had claimed McMilne had put a business rival in a coffin, buried him alive. The bloke had been dug up long after the worms got to him and McMilne was in the frame. A lot of hacks were chasing the story and at the time, I was one of them. We were all guilty of building up the Undertaker's rep in the papers. The filth were furious but they couldn't do him for the murder.

Every so often someone gets worked over in the city and the Undertaker's mentioned. His name was linked to grievous like the Colonel was linked to fried chicken. He'd built up a nice little empire on the back of knuckle-breaking too – few bawdy hooses, more than a few nightclubs, and he ran the lumps for every door in Edinburgh. I'd also heard that lately he'd become the go-to man on any kind of knock-off merchandise in the town. Touched just about every racket, except skag. That was a different game entirely.

As I got in the tenement I rested my back on the door, sighed.

Usual raced away up the stairs before me. I heard him scratch at the door. Debs let him in, made a fuss over him.

'Gus, that you?' she yelled.

'Yeah. Yeah . . . just coming.' I got moving. The stairs reeked again; another bastard had taken a slash while I'd been out. I covered my nose with my coat sleeve on the way up. I raged inside. Tried to make sense of the Undertaker's appearance and what he might be after. I didn't want him to show up at the flat, but I figured it was a long shot that he'd know where I lived. He'd obviously been asking about, heard I had the Wall once and chanced his luck. Still, the idea of being measured for one of his coffins didn't exactly thrill me. This turn of events spelled bad shit, in block letters. How it connected to Michael's murder, though, that was the question I wanted answered the most.

As I reached the landing Debs spoke: 'We're going to Jayne's.'

'What? *Why?*'

She frowned. 'God, do you need to ask?'

I needed a hit of speed, played for a diversion. 'Well, you better feed Usual first.'

Debs turned away, got back to fussing over the dog as I slipped the speed out of my coat pocket and headed to the cludgie. I shotgunned a couple of wraps, rapid style. I inflated the bag, then retied it. It held watertight as I opened up the cistern and sat it next to the ballcock.

Debs was standing in the hall when I came out. 'You set?'

The car's engine was still warm, it started first time. Debs fired into me about the therapist as we drove. I held schtum. Thought I might start prattling on with the speed coursing through me and I didn't want to give her any more ammo. She got the message. By the time we hit the Grange, she'd more to think about.

A huge Christmas tree lit up the front room in my brother's house. It shone through the window. Looked to be such a happy home. Thought: How could anyone doubt it?

'Beautiful tree,' said Debs.

'Yeah, she must have just got it in, wasn't there before.'

'How can she do it? God, that's so brave.'

I parked, two wheels up on the kerb. 'It'll be for Alice – she always loved this time of year.'

Debs leaned over, touched my arm. 'Remember we used to take her sledging when she was really wee?'

I smiled. 'Yeah, I remember.' Poor Alice, this time of year would never be the same for her. The thought of what this had done to her wounded me more than anything. It was another life damaged, in my battered family. Debs put her arms round me, held tight as we walked to the door. Somehow it didn't seem right, me being so happy to have Debs back in my life and my brother's family destroyed.

A heavy frost was beginning to settle as Debs pointed to the house, said, 'Who's that?'

On the path round the side, next to the wheelie bins, stood Vilem. He was leaning against the wall, smoking a cigarette and staring straight at me.

'That's the lodger,' I said.

'The what?' Debs edged forward, squinted.

'Apparently Michael took in a lodger a little while back. He works . . . worked for him.'

Vilem realised he was being talked about, dowped his tab, a shower of orange sparks hitting the ground as he stamped it out.

'Look, go on ahead without me, I want a word with him.'

Debs looked unsure. 'Gus, we came together . . .'

'Yeah, I'll only be a minute. On you go.'

I jogged away from her, left her to go inside by herself. As Vilem clocked me coming for him, he turned down the path.

'Hey, not so fast,' I yelled.

He kept on. His limp had eased a bit now, but the shifty demeanour was still in place. He picked up his pace a little, tried to pair it with a casual air, but it wasn't working. I hooked my fingers in his collar, yanked good and hard. He stopped dead. As I spun him I made sure Debs was out of sight – she'd gone indoors.

'Bit jumpy aren't we, Vilem?'

'Get your hands off me.'

I showed him my palms. 'Not touching you . . .'

He bristled, flared his nostrils. 'What do you want with me?'

'Och, c'mon . . . I think, by this stage, you know fucking well what I want, boyo.'

He spat. I watched the corners of his eyes contract as he tried to assess me. Like I was playing. I spun him towards the wall, put my forearm under his chin. He went up on his toes – his eyes widened now. 'Have I got your attention, fuckhead? . . . I mean your full attention?'

He tried to nod, realised it was gonna choke him, gibbered, 'Yes. Yes.'

'Good, then listen . . . real carefully.' I leaned in close, made sure my breath was hitting him. 'I've got your little game sussed, well and truly . . . Now, I don't know who's pulling your strings yet, but soon as I find out, someone's going to pay for my brother's death. You can pass that on. And while you're at it, let them know I won't be as easy to shut up as Ian Kerr.'

The name hit home. I could see the flash of recognition in his face. I thought for a moment he was about to speak, that I'd done a job on him, but there was a shriek from the back yard. It was Alice.

She stood plugged in to her iPod, obviously

shocked. She seemed to tremble. Her eyes looked red, like she'd already been crying. She pulled the sleeves of her baggy striped top over her hands, wiped her nose on her sleeve.

I let Vilem down, said, 'Alice . . .'

She looked at me, then bolted.

Vilem got a shot of bravery, pushed me away as he ran for the house. For a second I was torn, but knew I had to go after her.

'Alice . . . Alice!' I shouted.

She was off running, bombing it down the path and onto the street.

As I got into the car she was already out of sight. The roads were treacherous. A bloke in a Honda Civic flashed me at the lights; he had right of way but was wary of tackling the icy road with me sitting so far out of the junction. A slight loss of traction and his rear end was likely to go crashing into my grille. I waved him as I passed and got a nod back.

I drove around a few streets but she'd lost me. Must have spent an hour looking; knew, by now, Debs would have blown a fuse.

Banged the dash. '*Shitballs.*'

I pulled in at the late-night Spar to get some tabs. A crowd of teenagers were hanging about on the steps. Skinny jeans and T4 haircuts all round. Arse-cracks showing above their belts. I thought they must be insane in this weather to go about exposing themselves. They looked a right bunch of twats; even the blokes had kohl round their eyes, and one of them was making his way straight for me.

'Got a ciggie, my squire?' He was three sheets, grinning at me from beneath a Wookie-barnet, waving a palm in a circular motion. It was the most effete bit of begging I'd ever seen.

Said, 'Get fucked.'

His friends woop-wooped. I had him pegged as a student, regretfully one of our home-grown lot – around here they breed these invertebrates as effectively as the ones the English ship into the New Town every year.

I looked him up and down, waited for a put-up, got none.

He slunk off to his wooping buddies, showing me some red scants sitting above his kecks. They high-fived and handed him a tin of Scrumpy Jack for the performance.

I'd never wanted to drink alcohol less. I'd be hoarding this memory, bringing it back in widescreen the next time I felt tempted by the bevvy.

In the store I got my order in. 'Can you give me forty Marlboro?' Bloke on the till went for the yellow pack, the lights. 'Eh, no . . . the red ones,' I said.

He put them back. 'The heavy hitters!'

Smiled, went, 'Aye.'

'It's usually the others they go for round here . . . Saturday smokers, y'see.'

He grinned; a line of stained teeth showed me

he was a big-time tobacco fan. He dropped his smile quickly as he caught sight of a ruckus in the back of the shop, shouted, 'Hey, you gonna pay for that?'

I turned to see two of the yoofs from out the front and a young girl. They shoved a bottle of weapons-grade cider up her baggy striped jumper. I knew at once who it was. 'Alice!' I yelled.

She dropped the bottle and it bounced off the floor, then it burst, spraying out an arc of frothy liquid. The bloke behind the counter started shouting. The yoofs and Alice ran for the door. I went after them.

On the pavement I caught sight of their skinny arses chanking it up a close. They had their hoods up, laughing their guts out, slipping on the icy streets as they went. I made a sprint of a few steps but felt a stitch as I reached the corner, watched them disappear into darkness.

The bloke from the Spar came up behind me, panting, his cheeks going like bellows. 'Did you see them?'

'Gone,' I said.

He toppled over, put his hands on his knees. 'I'll need to get your details for the police.'

'Police . . . they never got away with anything.'

He stood up, still panting. 'I need to tell them. We lost stock, that's a bottle we could have sold.'

I passed him a fiver, said, 'Write it off.'

He shook his head. 'No, can't do that. Who was that girl?'

I shrugged my shoulders.

'You knew her name, though.'

I walked away. 'I was mistaken.'

'You called her Alice.'

I kept walking. 'Alice . . . Alice . . . Who the *fuck* is Alice?'

CHAPTER 14

Loud thumping on the door of the flat woke me. Usual kicked off, barking his best. I dragged myself from my pit; Debs had left for work hours ago, without a word. Figured I'd have to get used to that for the foreseeable.

I opened the door. Was the guy with the mop and bucket again. He said, 'Stair money.'

My eyes weren't fully open, my mind barely sparking. '*You wha'*?'

The bloke scratched his head through the beanie. 'I just cleaned the stairs there.'

I found my voice, some marbles worth throwing about. 'Didn't I speak to you about this just the other day?'

He stopped scratching. 'Aye, well . . . stairs were needing cleaned.'

He wasn't wrong, but I wasn't giving this schemie daytripper a button. 'So what?'

He held out his hand. 'Three pounds, chief.'

I closed the door on him. I got two steps towards my bed when I heard him knock on the auld wifey at number three's door. I returned to the spyhole. She was parting with her poppy again. I wasn't sure I was happy about this, made a note to check it out later.

I showered. We were out of soap, had to use Debs's Clean & Clear facial wash all over. Left me feeling clean, if not clear of anything. I'd finally found some music I could listen to: Jeff Wayne's *War of the Worlds*. There was something about Richie Burton's whisky-soaked tones that touched the void in me. The only trouble was the recording drove Usual mental. Every time the turning of the cylinder sounded, the dog went off his scone – barked and snarled like we actually had the Martians in our gaff.

I was wondering what my next move should be when my mobi rang.

Voice said, 'Dury . . .' It was Fitz, a croak in his throat as he spoke. 'I thought I better give you a call.'

He had my attention. 'You did?'

'I, eh, there's no easy way to tell you this, Gus, so I'm just going to come right out with it.'

He'd went back to using my Christian name again; it still unnerved me.

'I want to let you know that your brother's death is no longer being treated as a mugging gone wrong.'

This meant little to me; official or otherwise, it had been fucking suss to me from the get-go. 'That's what you've decided, is it?'

Fitz chose his words carefully, muttered a bit, shuffled the phone about. ''Tis all I can say.'

I wanted to know what had changed his mind. But he played coy. Fitz knew there was no way I'd let him call me up like this and leave it at that. I pressed him: 'So what's changed your mind?'

Now he went overcautious. I could imagine his gaze flitting about the room, looking for a distraction to light upon. 'Really, for sure, there isn't another thing I can give ye, Gus.'

'But this is all quite a leap from just another Meadows mugging.'

A sigh. Followed by another. 'As I say, I'm not at liberty to disclose any more of the relevant facts at the moment.'

'*Relevant facts . . . at liberty to disclose*: have you got a fucking media release in front of you, Fitz?'

The line went quiet. When Fitz spoke again he put a finality in his words that said *Don't push it*: 'I've got to tell you that, for now anyway, we won't be able to release the . . . remains.'

The word stung me. *Remains. The remains*. All that was left of my brother. I held my breath. Not consciously, my breathing just stopped.

Fitz broke in: 'Gus, are ye there?'

I was, but only just. 'I want to meet.'

'I don't think that will be poss—'

'Don't jerk me off, Fitz. I want to see you, today.'

His tone rose: 'I have a desk full of paperwork in front of me. There's no way I can get—'

I didn't listen, broke over him: 'Round the back of the parliament there's a place – Beanscene.'

He snapped, 'What's that, some fucking dyke hangout?'

For a copper, he wasn't very community aware. 'It's a coffee shop.'

He wasn't pleased by the proposal, but I could tell he was thawing. '*Beanscene* . . . by the holy . . .'

'One hour.'

Hung up.

I put on the radio as I dressed. Prime Minister Hash Brown was on the news, promising to do everything in his power to protect the stability of the banking system. I almost laughed. There was fuck all stability in the banking system – it had gone tits up. And the rest of us weren't that far behind. The man's arrogance astounded me: there he was strutting the world stage, talking up his role in the great economic rescue of the world and forgetting totally the part he and the swinging dicks in the City had played in getting us here.

'The jobless figures are now greater than two million,' said the newsreader. 'And now to other news . . .'

Other news! There was no other fucking news. Try putting food on the table without a job. I flicked the switch to off. The standard of reporting on this financial storm had been piss poor; as a trained hack it terrified me. Worse, got me ranting. 'I could do his job,' I roared, 'read the fucking news! Christ, I could write it as well.' I sounded like Yosser Hughes, wondered how far I was from the 'Giz a job' speech.

I dressed in a pair of grey cords from Next, and a black Stone Island top that Debs had bought me. The top fitted like a dream, definitely a touch better than I was used to wearing. I played with the zip on the front a few times; the noise it made was poetry, could never get used to that. My Docs looked decidedly down at heel. If I had the Gene Tunney I'd have sprung for a new pair by now; Debs had offered to get me some Caterpillar boots but I'd said no. She'd even suggested a pair of pointy numbers that wouldn't have looked out of place on Donald and Davey Stott, but I declined. I'd be sticking with the Docs, no matter what was in fashion.

Suited and booted, I took a quick delve beneath the cistern in the bathroom, got out my wraps of speed. I had a quick blast on a couple and sealed up the bag again, returned it into hiding beneath the cistern lid. I knew if Debs found this it was lights out. But I also knew she wasn't as suspiciously minded as me.

I had to leave Usual behind. Chucked him a couple of Bonios and said, 'Mind and behave . . . No digging on the couch!'

Arthur's Seat was covered in snow as I schlepped down to the half-a-billion-pounds parliament. It was our national shame; well, one of them. The cost had been the cause of massive anger and political recriminations, but none of the main players had lost their hats. I'd read in the paper recently that, at night, the forecourt of the place had been taken over by skateboarders. I saw their tracks now: wheel marks, skids and doughnuts on the concrete. A half-billion skate park – money well spent.

Out the back of the parliament a Marks and Spencer food van was being unloaded. Christ, this got my goat – did those bastards deprive themselves of nothing? Fucking Markies food deliveries whilst half the country is on bread rations. It boiled my piss.

I saw Fitz up ahead, outside Beanscene. I wondered why he hadn't gone inside. As I drew closer I saw the place had been shuttered. Another victim of the economic catastrophe.

'This place gone to the wall?' I said to him.

He seemed pleased. 'I didn't like the sound of it anyway . . . *Beanscene*: fucking hell, amn't I in the wrong get-up entirely without the dungarees?'

For a man in his exalted position, I was amazed at his lack of political correctness; I thought it had pervaded every hierarchy in the country by now.

'Come on, then, up to the Mile.'

We stationed ourselves in as near as you got to a greasy spoon on the city's main tourist thoroughfare. Fitz ordered a coffee for me and a pot of tea for himself. 'God, I used to fooster my days away in these places when I was on the beat.'

We both knew those days weren't so long ago – Fitz had ascended the ranks rapid-style with my help. I'd handed him clean arrests aplenty. I'd turned his success to my own advantage more than a few times, though.

The drinks came. Fitz took the lid off his teapot, stirred. I spooned the froth off my coffee, said, 'So, here we are.'

'Here we are indeed.'

There didn't seem any point messing about. I went for the jugular: 'The other day, when you told me to be careful.'

Fitz played it cool, kept stirring. 'Uh-huh.'

'You told me Davie Prentice was connected.'

'Did I? . . . I don't remember.'

I grabbed his hand. His eyes went to mine. 'Fitz, put the fucking spoon down – it's stirred already.'

He lowered the spoon, replaced the lid of the teapot. 'Stirred it is.'

I had his attention now, said, 'I had a visit . . . not the kind of visit I like to get.'

'Now who would that be from?' Fitz's meaty neck quivered above his shirt collar. He tried to play it casual but his colour flushed a little too much to make the move convincing.

'Ronnie McMilne.'

He ran his tongue over the front of his teeth, spoke softly: 'The Undertaker.' He said the name all too casually, as if it had been one he'd batted about quite a bit recently.

'The very same.' I sipped my coffee, lowered the cup again. 'Now, I'm taking a wild guess that when you told me to be careful, when you told me that fat Davie was connected, you were thinking of . . .'

I lowered my voice to Fitz's level, 'our man with the interest in coffins, the Undertaker.'

'All right, Dury, we've heard the name, don't think there's any need to mention it again.'

In the years I'd known Fitz, I'd been impressed with the way he had grown. The man of old would have been cursing and blasting me for presuming to have sussed him out like this. The mature Fitz had learned to keep schtum – he'd picked up a few tricks at all the meetings and seminars.

'No need at all,' I said.

Fitz poured out his tea. We had a routine for the exchange of information. I gave him something, he gave me something and nothing. This time the rules were different. Fitz knew I wasn't working an angle on him, he knew all I was after was peace of mind. I could see the years we'd known each other accounted for something with him; he felt for my loss.

'I have taken control of the investigation myself,' said Fitz.

'You have?'

He reached for the sugar bowl. 'It's, er, well, let's just say it touches on another aspect of my current portfolio.'

'Cut the shit, Fitz. I don't want a PowerPoint presentation.'

'Y'what?'

'Gimme it in plain fucking words . . . minus the management speak.'

He spooned in some sugar, stirred it up. 'Our

man – the McMilne fella – we have a task force that's been following him about and they report to me.'

'How did you make the connection to Michael?'

'By chance . . . Isn't it always the way.'

'Go on.'

'There were some reports of . . . intimidation of workers.'

I'd seen the workers: couldn't imagine any of them raising police complaints when they were living under a crime lord in a Leith kip house. I let this slide, wasn't about to overburden Fitz with information when I didn't know how he was going to use it. Plus, I wanted to keep his focus on the Undertaker: figured he'd have a better chance of success there than I would.

'Intimidation of workers . . . reported to the force?'

'After a fashion.'

He had a snitch. Someone on the inside was talking. 'Are these workers still employed by my brother's firm?'

He shook his head. 'No. No. These are people that have moved on.'

People like Ian Kerr. 'You mean they were punted . . .'

A nod. 'That's about the size of it.'

They knew something that they shouldn't, that was clear. 'So, McMilne gave them a scare. Why?'

'My information was that our fella was running a racket through the factory's transport channels.

Some of the drivers played along, some didn't. In the end, they all did.'

Until a few days ago, I'd thought my brother's business was totally kosher. I couldn't conceive of any kind of dodge, least of all one in league with the criminal underworld, one that had cost lives. 'What're you saying, Fitz?'

'They were trucking in contraband in the company vehicles.'

I couldn't take it in. The Undertaker didn't touch the drugs game in the city, I knew that. 'Trucking in what?'

Fitz took a sip of his tea. 'You fucking name it: fags, booze, Tommy Hilfiger knock-offs . . . anything they could get their hands on. Black market's exploded lately.'

My mind burned. Did Michael know about this? I couldn't believe it. Sure, there were the red letters looking for payment, Jayne joking about straitened times . . . but cosying up to Ronnie McMilne? I just didn't see Michael being capable of it. 'If you know about this, why haven't you shut it down?' I said.

Fitz looked to be clamming up again. 'This is all, what you might say . . . recently acquired information.'

I ran my hands through my hair. My head hurt. I felt blood rising in me. I squeezed my fingers; the pressure piled on my skull.

Fitz sipped at his tea, lowered the cup and added some more from the pot. I felt tempted to smash the lot over his head, not out of any anger towards him but out of my desperation to know what he knew.

'I want the name of your snout,' I said.

For the first time since we'd met up, Fitz lost his cool. His face inflated. 'Are ye out of yer feckin' mind?' The Irish in him came to the fore: 'I'm no feckin' informer, Dury. Ye can forget it! Go way outta that!'

I stood up so fast that my chair scraped noisily along the floor, attracted glances. 'Okay, I'll go it alone . . . But expect more blood.'

I went for the door.

He called me back: 'Dury.'

I halted.

Fitz rose, walked to within inches of me. 'Stay away from McMilne.'

I tutted, 'Shuh . . . thanks for the warning.'

As I turned he grabbed my coat sleeve, 'I'm not kidding: the man's . . . lethal.'

I snatched back my arm. 'He's not the fucking only one.'

CHAPTER 15

I tanked it up the Mile, each step on the cobbles an explosion. I held the Grouse bottle in my pocket so tightly that I thought it might shatter in my hand. I didn't care. I would have blood on my hands soon enough. I was ready to kill for my brother. The Undertaker, fat Davie, some unknown fucking Czech crim working out of the factory Michael built up – I didn't care.

A car sounded a horn at me – I'd walked on the road, shouted, 'Go fuck yourself!' I turned to see a school-run mum in a Stockbridge tractor. She had the revs up too high, but that engine was way behind me in the burn stakes. I brought my fist down on the bonnet. She gasped at me, ready to raise herself and confront me, but something in her advised against it. She put the foot down and forced me to jump aside; I let out a kick at the back fender as she went. Called after her, 'Fuck off, you snooty cow!'

Eyes lit on me, all the way up and down the street. A daft-looking tourist in a tartan cape dropped jaw.

'What? Anyone else fucking want some?' I yelled.

People took off in every direction. I got off the road, headed to the World's End pub. I stormed through the door, straight to the bar. The place looked dead. Usually this deep in the heart of tourist central was stowed out.

Barman came over. 'Yes, what can I get you?'

'Whisky.' I said the word before I felt its consequence register on my mind.

I watched the barman. 'A blend or a malt?'

I didn't care. 'Whatever.'

He creased his brows, went to the wall behind the bar. I watched him put a glass to the bottle of Teacher's, fill a measure.

He placed it before me, gave me a price.

I grabbed a crumple of bills and coins from my pocket, dumped the lot on the bar. He fished out the right amount and left me.

I stared at the glass of scoosh. I didn't need to raise it to my nose to pick up the aroma. I could have guessed this blend in a room of one hundred others. I felt the essence of it seeping into me. I was calmed by it. I knew this was my proper place. I knew I was home. I raised the glass and stared at it in the full light. One sip, that's all it was going to take. One little, insignificant sip of liquid. One moment on the lips, in the mouth, and over the throat. One second in the stomach, and then . . .

I lowered the glass.

Picked up my money.

The barman looked at me as if he considered calling for assistance.

I turned away, left the bar.

On the street a piper was playing now. The skirl of the pibroch attracted a crowd of tourists, but it left me cold. I wanted to be away from all things familiar. I wanted to be in a new place, where there weren't memories on every street wherever I looked. I needed to escape my past, but my future didn't seem to hold any alternatives.

I put up the collar on my Crombie and schlepped up the Mile. At the Radisson Hotel I got in a taxi and gave the driver the address for the Burlington Practice. He checked me in the rear-view mirror; obviously the name registered. Edinburgh cabbies know better than to make conversation with nut-jobs – they have enough experience of ferrying them about in a city full of them. I was grateful for his silence.

I fell into a state of high anxiety; figured Dr Naughton had sussed this tendency in me right from the off. I thought about my meeting with Fitz, what it meant. I was heading down a dark path. The Undertaker had an interest in my brother's affairs – fucking hell, Michael, what were you thinking? I wished him alive so I could grab him by the shoulders, shake some sense into him. I saw his face before me, questioned what level of desperation drew him to get into such a racket of shit. Did he know what he was doing? Surely he did, my brother was nobody's fool. I wondered how bad things had got for him, could see the escalation of the stakes as he got in deeper and deeper . . . and then what? I needed to know the how and the why and the who. I wasn't giving up until I did.

The taxi pulled up. I passed the cabbie a ten-spot, schlepped to the door of the practice. The path had been cleared of snow, but icicles still hung on the railings. Inside, my doctor was impassive, a bland, unreadable expression on her as she greeted me.

'Don't you want to take your coat off, Mr Dury?' she said.

'I thought you were going to call me Gus.'

She didn't respond to that. I kept my coat on and she brought me a bottle of water. I refused to take it and she placed it on the floor beside me. I acted like a child; I felt as helpless. Her hair looked wet. It smelled of apples; the thought of it made my eyes moisten, reminded me of a vague sensation from childhood. Scrumping for apples – how old was I when I did that? Where was Michael at the time? God, why did I have to think of that now? Was there a single moment in my past I could face again?

I looked at the pine shelves with the doctor's slim collection of books on them, tried to read the titles, distract myself. 'I thought you'd have more books.'

She smiled at me, grateful I was becoming more chatty. 'Everything's online now.'

I hadn't thought, said, 'I see.'

She put her hair back in a band. 'I'm sorry: tried to cram in a trip to the gym . . .'

That explained the wet hair, the smell of apples. 'What shampoo is that?'

She blushed – seemed out of place for her, 'Palmolive.'

'Oh, right . . . It smells familiar.'

I calmed down a notch. Got up, removed my jacket. The cycle helmet and Karrimor still sat in the corner.

As I returned to my seat, Dr Naughton spoke: 'I wanted to ask you about the kind of people around you at present.'

'Okay, go on.'

'What are they like? . . . Affectionate? Impatient? Bad-tempered?'

I shook my head. Who did she want me to think of? Debs, Mac, maybe Fitz? Said, 'Some are, some aren't.'

The question wasn't the opener she'd hoped for. She paused a moment, then tried again. 'I was thinking about what we spoke of towards the end of the last session.'

'Oh, yes.' We'd spoken about Michael.

'Would you feel comfortable telling me something about your brother?'

I shrugged. I felt strangely drawn out of myself now I was here, said, 'Guess so.'

'Could you tell me about something that happened to you both?'

'What kind of thing?'

'Perhaps something from your childhood.'

I remembered something. It was the smell of apples that reminded me.

'I robbed an orchard when I was about twelve, brought home bags of apples. They were cooking apples and when my father came in from the pub, utterly blootered as usual, he tried to eat one. He spat it out and then threw the whole lot in the midden at the bottom of the yard.'

Dr Naughton seemed interested. 'Is there more to the story?'

Was there ever. I went on, 'The next day my brother, he was only young, about four, found all the apples spilling over the midden and I told him the fairies had left them . . . My mam had told me the midden was a fairy rath when I was his age, that's where I got the idea.'

Reliving the memory now, in front of the doctor, didn't seem so hard. I felt a glow remembering my young brother. 'So Michael must have spent the day digging in the midden, looking for the fairies, and about dinner time he appeared at the table in tears. He was covered head to toe in muck and carried a hell of a stench.'

I could see him now, his face smeared black with soot and dirt. 'My father stamped his fist on the table: "What is this you are bringing into my house?" His voice trembled so much that it seemed his next word might hurl the plates and dishes to the floor.'

I smiled as Michael's words came back to me. 'My brother said he was looking for the fairies: "It's a fairy rath in the yard . . . Angus showed me." In a flash, all eyes shifted on me, then my father came racing towards me and lifted me from my chair. I knew I was in for trouble as he dragged me by the hair into the yard.'

I stopped talking.

Dr Naughton gently prompted me: 'Go on. What happened next?'

'My father grabbed my head, his whole hand fitted round it, and then he pushed me face down in the midden. There was the sound of shuffling as my mother and family came to see what would happen next and then my father roaring, "D'ye see them yet? . . . I'll fucking put you through it, I will." My mouth filled up with muck and potato skins, and he was roaring, "I'll put ye through it, I'll put ye through it." My mouth filled with dirt – I can taste it now. The rotting waste, in my nostrils and my eyes. Filled with thick black soil that stuck to me and choked me and then . . . the earth was frozen and hard where the midden ended.'

I looked at the doctor. Her mouth had drooped, her hand gripped the chair's arm. I wondered if she wanted me to stop. I carried on.

'I cowered from him. He looked lost in his fury, then a bizarre thing: a mouse scurried out from the midden and he shouted, "Vermin." Even with my eyes full of muck, I saw Mam and Michael and Catherine watching as my father's great boot stamped on the creature's head. The children screamed at the sight of it and Mam gathered them around her, led them back to the house.'

'I think that's enough,' said Dr Naughton.

I wasn't finished.

'I can still remember the way the mouse's little legs kept going – it wasn't dead yet. He brought down his boot again, and again, until the mouse was just a bloodied tangle of flesh, and tiny white bones.'

The doctor rose and wheeled her chair back behind her desk. 'I think we'll leave it at that, Gus . . .'

CHAPTER 16

After the visit to the shrink I spent two days in dock. Moped about the flat, doing the one thing I knew I shouldn't: thinking. I'd once asked my brother why he worked so hard. His answer had shocked me: 'It stops you thinking.' I knew at once what he meant, but I'd never been able to apply the wisdom. Only way *I* knew how to switch off the white noise in my napper was with drink. In the last few days I'd grown fixated on the whisky brands with which I'd once obliterated my thoughts. I'd come close to the World's End incident again, had even broken the seal on the quarter-bottle of Grouse I carried in the pocket of my Crombie, but my lips never touched the rim.

The visits to Dr Naughton had spurred my memories. I was deluged with events from the past. I thought of Michael and I thought of myself. I thought of how different we were, and also how similar. We were both men who had gone through a brutal upbringing. I never understood all those people who whined about a loss of youth, or complained about the surrender of dreams to maturity. Just getting to adulthood was achievement enough for us both. We weren't trading in any excitement for the drudge of the workaday world – we were escaping to it.

My brother wanted better for his family, but I worried that his passing had put any easy happiness out of reach for them. I'd kept schtum about Alice's performance at the Spar; I didn't want to bring the girl any more grief than she already had, but clearly something needed to be done for her.

I picked up my mobi. Jayne had gave me Alice's number, asked me to have a word. Apparently I was the only one in the family the girl didn't rate an old grunter.

I dialled.

Ringing.

She answered, 'Yeah, hi.'

'Alice, it's Gus.'

'*Who*?'

Bad start, said, 'Gus . . . your uncle.'

'All right. Whatcha want?'

She had that 'am I busted?' tone to her voice. I cleared that up for her: 'Well, I'm not phoning to blast you for the shoplifting attempt if that's what you think . . . I've snaffled a few bottles of Woodpecker in my day.'

She giggled. 'Mum would go spare if she found out.'

I knew she was right. 'Look, so how you keeping? Are you sorted?' I winced on the last word – I sounded like Jonathan Ross, like I was trying too hard to be *down with the kids*.

'Yeah, guess.'

'You sure, there's nothing . . . bothering you?'

A gap on the line. Then, 'I have to go now.'

I'd only just called. 'What do you mean? I just got you.'

'I have to go.' Her voice trembled.

'*Alice . . .*'

She hung up.

I looked at my mobi. The 'call ended' counter flashed; our talk's duration was fifty-seven seconds.

Said, 'That went okay.'

My niece wasn't handling her father's death at all well, that was clear. Something would have to be done to stop her becoming seriously troubled, or worse. I toyed with the idea of talking to Jayne or maybe one of her friends but I didn't feel capable. I mean, who was I, fucking Oprah? I felt a stab of guilt at not being able to do anything for her, but what could I do, save keep an eye out for her and offer the odd word of support? I knew we were all on our own, after a certain point.

There had been a story in the newspaper about parents buying Kevlar-lined blazers for their children at a city school – they were worried about a rise in crime being a by-product of the economic crash. It seemed like paranoia to me, but it did show they cared. Could you care too much for a child? I definitely wasn't the man to answer that – I had no experience on that score.

I dropped my breakfast dishes in the sink, threw Usual a spare crust. He snatched it in mid-air. The water in the taps felt cold, but I saved on the immersion heater and washed up with it anyway. Easter Road stadium glared at me through the window as I filled the sink. It was a view that unsettled me. My father had played there many times. As I watched the grey clouds coming in off the sea at Portobello I found myself cursing him all over again.

'None of us matched up to you, did we, Cannis?' I threw in the dish mop and went for my coat. The dog was watching as I closed the door.

I drove to Newhaven, my mind turning faster than the wheels, even when they spun on the ice. I'd lost two days to self-pity and I wasn't about to give up on finding Michael's killer. Outside the factory gates I put the car up on the kerb. Parked on double yellows – like I cared. A couple of snoutcasts chugged on their smokes by the front doors. I could see the young receptionist on the phone, but I didn't want to bother her; she was far too jumpy for my purposes.

'All right.' I rocked up to the smokers. 'I'm looking for Andy, foreman fella . . . Heard there might be work going.'

The pair looked at me, sussed me as a schemie

or a dole mole and bought the act. Bloke with a quiff, polo shirt buttoned up to the top, said, 'Aye, I'll give him a shout on the way in.'

I thanked him: 'Nice one, mate.'

He dowped his tab, went inside. I took out my Marlboro and asked the bigger bloke for a light. He was just about smoking the filter, gave me the last millimetre of lit tip – 'Chuck it when you're done.' He went back to the factory, leaving a trail of slushy footprints.

My hands were turning blue when Andy showed up. He recognised me right off, gobstopper-eyes the giveaway.

'Hello, Andy,' I said.

His steps faltered on the tarmac – there was a bit of ice. 'Hello.' He put his hands in the pockets of his starched white dustcoat. I saw his brow crease up; he had more lines than a Notting Hill dinner party.

I offered him a smoke. He declined, took out a packet of Royals, the Superkings. 'I'll stick to these, can't hack the Marlboro.'

I nodded, said, 'They suit me fine . . . But I'm made of hard stuff.'

He laughed up. 'Aye, aye . . . you and yer brother both. I mind seeing your old boy play. Christ, he was a hooligan!'

I got this kind of thing from everyone who had seen my father play. I never enjoyed hearing it. 'That's the word for him.'

Andy lit up, coughed on his first drag. 'Your

brother wasn't that fond of hearing about him either.'

'I bet.'

Andy leaned against the wall, rested a foot on the storm drain, a faraway look forming in his eye. 'I really was very fond of . . . Michael.'

'You said.'

He held his smoke like a dart, then pressed it in his mouth. As he spoke, the cigarette rose and fell with his words. 'He was very good to me, took me off the wagons when my back went.' He smiled, the cigarette wobbled at its tip. 'Even kept me on through all this nonsense.'

I put my shoulder on the wall, faced him. '*Nonsense*?'

Andy seemed to clam up. He took the tab out his mouth and stubbed it on the sole of his shoe. 'Aye well, we've no work.' He put the half-dowped tab behind his ear. 'So that'll be you off now.'

I watched him but said nothing. He knew what I was thinking, and why I was there. Two more workers came out of the factory. They spoke in Czech to each other, laughed and passed out the tabs.

'I have to be getting back.' Andy's breath came white against the cold air.

'Okay,' I said.

He leaned over, lowered his voice: 'Look, I've nothing to tell you.'

'I hear you.'

'I'm serious . . . I have a family to think of too.'

I dropped my gaze, said, 'We've all got families, Andy. My brother had a family; Ian Kerr had one too.'

The two Czechs pulled up beside us, nodded to their gaffer.

Andy raised his voice: 'So, thanks for dropping by. I'm sorry we've no work for you.' He took me by the arm to the edge of the car park. I watched his gaze shift edgily, left to right, as he walked. 'The backshift comes in a couple of hours. Give me five minutes to sort them out and then I'll see you over there.' He pointed to a boozer – it was old school, proper Edinburgh.

I thanked him: 'I won't forget this.'

I moved the car off the double yellows; even in an industrial area, you couldn't be guaranteed the ticketers wouldn't be out – it had become a real cash cow for the city. I got parked on a side street. Children were throwing snowballs all about, young kids, only about seven or eight. They sang a bawdy old rhyme:

Olé, olé, olé,
Tits in the trolley,
Balls in the biscuit tin.

The words came back to me from my schooldays. I used to think it was just a street saying that got passed around by the kids. Now I disinterred a deeper meaning, a significance: life was just a constant struggle, projected in our physical and mental deterioration. But even so, it was the only game in town. Graft, or go under.

I crossed the street to the drinker. A portable telly sat on the bar, no flat-screen here. The barman was watching *Countdown*; he could hardly drag himself away as a Geordie bloke asked for a vowel and then a consonant.

'Can I have an orange juice, please?' I said.

Cautious looks from a toothless jakey in a baseball cap to my left. I knew the territory: there was a time when I wouldn't have trusted someone coming into a pub and ordering – that worst of things – a *soft* drink. My father would be roaring laughing in his grave.

I took my glass to a table in the corner, where I could keep an eye on the front door. I still heard *Countdown* blaring from the portable, the clock ticking to the end of the round.

I found a newspaper sitting on the next table, flicked through it, eyes half shut. Full of celebrity pish, no content. One story struck me though: today tattoos had officially become uncool – Nigel Havers had got one.

I sipped at my orange and watched the clock begin again on *Countdown*. I wondered about buying another drink when in walked Andy. He wore an old Lord Anthony ski jacket; the shiny collar was turned up, his thin shoulders poked through. He had a look about him that fitted many a Scotsman of his class and generation, the word is *puggled.* A lifetime spent keeping body and soul together had taken its toll. Left him worn out.

I greeted him with a nod. 'What can I get you?'

'A wee nippy sweetie.'

I took myself to the bar, ordered a dram. I switched off my mobi – didn't want to disturb Andy if he started to rabbit. He scratched the stubble on his chin as I returned. 'We no' a bit close to home for you in here?' I said.

He tutted. 'Nae danger . . . None of that shower come in here.'

It was my experience that a workforce piled into the nearest pub after every other shift. 'How come?'

Andy rubbed his chin again. 'No' allowed.'

This threw me. '*Y'wha'*?'

He took up the wee goldie, sipped. It made his eyes widen. He had very large eyes, dark, with an excess of white surrounding them, said, 'The set-up in there is the workers get bussed in and bussed back. Bus doesn't stop at the pub.'

I saw Andy might be ready to unburden himself, but I thought I still had some persuading to do.

He drained his glass.

'Another?'

He pressed his lips together. The tip of his tongue darted out. 'Aye . . . please, son.'

At the bar the jakey watched me order another whisky with something close to envy glowing from him. He tried to engage me in chat about Carol

Vorderman having refused a cut in her million-a-year salary: 'A fine bit ay stuff, mind . . . for an older woman, like.'

I blanked him. Returned to my table.

Andy kept his jacket on. I noticed there was a little snow on the shoulders; as I glanced out the window I saw another deluge had started.

'Here you go.'

He took the glass, fired a good mouthful. '*Slainte mhath.*'

I watched the burn of the whisky settle his mind. I envied him, but knew I needed to stay the course.

'Andy, do you know why I came to see you today?'

He nodded. 'I have a fair idea.'

'You strike me as a decent sort.'

He laughed. 'I don't know about that.'

'Well, *I* know.'

He looked at me, quickly turned back to his glass.

I said, 'Andy . . . my brother was murdered. I don't know what you heard about that, but I know that something fucking shady's going on over the road . . . I think Ian Kerr knew that too. I need you to help me join the dots.'

The words didn't seem to have the impact I'd expected them to. Andy looked unfazed, but then he hadn't seen the kip of Kerr.

He sighed. 'I'm very sorry for your pain. Really, I am.'

I didn't want his sympathy. 'It's your help I want.'

He tipped back the last of the scoosh. 'And what about the way Big Ian went?'

'You want them to get away with that?'

He huffed.

'Someone wanted Kerr to stay quiet . . . Someone's got a lot to lose,' I said.

'Oh, I'd fucking say so.'

I held back for a moment, let the thought of Ian Kerr's death settle between us. 'I need information about the set-up over there.'

'What information?'

I smelt the whisky on Andy's breath; it made my pulse race. 'I know about the Czechs, the labour racket . . . Fucking hell, let's call it what it is: *slavery*. And I know about Ronnie McMilne.'

The mention of the Undertaker put the shits up him, I could see that. The idea of being buried alive was universal. Something leaped in him. 'I was on the trucks when McMilne came in . . .'

'Go on.'

'It was low-scale at first, bits and pieces added to the loads.'

I checked him: 'The loads . . . Rewind a bit there, mate.'

Andy sketched out the way the business worked, shipping components from all over Europe to assemble in the city factory. There had been cash-flow problems, trouble paying wages, creditors giving agg. The banks had been no help.

'That's when Davie took up with this McMilne geezer,' said Andy. 'The idea was the truckies would load a few extra pallets on the wagons and customs would be none the wiser if the paperwork was sound.'

'And no one said shit about it?'

'One or two drivers got lippy and were sorted out, but the rest got a right good drink out it. You've got to remember they were bumping folk left and right at this time . . . The boys had to put steam on the table.'

'So where did it all go wrong?'

'This fella . . . McMilne, he was pushing for more and more, wanted whole loads carried, all this Polish vodka and ciggies, container-loads. The boys got worried. That's when it got kicked upstairs . . . to Michael.'

'He didn't know?'

Andy returned to his stubble, ran his palm over his chin. 'No, your brother knew, I'm sorry to tell you. He had no choice – the firm was going under.'

It came as a jolt to hear Michael had been involved with the Undertaker, but who was I to judge? Hadn't I done a million times worse myself? My brother was only trying to protect his livelihood, looking after his family, and quite a few others.

'Then what happened?' I said.

'We took the full loads.'

I shook my head. I could see the Undertaker had his hooks into Davie and Michael. Running some knock-off was one thing, though. I just didn't buy my brother going for the labour racket, that would be a step too far for him. ‘Tell me, Andy, where do the Czechs come in?’

His face blackened. ‘Bunch of cu[illegible]’ He spat on the floor. ‘That’s where it all went fucking crazy . . . I wanted out, but they told me no way.’

‘Who told you?’

‘Davie – the Czechs were his idea . . . McMilne brought them in by the lorryload but that was all we had to do with them at first. It was fat fucking Davie who saw the benefits of putting them to work over the road.’

I knew it. Davie had been led by the wallet. ‘Punt the loyal workers and replace them with a cheaper lot . . . and turn a blind eye to why they were so cheap.’

‘Said the wages bill needed cut doon. The Czechs told him they were the answer to all his worries, and he believed them.’

‘Fucksake, did he buy any magic beans off them as well?’

Andy snorted. ‘It all backfired on fat Davie, though . . . when he punted all his workers, the Czechs took over. And they wanted fuck all to do with McMilne.’

I couldn’t see the Undertaker being too pleased about carving up his venture. ‘So they edged him out?’

‘Too fucking right they did. Took over the runs themselves.’

It sounded like an act of war to me, said, ‘I bet that didn’t go down too well.’

Andy nodded, let out a nervous grunt. His eyes grew even wider as he looked to the window and across the factory yard. 'I'm surprised we're no' all in the fucking ground.'

I shook my head. 'There's time yet.'

CHAPTER 17

I sat at the lights on London Road. Didn't realise they'd changed to green, and then back to red, until some bell-end in a white van started blasting me with his horn. I turned round to eyeball him through the back window, and he pretended to talk into his Bluetooth earpiece.

An excuse, even a slight one, and I was going postal.

My mind was awash with what Michael had been through in his last months. He'd built up an international business, had made the kind of life for himself that most of us could only dream of, and it had all been snatched away from him. The masters of the universe he called neighbours had crashed the banks and took his business down with them. The bankers were all right, though: the government had insured their fuck-ups, even managed the kind of bailout that would see some of them paid bonuses like nothing had happened. The world had gone mad. How could I blame my brother for losing it too?

Nightly, the politicians – our supposed leaders – strutted out, chests puffed, PR-advised smiles plastered on their coupons and assured us they had everything under control. Like fuck they did. They were in a spin, pumping the gas then the brake in ever-increasing desperation to stop this rig from hitting the wall.

'Fucking bastards,' I mouthed.

I'd never felt more helpless; I knew how the workers, the truckies and the line operators that fat Davie punted must have felt. The suits had brought us to this crash, but it was the working man who was going to feel the full impact.

I parked up on Easter Road and braced myself for the Arctic blast I saw blowing the litter up the street at a hundred miles per hour. I wondered if the scaffies were on strike again; if they were then, for the first time, I didn't blame them. We needed more protests. We needed to get the fucking tumbrils rolling.

Outside the flat there was a cold-looking cat stood on a window ledge. It screeched to get inside but there was no one home. The animal looked frozen, like the one Victor Meldrew found in his freezer. I picked it up and brought it into the stairwell. It raised tail and prowled before the door of the ground-floor flat it called home.

As I took the steps I sensed movement, looked down to see a yellow trickle rolling over the stair. I knew at once what it was from the smell. As I turned the corner I caught the schemie who'd been round asking for three quid to clean the stairs. He stood with his tackle out, a grand arc of pish flowing from him.

He clocked me, made a mad fumble to zip up.

I took the stairs slowly. The blood-pumping so loudly in me that I could hear it. 'You fucking skanky piece of shit,' I said.

He looked up at me. His beanie was pushed back on his head; a couple of grey teeth protruded above a scabby lip. I waited for a reply, got none. He obviously took being rumbled as a professional risk – sauntered past me onto the steps with a shrug.

I wasn't having it. Launched a rabbit punch to the back of his napper. He flew into the wall, collapsed in his own urine. As he turned I saw his teeth had made contact with the plaster, dislodged a chalky hole that fell like dust over him. He tried to get up but slipped in his own pish.

I moved above him. 'You little fucker . . . Think this is the way, do you?' I slapped him across the puss, forehand then backhand. 'Nice little fucking earner, was it?'

I yanked open his jacket, ripped into his inside pocket. Found his cash and yanked it out.

He spluttered blood from his mouth as he tried to speak, made a weak attempt to snatch back the notes.

I showed him the back of my hand again, he recoiled.

'I need that,' he said.

I couldn't believe I was hearing this. I counted

the notes. 'And what, you think the folk in here don't?' It was only twenty-six pounds: enough to fill the tank at the pub and come back for more.

'But . . . but . . .'

He watched me pocket the cash. His mouth still drooped open, dripping blood. I slapped the side of his head, the beanie went for a flier. 'Now, listen up, you daft little cunt. I catch you in this stair again, the only pissing you'll be doing is into a fucking bag, you get me?'

He eased his way along the wall then made a stumble for the stairs. I heard the cat yelp as he passed the bottom flat, then the door slammed behind him.

I chapped up the auld wifey at number three. She took an age to answer. 'Hello there,' I said.

'Oh, it's you. I thought it was the stair fella again.'

I dug in my pocket for the notes. 'I don't think we'll be seeing him any more. He's shut up shop, and, well, he's given us a refund.'

I handed over the twenty-six pounds.

She had glasses on a chain around her neck, she put them on, 'Oh, I think he's given me too much.'

I smiled, gave her a wave as I turned to my flat. 'Treat yourself,' I said. This wealth distribution felt good. Knew it would never catch on.

Usual barked and jumped onto the couch at the sight of me, barked again and dropped back down. He stretched out his front paws and lowered his chest to the floor. I was grateful for the welcome but thought I deserved none of it.

'Down, boy, down.' I patted his head, watched his tail wag as I took out my mobi; I'd had it switched off since my meeting with Andy and there were half a dozen missed calls from Mac.

I pressed 'return call'.

He answered on the second ring. 'Where the fuck you been?'

'I owe you a tenner,' I said.

'*Wha'*?'

'Just caught the stair pisher . . .'

He didn't even laugh. His voice came low and flat: 'Gus, there's been some developments.'

'Such as?'

'Hod got into a bit of bother . . . got himself a bad kicking.'

I didn't like the sound of this. I'd asked Hod to look into the Czechs. He had a rep for Ramboing. 'Spill it.'

'There were words exchanged . . . some boxing.'

Knew at once he'd been hurt. 'How bad?'

'He's up on bricks.'

'I'll be right round.'

Mac raised his voice: 'Gus, he's not here. He's at the hospital.'

I felt empty.

Hung up.

The thought of Hod being worked over felled me. I headed straight for the cludgie and took out my bag of speed. I'd been hammering it; the wraps were going down. I got tanked into one, then another. The dog watched me. He knew I was up to something, wore that 'Debs won't be pleased' look of his. I yelled him off. He flattened ears and went to his basket. 'Like I could feel any worse,' I told him.

I took myself to the hall, then back to the kitchenette and opened one of the cupboard doors. My mind was working so fast on all the possibilities that I hardly noticed my movements speeding. I dished up some Pal for the dog and grabbed my Crombie from the hallstand.

It was rush-hour traffic, roads clogged with double-deckers. For half an hour I sat in a stationary lane next to a ten-foot poster of Carol Smillie flogging the chance to win a million quid on the Postcode Lottery. When I finally made it to the Royal the sky was dark and the temperature well below zero. I got the ward number from reception and headed for the lift. I still felt like I was speeding out my face, the blood pushing behind my temples as the bell pinged and the doors opened.

Mac sat on the end of the bed. As I clocked Hod he looked to have been solidly worked over. Both his eyes were blackened. His nose wore a white T-bar where the doctors had tried to reset it; I knew from experience it would never be the same. I was relieved to see his limbs had been spared. Thought: Christ, how bad is it if you're grateful his kneecaps are intact?

'All right,' I said as I walked in. I eyed some fruit sitting by his bedside, a bottle of Lucozade and a couple of cards. 'I, eh, haven't brought anything . . . sorry.'

Hod shrugged. Immediately a wince spread on his face and he touched his ribs. 'Don't sweat it, I've been promised jelly, I'm rapt.'

I smiled, glad I wasn't being blamed for this. Least not by Hod.

Mac spoke: 'Where you been all day?'

It didn't seem the place to talk. There was an old geezer in the next bed, sitting up in striped pyjamas, reading the *Hootsman*. I tried to appease Mac, hunted in my pocket for a tenner, handed it over. 'Here you go . . . Your winnings.'

He grinned. 'Stair pisher got you as well, eh?'

'What's this?' said Hod.

We both shook heads. Mac said, 'Fancy a donner down to the day room?'

Hod hauled himself out of bed. 'Aye, c'mon . . . Grab a coffee, eh.'

Hod hobbled down the corridor – wouldn't take any help. In the day room we bagged some industrial-issue chairs, bright orange hoseable numbers that looked like relics of the seventies. Thought they wouldn't have been out of place in our rental flat.

Mac carried over three cups. 'Only got tea.'

'I can't drink tea,' I said.

Mac looked back to the vending machine. 'There's soup – mushroom, I think.'

'I'll go without.'

When I got a closer look at Hod's injuries I saw

his knuckles were scraped to bits, swollen and bruised. 'You got a few good biffs in, then,' I said, pointing to his hands.

He grinned. 'Some fucking belters.'

Mac sipped his tea, tore back the corners of his mouth. I guessed I'd made the right move crying off it. Went, 'So, what happened?'

Hod drew fists. It looked difficult for him; the tendons in his wrists showed as he spoke to Mac. 'Did you give him it?'

'Nope . . . first I've seen him since.'

I looked between them, tried to piece together their thoughts. 'I'm guessing this was the Czechs. Right?'

Mac returned to his tea, blew on it. He shook his head. 'Tell him from the start.'

Hod's shoulders rose and fell beneath his gown. His face portrayed every painful movement. 'I haven't got started on the Czechs yet, Gus.'

That only left one other option. The thought stuck in me like a blade.

'You haven't?'

Hod spoke: 'I was planning to, but got a bit side-tracked.'

I took the blow. 'Wasn't meaning . . .'

'Don't worry. Can I get on with this?' He leaned forward, took a sip of tea. 'Christ, that tea's rough . . . Anyway, I was locking up and there was a bloke standing over the road, staring in. Just giving me eyeball, y'know. And I thought, What's his fucking problem? So I says I'll go have a word, and he gets the same idea, started strutting over like the Big I Am, yeah . . .'

I couldn't see that going down well with Hod. Man works sites in all weathers, he develops a certain amount of hard.

'I thought he was casing the bar, or had his eye on the till . . . or fuck, I dunno, maybe I'd put a line on his bird or something. So I went out. He was a big lad. Y'know, skinhead, fucking rocks in his head more like. And I said, "What you playing at, mate?"'

I felt Mac's eyes on me. He was waiting for my reaction to the next bit.

Hod went on, 'So then he goes, "Nice pub. Gus Dury still run it?" I told him I was the fucking owner and what's he asking about you for, and the cunt starts to laugh.'

I glanced at Mac. He was nodding, said, 'It gets better.'

'So I asked him what was so funny,' said Hod, 'and then he walks off. I was half tempted to panel the prick, when he got into a big Daimler and who's in the back but—'

I cut in, 'Ronnie McMilne.'

Mac and Hod looked at each other. 'How did you know that?' said Mac.

'I had a visit myself.'

Hod tutted. 'Not one like mine you didn't.'

I thanked my stars for that. 'So, then what?'

'I went back to the pub, cashed up. I was about to go and put the shutters up when the skinhead came in, dropped a packet on the bar and walked off.'

Mac took something out of his pocket, handed it to me. It was a Marlboro packet. I opened it up – all the cigarettes were still inside, except one. It had been replaced by a long bullet, kind you put in an assault rifle.

I closed the box. 'He gave you this for me?'

Hod nodded. 'I opened it up and he said, "That's for Dury" . . . I just flipped. I ran after him, had him in the street, grabbed his coat over his head and was weighing into him. Was battering ten bells out the cunt when the Daimler screeched up and another lump got out.'

I didn't know what to say. I felt my spine straighten; as it did so a single bead of cold sweat ran the length of it. I reached out to Hod, put a hand on his shoulder. 'Mate, I'm truly sorry. You can't imagine how mad this makes me.'

Hod brushed away my hand, leaned over and put an eye on me. 'Gus, don't get mad . . . get fucking even.'

CHAPTER 18

When I broke the news about Hod to Debs she went apeshit. Her concern about how I was handling my brother's death was now replaced by her greatest fear – that I'd soon be going the same way as him. I knew she wondered what I'd let myself in for; Christ, I did too.

'Gus, this has got to stop,' she yelled. 'Now, before anyone else gets hurt.'

I put my hands on her shoulders. She was shaking with fear, hurt, maybe both. 'It will. It will.'

'But how? With you in the ground?' Her face contorted, twisted into a mask of anguish and then her lips quivered as tears came.

'No, Debs, I wouldn't put you through that.'

'Oh, you think you'll have a fucking choice.'

She ran from the living room, slammed the door behind her. I thought to follow, try to explain, but I knew there was no explaining. I had let Debs down again – I wondered how much longer she would put up with it.

I took down my Crombie and the car keys.

The flat was too small for both of us when the atmosphere turned this sour. I knew things were bad now. 'Debs, are you okay?'

No answer.

'Debs,' I knocked on the bedroom door, '. . . hon, I'm sorry. I know you're sore at me.'

I heard her jump off the bed, the door jerked open. 'Sore at you . . . Sore at you! . . . Gus, you have no idea!'

I wanted to say something but nothing sparked in my mind. I made another weak play: 'I'm seeing Dr Naughton tomorrow. I'm doing that for you.'

Her mouth widened, I saw her teeth white against her tongue. 'You're doing that for *you*, Gus . . . You're doing that for you.'

'I know, I only meant—'

'You don't know what you meant. You don't know anything any more, Gus . . . All you know is how to hurt. How to feel hurt, and how to spread hurt.'

She started to sob into her hands. I dropped my coat and reached out to her. 'Debs, come on . . . don't say that.'

She only cried harder. She pushed me away with her fists and went back to the bedroom. I watched Usual come through from the living room and lie down at the door. I wanted to tell Debs she was wrong, that I wasn't like that, but the truth was – she was right. I left her alone; she was better off without me.

I picked up my coat again.

Outside it felt colder than I ever remembered it. The air seemed to crackle in front of me as my breath touched it. My ears and nose nipped, my lips dried and hardened. As I walked to the car the icy surface of the pavement crunched underfoot, the frost sticking to the soles of my Docs. I felt my knees twinge on every step as the cold blasts from the street cut at my shins.

I stood in front of Meadowbank Stadium waiting for Mac to collect me. The temperature was far too low to hang about and I was relieved when I saw him driving down in Hod's Toyota Hilux; I raised a hand in a wave. The truck slowed, stopped in front of me. I jumped in the cab. It was warm inside, the heater blasting. Bit of Big Country blasting too. I turned it off – couldn't face guitars that sound like bagpipes.

'Hey, I was listening to that,' said Mac.

I shut him down: 'Gimme the SP.'

Mac had been trailing Davie Prentice since the night before. I needed to know what he'd found out; it could be useful for when we pulled him again. Things had started to get desperate after Andy talked and Hod got worked over. I knew I needed to move fast. Fat Davie had already whipped up a shit storm between the Undertaker and the Czechs – I knew it wouldn't be long before I was battered about in the eye of it.

Mac spoke: 'Well, for a kick-off, he's got some tart up in Restalrig . . . A right Boaby Moore, got her set up in some rathole flat by the look of it.'

I asked for the address, stored it away.

He continued, 'The fat prick headed off there at knocking-off time last night.' He laughed at his unintended joke. '*Knocking-off* time – see what I did there?'

I gave him a slow hand-clap, said, 'Go on.'

'He was up there again this afternoon, took a carry-out from the Cantonese. Came back out with a bag of prawn crackers and a grin on his face you could have crossed the Forth on.'

'Prawn crackers . . . How the other half live, eh.'

We hit Queen's Drive. It stunned me to see people out running in this weather. At the roundabout Mac drove straight through, followed the Holyrood Park Road traffic to the lights outside the Commonwealth Pool.

'So where is he now?' I said.

Mac put on the indicator, turned left down Dalkeith Road. He pulled through the gears, then slammed on the anchors for another sharp left. We headed for Prestonfield Golf Course.

'On the links.'

'You jest . . . It's six-below out.'

'He's on the nineteenth hole, mate.' At Prestonfield House, Mac parked up. Davie's big old Citroën was in the space next to us. 'Want me to haul him out?'

'In front of his golfing buddies . . . that would be unkind.'

Mac opened the door, slid out. As he was about to leave he turned back. 'There's something under there for you. Thought you might thank me for it.'

I ran my hand under the front seat, felt something cold: a plastic baggie. I pulled it out. Was just what I needed – had been running low on amphetamine support. I took a wrap, fired it, tucked the rest in my jacket.

A few moments later fat Davie appeared, stumbling out of the front door. Mac walked behind him, prodding him in the back with his hand. If anyone had seen this performance they would have thought Mac was a carer, mistreating some half-witted care in the community patient. Fat Davie slipped and stumbled on the scree; it might have been comical if the consequences weren't so serious now.

I got out of the cab, called out, 'Hope you're feeling like a wee drive, Davie . . .' Mac poked him between the shoulder blades, pointed to my side of the vehicle. As he reached me Davie hesitated, looked like bolting for the fir trees. I grabbed him by the collar. 'Get in there, and be quick about it you little shitkicker.'

Mac got in his side of the truck. I dived in after Davie, sandwiching him between the pair of us. The speed was coursing through me. 'Now, isn't this cosy,' I said. I watched Davie's face contort; he looked first to Mac then to me before he got thrown back in his seat as the wheels spun on the scree.

'Jesus, what are you playing at?' he yelped.

I flicked a backhander over his flabby cheek, said, 'Haven't decided yet.'

As we drove, we fell into each other on the bends. We stayed silent but the air in the cab soon became foetid.

'Fucksake, Davie, have you let loose?' said Mac.

'Be that Cantonese,' I said. 'Must play havoc with the digestion at your age.'

I opened the window. Davie spoke: 'How do you know I had a Cantonese?'

I felt hyped – the drugs firing in me – I grabbed his face in my hand, squeezed hard. 'There are many things we know about you, Davie. Many, *many* things . . . Isn't that right, Mac?'

He crunched the gears. 'Too fucking right.'

Fat Davie's meaty neck started to quiver. His eyes widened on the road ahead. He looked as if he was travelling on the roof of a train, grabbing on to the seat with his fingernails. His mouth was a plughole, set too far back in his head, and his face was the wrong colour for a normally ruddy-complexioned tubster.

We drove back the way we'd come, headed for the Craigs. Mac had to drop the gas as the roads got icier. It looked dark for the time of day, the frost on the hills and the lying snow adding a surreal tint to the topography. As we climbed to the top of the hill it got even darker, the winding road gave out. I watched Mac kill the engine, then the lights. We sat in almost perfect stillness; save for the dim flicker of street lamps from the city below, nothing moved.

Then, 'This is where Billy Boy copped his whack, is it no'?' said Mac. He was referring to an old case of mine. Tragic shooting.

I took up the baton: 'Shot in the face.' I rattled Davie: 'Not a nice place to end your days . . . Dying out in the cold.' I pressed the point: '. . . Last sight, a shooter going off.'

Davie played with his shirt-cuffs. I watched his row of chins tremble with the movement. I spotted a little bit of tissue paper sticking to the edge of his collar, held on with a spot of blood. A razor nick; he had fucking more to worry about now.

He spoke: 'Look, I don't know what you want with me . . . I don't.' His voice sounded strangled, the words lost in the tightness of his throat.

I grabbed his tie, pulled him closer to me. 'You're holding out on me, Davie – that was your second mistake. Your first was thinking I'd let you get away with it.'

Mac started to drum his fingers on the steering wheel: Davie took his gaze off me – I grabbed his jaw, jerked back his head. 'I know you were running knock-offs for Ronnie McMilne,' I said.

He held it together. 'Your brother knew all about it . . . Michael was totally aware of—'

I slapped him on the brow with the heel of my hand. I didn't need telling by this sack of shit. 'Don't even fucking presume to know more than me. I know about you, Davie, I know about the Czechs as well. The Undertaker must've took some hump when you cut him out of that racket!' I yanked hard on the tie, smacked his brow into the dashboard.

Davie stayed down, dropped his head in his hands, lost it. He whined like a trapped animal. Mac edged round in his seat – the noise made Davie jump again.

'Get this cunt oot before he shits himself.' Mac pushed Davie towards me. I grabbed his tie again, jerked it tight as I backed out the door.

'Better talk to me, Davie, I'm your best option. Did Michael kick off about the Czechs, was that it? Did he protest about your plans?'

The fat fucker fell on his knees, quite a clatter. I watched his face lose more colour as he started to stammer, 'N-no. No . . . there was nothing like that. Nothing like that.' He was sweating now, it came off his broad head in cobs. His face turned grey, the moisture adding a waxy sheen to him.

Mac slammed his door, walked round to join us. He stood over fat Davie for a moment then grabbed his hair. I gave him a slap with the back of my hand. Mac pulled him from the ground, forced him to face me.

Davie knew he was in Shit Street, his golf-club bonhomie was no good to him here; he reverted to the squealing little wimp he must have been in school. Mac and I were the playground bullies, taking his dinner money. He yelped a defence: 'Ronnie was mad . . . furious. Michael went to see him, to try and talk some sense to the man.'

I barked at him, 'When?'

'The night he died.'

'Are you saying McMilne killed my brother?'

'I-I don't know . . . I don't know.'

My synapses jumped. 'It sounds like it to me, Davie.'

'I'm only telling you what I know . . . You asked me what I know and I'm telling you.'

None of it made sense. Davie was trying to save himself. 'If McMilne killed Michael, then why's he left you alive?'

Davie's breath shortened. His face grew so pale I thought he might have a coronary. 'I don't know, I don't have all the answers.'

I smelled bullshit. 'Is it because you have protection, Davie . . . is that it? Who's protecting you, the Czechs? Or is it the filth?'

He shook his head, panted, gasped for air. 'No one's protecting me.'

I was ready to see this fat fucker keel over. I grabbed his tie again and hauled his face to mine. I bawled at him, 'Someone's fucking looking out for you, only I wouldn't count on them saving your arse. There's a rat in your outfit cosying up to plod and given you've only got Czechs on the payroll it doesn't look like you've many true friends.'

Mac stepped in, separated me from Davie. I was out of control, had said too much and I knew it. He hosed me down, put a hand on my chest and said, 'Watch it.'

I took the hint, walked to the edge of the road and sparked up a tab.

Davie spoke: 'Gus, Gus . . . I was Michael's friend, can't you see that? We were partners. I wouldn't have done anything to hurt him . . . I wouldn't.'

I drew deep on the cigarette. It stilled my heart rate, but not my rage. I said, 'Tell me who killed Michael and I'll make it all go away. You'll get me off your back and you'll get whoever killed him off your back at the same time, because I'll do them, and you know it.'

I walked to the truck, opened the door. A fierce wind blew up from the sea, hit like a blast. I watched Davie turn in the road. He fell on his knees again. 'I don't know who killed Michael, I don't . . .' He was close to collapse. 'I don't. If I did, I'd tell you. I would . . . I would.'

'You're fucking lying to me.' I was sure of it: he was protecting someone. That he'd told me McMilne saw my brother the night he died made me think the Undertaker had Davie's nuts in a grinder – but it would be me turning the handle soon.

Mac walked around him, scowled, and returned to the truck.

I got in and closed the door. As Mac started

the engine I lowered the window, said, 'Think about what I said, Davie. Because only when I know who killed my brother will I leave you in peace.'

CHAPTER 19

There was less than a week till Christmas. I got my first card of the year – from my mother. I put it on the string above the mantel with the fifty or so that Debs had received. Time was when we got cards addressed to the both of us; not any more. It would take a while before it registered that we were a couple again. I wondered if we would last that long.

Debs wasn't herself. There'd been tears, shouting. She knew I wasn't about to let up on the case; she understood I couldn't. It came as a heartscald to her, because it was a red-flag warning that the Gus of old was still with us. Much as I wanted to change, much as I'd made promises and real progress, my old self was still there. Like Yul Brynner's faulty android in *Westworld*, you couldn't kill him with an axe. Just kept coming back at you. Again and again.

I'd pledged to keep up the sessions with the shrink, but I doubted their worth. I wasn't sure all this psychobabble wasn't just dredging up more hurt, exposing me to memories and emotions I'd buried for years. My past had been something I'd kept locked away, sealed in a jar. When it did present itself it took another kind of jar to wash it away. I wasn't sure all this introspection wouldn't have me reaching for the sauce soon. I felt the pull of it growing stronger by the day.

The dog came over to me on the couch, jumped in my lap. I patted his head, said, 'Least I still have you, boy.' The words seemed to pump me up. I didn't want to lose Debs again, after all we'd been through. I didn't want to go back to that lonely place, the late-night lock-ins, the obliteration of drink, the longing for a new life. I had another chance, but did I deserve it? Christ, it was more than Michael had. The thought wounded me. The old Presbyterian guilt rose. Was God toying with me? Giving me a glimpse of happiness to make the return of misery more painful than ever?

I felt sure of only one thing: I couldn't go on like this. Something had to give. And soon.

My thoughts spiralled away from me, then my mobi began to ring; brought me back to earth.

Picked up. 'Hello.'

'That you, Gus?' I half recognised the voice. 'It's Mr Bacon.' My former boss on the newspaper, Mr Bacon – or Rasher, as I called him. He went on, 'I was sorry to hear about your loss, Gus . . . so very sorry.'

I didn't want to hear this; I knew at once why he had rung.

'You got the scoop, then . . .'

He gave a little cough. 'Erm, that's not why I called at all. I just wanted to say . . .'

I wasn't buying his bullshit. Hacks have little compassion when there are headlines involved. He was using his best 'in' to get a comment. I said, 'You wanted to fake concern to see if there was a better line on offer, that it?'

'Gus, I-I never . . .'

I sounded harsh. Like I gave a shite.

'Fuck off, Rasher.'

Hung up.

My mobi smelled of Marlboros. As I held it in my hand I knew I needed to get moving. If the press were onto the murder story, time was a bigger factor than ever.

Dialled Jayne.

The answerphone came on, inane preamble followed. I was about to leave a message when she picked up: 'Hello.'

'Jayne, hi . . . It's Gus.'

She spoke fast, sounded manic: 'I was just doing some cleaning up – I don't know where all the dust comes from.'

I skipped the chit-chat. 'So you're not tied up, grand. I was wondering if I could pay you a wee visit.'

She faltered. 'Erm, yes, I suppose . . . Was it anything in particular?'

I felt my eyes roll in my head. Of course it was something in particular! Wanted to say, *Well what do you fucking think?* Went with, 'It's about . . . Michael.'

She was fiddling with the answerphone, I guessed running a duster over it. The woman was coping the best way she could. I felt guilty for being short with her, even if it was only in my imagination.

'Yes, that should be fine.'

'Okay, I'll be round in an hour.'

Clicked off.

Got booted and suited. The dog trailed me down the stairs and onto the street. At the top of Easter Road I saw something I hadn't seen in years: a man carrying a sandwich board. It read, FREE CHIPS WITH EVERY PIE. As he passed I looked to see what was written on the back, CHIPS AND A CAN – ONLY £1. Had we really slumped this low? We had returned to Victorian advertising practices. I shook my head. Don't know why I was getting so het up – we had been recycling Victorian work practices for years now. I wondered how far we were from seeing a man in a sandwich board that read, WILL WORK FOR FOOD.

I'd parked the car next to a communal dumpster that had been filled with a burst couch. Some massive floral eyesore, beige, but worn black at the arms, and spilling industrial foam onto the street below. It had been introduced vertically – a real challenge. I almost admired the arrogance of the fly-tippers.

As I put the key in the car door a bloke in a council van pulled up, started taking photographs of the couch. I couldn't believe this, thought: Of course, they'll be collecting forensic evidence to catch them. Laughed, shook my head for the second time in five minutes.

An old gadgie appeared at my back, said, 'He's wasting his time.'

Did I want to engage this bloke? Tried a 'go away' smile.

He went on, 'They'll have that oot there in no time.'

I knew he wasn't talking about the scaffies – the council would have a cherry picker in the street before risking someone putting their back out, health and safety regs and all that.

'Who will?'

'Some mug after a sofa. Can't leave anything on the street now. Shit-stained mattress isnae safe these days!'

True to form, a blue Bedford pulled up, couple of blokes got out and eyed the couch.

The gadgie watched. He had no upper teeth, just two in the row below. 'Told you . . .'

I saw him on his way with a salute. 'You weren't wrong.'

I opened the car door and Usual jumped in.

The journey out to the Grange was treacherous; black ice had put a few cars off the road. A bus had bumped a left-hand drive-Beemer, pushed it onto the kerb at York Place. All the buses had been taken off Princes Street to get the new tramlines down and there was a tailback that stretched the length of George Street. We had to be the most congested city in the world. Nowhere else had a look-in, surely. It seemed utterly pointless owning a car; but then, that's what The Man wanted. So fuck him; I revved it up.

As I pulled into my brother's drive, I noticed someone had been busy: a snowman had been built in the front garden. It seemed out of place – I wondered who had felt jolly enough in the home to do it. I got out of the car, watched Usual settle in my vacated seat, then a loud scream came from the back garden.

I slammed the door and ran to the gate.

It was Alice.

I thought she was in trouble, visions flashed. They were all wrong.

'Alice!' I yelled.

She looked across at me. She had a snowball in her hand, taking aim at the lodger, Vilem. They both looked flushed and red, covered in snow. She opened her mouth a little, derived something from my expression and dropped her snowball on the ground. She pulled off her mittens as she ran to the back door. Her lope was girlish and knock-kneed.

I called to her as she passed me, 'Alice. Alice . . .'

She ignored me and went inside.

I turned back to Vilem. He looked smug, pressed down the corners of his mouth in a smirk, shrugged.

I said, 'I'm keeping a close eye on you, fuckhead.'

He tossed his snowball between hands, then threw it at the wall. It exploded on impact. He didn't answer me, followed Alice's footsteps through the snow as he walked back to the house. He knew he was protected as long as Jayne was around; he'd done quite a number on them, but it couldn't last.

I still felt nervous having this guy around my brother's family. 'A real close eye . . .' I said, 'remember that.'

I went round to the front, knocked. Jayne opened the door in an apron and Marigold gloves. As she waved me in she looked over the handle and letter box, 'I'll need to get some Brasso on those.' She tugged at a rubber glove; it twanged as she removed it. She repeated the motion for the other one, spoke rapidly: 'Can I get you some tea, coffee?'

'Eh, coffee please.'

Jayne's quick steps on the parquet floor sounded like rifle fire as she went. I watched her remove the apron over her head in one swift, deft movement. Right away I saw she was hypo. I hadn't known her to behave like this before. My brother and Jayne were the most together people I knew; it was a knock to see it. Made me wonder how much you really ever know anyone.

I settled down. She soon returned with a tray, set with cups. Sat down herself. 'Oh, the biscuits.' She jumped up again, ran through to the kitchen. I grew exhausted watching her.

When Jayne returned I let her pour the coffee. 'So, how are you coping, Jayne?' I knew the answer to this question: it was obvious the answer was 'not well at all'.

She spoke so fast I hardly took in her words, found myself focusing on the delicate lines around the edges of her mouth. I'd never noticed them until recently.

'I'm fine, fine . . . just fine. Keeping myself busy, y'know. Around the house and what have you.'

I took my cup from her. 'That's good, Jayne.'

'Yes, yes . . . So much to do, this time of year.'

'Less than a week till Christmas.'

She looked like I'd slapped her. 'Is there? I mean, so soon.' She put down her coffee, stood up. 'My God, I'll never be ready in time.'

I patted the chair. 'Jayne, sit down.'

She took the hint. 'I'm sorry. I get carried away . . . And there's so much to do.'

I tried to relax her. 'Don't apologise. You're doing fine . . . How's Alice?'

Jayne dropped her gaze. She picked up a teaspoon and stirred her coffee. I thought for a moment she wasn't going to answer me. A silence stretched out between us, then, 'She's . . . coping.'

'You don't sound convinced.'

'We've had to pay a visit to the doctor . . . get her medicated.'

I got the hint Jayne was too; like I could comment. 'So long as it helps.'

A sigh. Deep breath followed. 'Yes, long as it helps.'

I thought to press her further, to ask about the scene I'd just witnessed in the garden with Alice and Vilem, but I pushed it out of my mind. Told myself I was being overly protective of my niece. I still had my suspicions about this character but this wasn't the time to raise them.

I sipped my coffee, told her it was great.

'You didn't come to talk about the coffee, did you, Gus?'

I felt heat rise on my chest. 'No, no I didn't.'

Jayne squared her shoulders, took another deep breath. 'What is it you want to ask me?'

I had a million and one things I needed to know. I saw by the state she was in that I'd have to tread carefully. Much as I wanted to protect both her and Alice, though, I had a duty to Michael to root out the truth. We were all hurting, we were all asking why, why us? I knew if I found some answers, even if it meant more pain in the short term, we would have some peace.

I spoke softly, kept my voice flat: 'Did Michael ever mention any trouble he might be in?'

Jayne tilted her head to one side. 'Trouble? . . . No. Never.'

I tried again. 'I spoke to Davie and one or two others and I get the impression that things weren't right with the business.'

She brought her hands together. 'Well, you know Davie . . .'

'What do you mean?'

She played with her watch strap. 'Michael used to say that Davie could sell the Pope a double bed.'

'He did? . . . Did he say anything else?'

Jayne looked away; an old memory played on her face. 'I think Michael regretted being tied to the partnership. He spoke about going it alone, but he never would . . . He'd put his heart and soul into that factory.'

I could see this was painful for Jayne. Her eyes misted.

'I'm sorry, I hate to put you through this.'

She shook her head. 'No, it's fine. It is, really. Go on.'

I drew breath, fired on. 'On the night . . . on the night Michael didn't come home, did you notice anything unusual?'

Jayne rolled her gaze to the ceiling. The tears in her eyes sat poised to fall as I watched her bite at her lip. I thought she might crumble, fold. She found strength, though, said, 'A man came to the door. I had never seen him before. I didn't think anything of it at the time, a lot of business associates come . . . *came* calling for Michael . . . but this guy was a bit strange.'

I pressed her. 'In what way?'

'When I answered the door he was already on the step, he seemed very anxious . . . He jumped back right away and apologised.'

'Did he come into the house?'

'Yes, he was here to see Michael. He had very

broken English. That's when I realised he was from the factory and I got Vilem.'

'You got the lodger?'

'Just to talk to him, whilst I got Michael . . . He'd had a long day and was in the shower. When we came back it looked like the man and Vilem were arguing, but I couldn't be sure, it might have just been the language I'd picked up wrong.'

I looked back to the kitchen door. There was no sign of the lodger. 'And then what?'

'That was it. Michael told me there was some problem at the factory, a conveyor belt or something had broken. He told the man how to fix it and he went away.'

'Did Michael go with him?'

'No. He went out later . . .' She paused. A tear fell down her cheek, she wiped it away with the back of her hand. 'That would have been when he . . .'

I wondered if this had been Michael's visit to the Undertaker that Davie spoke of – or if there had ever been a visit to McMilne. Here was Jayne telling me about a Czech calling the night he died. I found it hard to believe Davie didn't know about this too, but he'd chosen to leave it out. I saw Jayne'd had enough; I wanted to stop but I knew I might never get this chance again. 'The man that called, what did he look like?'

'He was tall, broad . . . dark-haired, I think.'

'Did you see his car?'

'I don't think so. I didn't look out the window. Oh, I don't remember.'

'Think. What about when you let him in?'

She seemed to be rallying. 'There was, now I think about it, there was one of those jeep things.'

'A four-by-four . . .'

'Yes. There was one parked in the road.'

'Was it a Pajero?'

She shook her head. 'Oh, Gus, I don't know cars.'

'What colour was it?'

'It was too dark to say. It was very dark, though.'

'Could it have been black?'

'I suppose so, yes, I suppose it could have been black . . . a black four-by-four.'

CHAPTER 20

Dr Naughton had been Christmas shopping. A little kid's tricycle sat in the corner of the room. She'd tied pink ribbons on the handlebars, secured them with a big bow. I couldn't stop staring. On my last case, a mother had told me of her murdered young child's love for such a tricycle. I couldn't believe that the sight of such an innocent object could be a trigger for so much misery. My demons were forever with me.

'It's safer away from prying eyes,' said the doctor. 'I'll take it home on Christmas Eve.'

I tore my gaze away, nodded. 'Of course.'

'Would you like to sit down?'

I removed my coat, hung it on the stand. I didn't know what to say; Michael had been the one with all the small chat. I smiled. Prayed we wouldn't delve into baby talk. I'd been frozen out of that subject a long time ago. I even stopped looking at small children as people – they seemed like accessories that the more successful adorned themselves with. I might have felt differently if I was a father, but the older I got, and the more

I found out about the world, the more relieved I was to be childless.

Dr Naughton put on her professional tone; she had her clipboard back: 'How do you feel today, Gus?'

It seemed a totally meaningless question, even as an opener. 'Fine. I feel fine.' Was I nothing. I burned inside. In the last few days I'd replayed a million and one scenarios that might have led to Michael's murder. Every one was possible, and every one twisted in my gut like a bolt.

She made that face of hers, one that says *Trust me, I'm a doctor.* I wondered if she practised it in the mirror. 'Do you think we made any progress in the last sessions?'

I nodded. She seemed a good person and I didn't want to upset her, but I thought it would take more than a few hours of chat to see any progress in my life.

'That's good.' She sounded pleased, one of her Kicker boots started to tap on her chair leg. 'Maybe you'd like to tell me some more about your upbringing.'

Or maybe not. I looked out the window. There were icicles on the railings. They'd thaw before I would, but I played along, said, 'What would you like to know?'

'Can you tell me something you remember from your adolescence?'

I had a store of memories from this time. The one I thought of first was when I met Debs. I toyed with telling her about that, about how she thought I looked like I'd been hit with a brick. The memory spiralled on to the time I took her home to meet my family, and it ended with another first: my raising a hand to my father. I decided against telling the doc.

'I, erm, went to university at seventeen,' I said. 'I was the first in my family to go. It was quite an achievement. My mother was just rapt . . .'

She sensed an opportunity to probe. 'And your father . . . How did he react?'

I huffed, 'He didn't.' My father was hacked-off – anything that took the sheen off his accomplishments was worthy of frowning upon.

She pressed: 'He never commented?'

I remembered his face, wanted to punch it yet. 'He did, yeah, about six months later . . . when I bailed.'

It must have been in her middle-class programming to attack me for that decision, but she held it back. Her face held firm, she let some distance settle between the years then continued, 'Do you want to tell me what he said?'

My palms itched. 'He laughed and said I had shown myself up. Not him, because he had told everyone I'd be back like a whipped dog before the end of the first year. Bastard knew exactly how to get me back as well – it was all his fault. He ruined my chance.'

Dr Naughton looked impassive. She kept a hold on the level of emotion in the room by remaining so calm herself. She said, 'What was the subject you studied at university?'

She never asked the questions I expected, the logical ones. 'Don't you want to know *why* I left?'

'Only if you want to tell me, Gus.'

I leaned forward in my chair, planted my elbows on my knees. 'He beat my brother so badly that he ended up in hospital. He'd duffed us all up for years but this was something else, this was savage. He'd kicked him about like a football.' The memory set off a tick in my brow; I smoothed it away with my fingertips. But the image still burned. 'He was so black and blue, his face such a horrific sight, that my mother woke up screaming in the night for months.' It wasn't the physical beating she'd upset herself over – it was the damage it had done him inside his mind. 'Michael was so ashamed, knew he couldn't hide his bruises like we were supposed to, that . . .' I wondered if I should tell her this. I had never spoken of it before, it was Michael's business and no one else's, but now he was gone. 'He put a clothesline around his neck and jumped from the back dyke. If the line hadn't been rotten through he'd have made a job of it.'

The doctor lost her composure – her hand jerked on her clipboard. 'My God.'

I had gotten to her, broken that steely reserve. 'I'm sorry, I didn't mean to shock you.'

My words helped her gather herself. 'You came home to protect your brother?'

I had been used to protecting Michael – this one incident aside, he had fared better than all of my father's children. 'I wouldn't want you to feel I resented him for that . . .'

She spoke softly, 'It's what *you* feel that matters here, Gus.'

I didn't know what to feel any more.

CHAPTER 21

Hod was due for release from hospital. I waited for the call. Mac had told me that Hod had some information to give me; apparently he'd come good. I'd already decided what my next move was going to be: if Hod had come up with the goods then it was time to do some serious head-stomping.

I sat in front of the tube, flicking, when I caught Gordon Ramsay calling a chef an arrogant twat, thought: Has the man no sense of irony? It was some 'reality' shite, couldn't watch more than a second. Had the notion to suggest Tyson as one of Gordon's next star turns – like to see him try the rough stuff on Iron Mike. Might even tune in for that.

Flicked some more, found an infomercial for a lateral thigh trainer. Kept going through the channels, hit the twenty-four-hour news. Some academic banged on about the end of capitalism, said we'd be binning globalisation and going back to small-scale economies. A bloke in the street had said something similar to me the other day: 'We'll see the horse making a comeback yet!'

I knew who I believed.

News said the oil price had slumped and Scotland was facing a whack to its offshore development. We'd lost our banks – some that were older than our dodgy Treaty of Union – our businesses were going to the wall by the hour, but I found something to smile about: the man who had been the country's one and only billionaire had lost his title as Scotland's richest man. His fortune had been slashed, he was even forced to sell his £50 million Cap Ferrat mansion. If I had any tears left I spent them laughing that he had to sell his £2 million yacht as well.

'Welcome to reality,' I said. Could see the day when some of the plutocrats that had been pushing the trickle-down economic model would be trickling down to the job centre. And it wouldn't be long.

My mobi started to ring.

'All right, my son,' said Hod.

'It's John Wayne!'

'I'll be fucking John Wayne Bobbitt if I have to spend another night in here surrounded by nurses.'

I laughed that up, said, 'Thought there was only two sure things in life – death and a nurse.'

Hod guffawed, 'Aye well, no' in uniform, that's for sure. The food's fucking awful as well; my belly thinks my throat's been cut.'

I saw where this was going. 'You checked out?'

'Aye, oh aye . . . Want to come and collect me?'
'I can hardly say no. When?'
'Now, mate . . . sooner if you can make it.'
I flicked off the TV, said, 'I'll get in the car.'
I left the dog behind, chucked him some Bonios.
The roads were still iced up. No sign of a gritter the entire route. I drove in the teeth of a fierce wind all the way to the hospital. When I arrived Hod was out front in a short-sleeved shirt, three buttons open. The dash said it was about two degrees above freezing, but he looked unfazed. His second skin poking out his collar did the job. He smoothed down the corners of his tache as I pulled in – still couldn't get used to the sight of it. 'You want to drop round Wyatt Earp's gaff to give him his mozzer back?'
'Shut it, man. You're just jealous of my manliness.'
'Ah-ha, of course, your manliness . . . that's what it'll be. And I thought I was just embarrassed to be seen with someone who looks like he's one of the Village People.'
He gave me the finger, said, 'Fuck off, I can take it.' We pulled out laughing. I was glad to have my mate back in one piece; didn't think I'd ever been happier to see him. We headed for the Wall but got stuck in a static lane of traffic.
'These roads are murder,' said Hod. He winced, went on, 'Sorry, didn't mean . . . you know.'
I put him straight: 'Don't be daft, I'm not that far gone.'
'Look, why don't you pull off the road, we'll

grab a coffee and a roll in there.' He pointed to a caff with a big open window. In front of it a bloke in a Honda indicated he was leaving his parking space.

I nodded, stuck the car into first.

The caff was a bit of a dive, peeling linoleum on the floor, peeling Formica on the tables. But it was a good solid Edinburgh scran house, and it suited us down to the ground.

Hod ordered up some rolls on sliced sausage. 'You put onions on them?'

The waitress was tipping sixty, a frame so delicate a sneeze might knock her to the ground. Her face looked broken by the years, her eyes watery. She was no heartbreaker, but one of a thousand like her in the city. She was what the Scots call *soulish*. 'You want sauce with yer onions?'

'Oh aye, brown sauce.' Hod rubbed his hands together, a bit too energetically: his ribs twinged and the pain played on his face.

The waitress left us, but her forlorn presence lingered.

I spoke: 'Mac said you'd made a few calls in the hospital.'

He nodded. 'Got on to some of the builders still in the game. Had big Brian Ingram pay me a visit as well – had lots to say.'

I was glad to hear of some progress. 'Well, spill it.'

'Your Pajero geezer . . . name's Radek.' He put his hand in his pocket, pulled out a note. It was an address overlooking Leith Links, written in carpenter's pencil on the back of a torn-up pack of Regal King Size. 'That's his kip.'

I smiled, waved the address about. 'This is good work, Hod.'

He shrugged. 'I've got my uses.'

'So, what's this cunt's story?'

Hod leaned in. 'Well, he's no fucking saint.'

Surprise, surprise, said, 'We knew that.'

'In fact, he's a bit of a nut-job by all accounts. Big Bri said he started out on the sites about a year and a half ago, was labouring, doing it hard as well. Double shifts on more than one site about the town. Was pulling a fair whack in poppy, but never happy, y'know the type?'

I nodded. 'Eye to the main chance, enough never enough.' No wonder he got on so well with fat Davie.

'He's got a bit of a rep as a boxer as well, going bare-knuckles and that. Got into a few scrapes on Bri's crew and he punted him. Mad bastard only went and pulled a blade.'

This all sounded very interesting. 'Mad indeed.'

There was some kind of commotion up the street, horns blowing. I looked out but couldn't see anything. The waitress reappeared. She crept towards the window and stationed herself there like a wobbly sentry. I watched her shake her head, bony fingers worrying at the front pocket of her nylon tabard.

Hod reeled me back in. 'Anyway, so Radek set

himself up, got a few homeboys around him, was pulling in some gigs here and there and the rest is, well, you know the rest.'

The horns got drowned out by a belt on a police siren. A blue light flashed into the caff. 'Aye, aye, it's the woodentops. What's going on here?' I said.

Hod looked like he was about to speak, his mouth began to form the words then closed like a trap as the door to the caff swung open.

In walked a couple of uniformed plod. 'On your feet, Dury.'

I turned. '*Wha'?*'

I felt a hand on my shoulder. 'Now come on, don't have us haul you along the street . . . On your feet. We're going down the station.'

CHAPTER 22

'Do you want to tell me what this is about?' I said.

Obviously he didn't: the uniform put his hand to his belt, took off his cuffs. I was spun by the shoulders and thrown onto the table.

'For fucksake!'

Hod was on his feet. 'This is out ay order.'

'Shut it,' said the flatfoot. 'I can easy take you in as well.'

Hod raised his hands. I saw the old waitress come back from the window to join the rest of the folk in the caff staring at me, mouths open, heads shaking. I thought, What the fuck have I done?

On the street I got passed to another uniform, heard the first one talking on his radio, 'Yeah, bringing him in now, guv.'

My head got pushed down as they forced me into the meat wagon. I protested and arced up, 'What the fuck is this about?'

'Shut yer fucking yap, Dury.'

It concerned me how well known my name had become, in all the wrong circles.

We took the ride to Fettes with the blue lights on. I thought this was a bit much, but there was no doubting their effectiveness on the Edinburgh traffic. I was thrown about in the back of the wagon; the cuffs dug into my wrists and stretched my arms from their sockets.

At the nick they hauled me in. 'Look, you gonna tell me what this is about?' It was ten minutes before the bastards took the cuffs off me, shoved me in an interview room.

Minding me was what looked like one of the force team's rugger buggers: flat nose, beefy chest, and thighs that meant his trousers required the special attention of a tailor. He didn't even glance at me, stared off into the middle distance, a dream of Murrayfield glory dangling before him.

I rubbed my red wrists as the door opened, a waft of air hitting me in the face. It was Fitz; he looked proper furious. The spruced look had gone – his collar open, the tie hanging like a noose. His sleeves were rolled up to the elbow and he was unshaven. I saw some burst blood vessels in his eyes when he looked at me.

'Dury, by the fucking cringe.' He slapped a folder down on the desk. I watched it fall; some pages escaped its edges.

I wasn't biting. 'Why the fuck am I here?'

He saw me rubbing my wrists. 'Did they try the rough stuff? . . . Sorry, I told them to go easy.'

It made little difference to me, the situation hadn't changed. 'Do I have to ask you again?'

Fitz pulled out the chair in front of me. It stuck on a table leg. He cursed it, yanked so hard the table shook. I leaned back and fixed eyes on him. He was aware of my glare but didn't respond. He ferreted in his pocket for a pack of Dunhill, found them, realised he didn't have a light, said, 'Ho, bonnie lad, you got a light?'

The uniform shook his head, pulled out his empty pockets.

Fitz said, 'Ah, a feckin' fitness freak.' He opened a drawer and located some Swan Vestas, sparked up. He offered me a smoke; I declined.

'Are you going to tell me?' I said.

He drew in. 'You don't know?'

This was insane. 'My telepathy's on the blink, Fitz.'

He peered into me, over the smoke; I knew I'd been tested. Maybe I was still being sussed out. Either way, Fitz's tone changed. He turned it up: 'Ye feckin' reckless young heller!' He jumped out of his seat and slammed the table.

I'd seen bursts like this before, some in this station. It didn't faze me. 'Sit down, man.'

He paced, turned to me again. 'You are one daft fecker, Dury. Daft as feck . . . Running about all over the shop, wrecking my investigation.'

Was this going somewhere? 'Look, do you want to fill me in?'

'I'd feckin' love to fill ye in, Dury!' He drew fists, ash fell from his cigarette. 'Nothing would give me more feckin' joy.' He stamped back to the desk, grabbed the folder and opened it up. He plugged his tab in the corner of his mouth, muttered as he turned pages to find what he was looking for. The folder held photographs. He picked them up, one by one he flung them at me. 'Feast yer eyes on that little lot . . . Jaysus, if it doesn't make ye throw I don't know what will.'

Fitz stamped away again, walked over to the wall. I watched him running his hands through his hair, then he hoisted up his trousers by the belt loops. He sighed and rubbed the back of his neck as he turned to watch me pick up the photographs.

'Oh, fuck no . . .'

The images were horrific. They'd been taken at a crime scene; nothing had been missed out. I saw a face robbed of its features, black bruises and deep-drawn wounds where you would expect a nose or an eye. The pictures were in colour, but seemed to lack the full spectrum: everything appeared black or white, the death-mask skin so pasty, the blood so dark. The only hint of colour I found was on the collar of the old Lord Anthony ski jacket.

Fitz stood over me, 'You recognise him?'

I nodded. 'It's Andy . . . from the factory.' I kept turning the pictures. There were wider shots, had taken in the length of his body. A particularly gruesome image showed Andy lying spread-eagled, on wasteland. There was a dark pool of blood behind his head, down his front it looked like another bucket of the stuff had been tipped over him. Something was pinned to his chest – I saw the hilt of a blade.

I pointed. 'What's that?'

Fitz leaned in, drew on his tab. 'That there . . . that would be the poor bastard's tongue.'

I felt a heave in the pit of my gut. 'They cut his tongue out?'

'I don't think the fecker did it himself.' Fitz stubbed his cigarette, moved round the other side of the desk, sat. 'I know ye spoke with Andy Gregory earlier in the week.'

I looked up from the photos, pushed them towards him. This was quite a turn of events. 'Have you been trailing me?' I knew he hadn't; I'd never met the plod who managed that trick without making it as obvious as a donkey's cock.

Fitz pointed a finger at me. 'Dury, don't feckin' quiz me on this investigation. Ye have already gone and bollixed it up.' He moved his finger to the photographs.

'You blame me for that?' The accusation jabbed me. Andy was a good man. He had helped me out, because he knew there were wrongs being done and because he respected the memory of my brother. I felt enormous guilt to have endangered him. All I could think about was what I had said to fat Davie on the Craigs, about having a snitch. Mac had held me back – I knew I'd fucked up. Had I caused Andy's death?

Fitz kept still, then spoke slowly: 'I don't know

the exact circumstances . . . Andy Gregory was obviously in over his head.'

It was time to tell Fitz what I knew.

I revealed everything I'd learned from Andy about the Undertaker's involvement. He seemed to know all about it, sounded like the factory had been under surveillance for some time, which told me how they knew I'd met with Andy. I told Fitz that I knew Davie Prentice was up to his nuts in it and that got nods. He didn't know what fat Davie had told me about Michael meeting with the Undertaker the night he died, and he knew nothing about the Czechs – or pretended not to.

'What else did you question Andy Gregory about, Dury?'

'The factory, y'know . . . what was going on in there.'

'And what did he tell you?'

'The Czechs had pushed out McMilne and he wasn't happy.'

Fitz reached for another smoke. I took one too this time.

'This is getting feckin' tribal,' he said.

I lit my cigarette. It tasted too mild after the Marlboros. 'It's only going to get worse. The Czechs are . . .' I was going to tell him about the visit to Michael's home the night he died, about the bloke with the black Pajero, but Fitz shot me down.

'Don't tell me how to do my feckin' job, Dury.'

I saw he had a boner for the Undertaker. Fitz was glory-hunting, he was imagining the headlines, knew he had a press favourite on his hands. It made me mad as hell. Another man had died – how many more would there be? 'If you did your fucking job I wouldn't need to tell you. And I wouldn't have a dead brother.'

That wounded him. Fitz rose from his chair, swept up the pictures and closed the folder. He walked to the door. Before he went through it, he turned. 'Leave this to the professionals, Dury, or sure as there's a hole in your arse you'll be joining your brother soon.'

CHAPTER 23

I walked home, struggling to keep a straight line. Nothing new for me there, however this time I was sober. My legs felt so limp, my knees weak. Every few steps a shiver came up from the street and rampaged through my gut en route to my heart. Another man had lost his life. A good man. Andy had a family, he'd worked hard all his days to keep them; now they'd be spending Christmas without him.

I couldn't keep Andy's face from my mind: not his troubled, forlorn, world-weary face, but the bloodied, brutalised mash I'd seen in the photographs. My life had taken another turn; the slow, ponderous descent into ruin had been hastened. I had another soul on my conscience.

The cold north winds scattered litter and leaves before me. Bodies bent into the onslaught and fought to stay upright. The entire city seemed to have been drained of blood, everywhere looked greyer, darker than usual. I couldn't focus on what had changed. Perhaps it was everything; perhaps it was me. My existence seemed futile. I held tight to the quarter-bottle of Grouse in my coat pocket.

It felt cold; my fingers clasped tight but there was no warmth to be had. I knew that bottle held fire, I knew it also contained answers, of sorts. Those who say, 'You won't find any answers at the bottom of a bottle' are dead wrong. The one and only answer was in there: oblivion.

I craved an escape from my life. I wanted to unscrew the cap on the bottle of Grouse and swill deep. I wanted to taste the heat of it, the burn of memory being obliterated, thoughts turning to smoke and ashes. I was lost. I knew I had no clue as to who had killed Andy, or Ian Kerr, or Michael. I had my gut telling me it was the Czechs one minute, then the Undertaker the next. I had Davie Prentice calling for a bullet out of sheer frustration, but I knew that was just my anger, my stupid lust for revenge.

The truth was, I had failed Michael; and now Andy had paid the price with his life.

Snow fell again. It came down quickly, deep and thick. It settled on the street and the walls and the railings. The rooftops turned white and the cars slowed as the roads filled with slush. No one seemed to be bothered by the downpour: they dashed in and out of shops with carriers and Christmas trees and rolls of wrapping paper as if nothing mattered save the coming celebrations. What happened to the crisis in capitalism? I thought. What happened to economic misery? To the great woes we had all embraced, the new-found common enemy? I wanted no part in readying myself for the festivities. I knew that in the next few days, three families would be gathering with empty chairs round the table. It didn't seem right. Nothing *was* right any more.

I schlepped through the town, along the main drag and onto Waterloo Place. On Regent Road I looked up at St Andrew's House, had a thought of praying to our nation's patron saint but let it pass. A weather-beaten saltire flew above the building. It was so faded I could hardly make out the cross on it. I tried to look at it, tried to raise my head from the gutter, but the snow kept filling my eyes.

I was wet and cold and tired. As I made my way back to the flat I stopped to watch a window cleaner, working a cake shop's front pane. Chocolate tarts, topped with strawberries and cream, sat on the shelf inside. I wanted to ask him: 'How can you do that without your mouth watering?' But I didn't have it in me. Michael was the man to stop and share a craic with anyone – I didn't feel capable of bringing a nice moment to another's life.

When I got to the flat and looked at the keys I realised I'd walked home in a daze: I'd left the car parked on the south side. I thought to call Debs and ask her to retrieve it on her way home from work, but I'd have to give her an explanation and that would cause more grief.

Usual went wild. He'd been cooped up all day – a walk would do him good. I shook the snow off my coat, said, ‘Okay, boy, soon, just let me get warmed up a bit.’ My solution was to take some speed from the cistern, got my heart racing right away. I worked through the wraps, dreaded to think the kind of shit storm this would raise if Debs found out.

I was losing her again, I knew it. I had lost her once before: we had been married and she’d divorced me. Why she gave me another chance I’d no idea. I wanted to make it different this time, I had tried and tried but things were slipping away. I knew Debs deserved more and I wanted that for her; maybe it would be for the best if she dumped me for good. I saw an image of me alone, drinking and wallowing in my misery. It was a picture of defeat. ‘Is that what you want for yourself, Gus?’ I mouthed. Knew I might not have a say in the matter.

I clapped at the dog. He seemed filled with joy, running to his basket to retrieve his favourite plastic hotdog toy. He bit it and made it squeak, ran with it to me and thwacked it off my leg. I took the challenge, held tight to it and watched as he tried to tug it away again.

‘If only everyone was so easily pleased, boy,’ I said.

I was stunned by the dog’s stamina, got the impression he’d be able to keep this up all day. Me, I needed wraps of speed to keep me in the game. I was coming round to the idea that things were as bad as they could get. I had been going in reverse for so long, perhaps it was time I changed gear.

I took out my mobi, called Hod. 'You all right?'

'Gus, fuck tae fuck . . . Are you down the nick?'

I snorted, felt my nose running. 'No, I'm out. Look, where are you now?'

'At the pub. Want to tell me what happened?'

I wiped my nose. 'Yeah, soon. I'm going to collect the motor. I'll get you at the Wall.'

Hod flared up, 'Ah, not a good idea. Remember that McMilne cunt's been round here looking for you.'

'So what?'

I heard him prepare a warning, tip the granite in his voice. 'Are you forgetting he put me in the Royal?'

I knew what Hod was aiming at, but the point was wasted on me. I needed to see him and Mac. I had an idea forming that might just lead to some progress. 'Look, Hod, if Ronnie McMilne wants to come dig me out he can . . .'

'It's a fucking grave he'll be digging if he gets hold of you.'

I hosed him down: 'Hod, that's just shite. The Undertaker's putting a threat on me because he wants something.'

'*Wha'*? . . . What's that then?'

'*That* I don't know, but I'm figuring it's not something I can't do if I'm in the dirt.'

Hod sighed. I could hear a punter ask if he was serving. 'I think you're taking an unnecessary risk.'

'No, Hod, every risk I take now is entirely necessary . . . I'll catch you in a half-hour. Try and grab hold of Mac, I'll need you both for what I have in mind.'

'And what's that?'

'Look, you'll see . . . Tell Mac to bring his hammer, though.'

'I like the sound of that.' I imagined him smiling into the phone.

Hung up.

Snow covered the car. Even the tyres. As I tugged open the frosted door Usual raced in before me. I took a sketch at the caff, saw the old waitress shuffling about inside. It crossed my mind to go in, apologise, but I thought it might just put a fright on her. I'd caused enough grief for one day.

The engine started first time, surprised me. The wipers struggled a bit on the windscreen, got snagged on all the snow. I went back out and wiped away a swathe, then I clocked the ticket. 'The fuckers,' I muttered. Leave a car parked in this city without a watch on it, you're getting ticketed. I thought to scrunch it, throw it into the street, but knew I'd get caught on camera, and done for littering. Pocketed the bastard and cursed.

It took the now mandatory time to get through the town. It shitted me, but I had grown used to it. When I got to the Wall, I parked up. Left an inch of window open for the dog; didn't think anyone would have the knackers to try breaking in with Usual on shoatie.

In the pub, Mac stood behind the bar. He wore a black T-shirt with a picture of David Hasselhoff that read, 'Don't Hassel the Hoff'. I nodded, gave him an 'All right, squire.'

'Gus, boy. What you having?'

'Give us a Coke.'

He frowned, watched the pint he was pouring fill to the brim. 'We're out of Coke.'

A pub out of Coke? Things didn't look good here. 'Well, give me whatever . . . juice, water.'

Got a nod and a wink as Hod came in; he seemed to have relaxed a bit. Planted a slap on my back. 'You right?'

'Yeah, yeah . . . What about you? You look on the mend.'

He tapped his pocket. 'Dr Mac there got me a few Harry Hills.'

Whatever it was, it was working. Hod clapped his hands together, pointed to the seats at the back of the bar. As we walked over Mac called through the kitchen hatch for somebody to mind the till. My eyes dropped to the uplighters in the floor. They seemed solid purple now. 'You got the mood lighting a bit severe today, Hod, have you not?'

'That's him,' he said, pointing to Mac, 'fucker's colour-blind!'

Mac reached a hand to Hod's mozzer, tweaked it.

'I'm not working in a pink palace just because the boss's a buftie, aw right.'

We laughed it up – Hod less so.

Mac spoke as we took our seats: 'So, you were lifted?'

'Aye, no charges or owt . . . Just had my collar felt.'

'So what was plod after?'

I filled them in on the murder of Andy. I left out the most gruesome details: didn't want to put the shits up them because I needed their help. Not that it would put this pair off – more likely it would incite them to damage of an altogether more serious nature.

'He was a nice bloke,' said Mac.

I agreed. 'He was.'

Hod smoothed down the edges of his moustache. 'So, who do you think did him over?'

I went into my back pocket, pulled out the torn piece of Regal pack that Hod had given me earlier. Mac snatched it, read, 'Radek . . . Who the fuck's that?'

Hod answered him: 'He's our Czech gangsta. Nasty piece ay work as well.'

Mac pried and Hod gave him a rundown on some of the stories that had followed Radek around, got him turfed off the sites. He managed to make him sound like Charles Bronson – not the actor, the one in Broadmoor.

'We should do him,' said Mac. He was serious as well. Completely unfazed by Hod's description.

'Oh, y'think . . .' said Hod. He was just as straight as Mac. The pair seemed ready to go, here and now. Was madder than *Death Race*.

I slapped Mac's shoulder. 'Will you cool yer jets? We're not doing anyone. You forget he's just out the hospital.'

Hod leaned back in his chair, spread his arms. 'Hey, I'm good to go. Those wee Mick Mills have done the trick.'

I told him to shut up. I needed a pair behind me that were useful in a pagger – but I wasn't going looking for a fight.

Mac tried a new approach: 'That was Ronnie's lumps that did Hod over; we're talking about going for the Czechs.'

'Whoa, newsflash! If you think the Undertaker's capable, I'd say these boyos are way worse.'

I gave them some more details about the state of Andy in the pictures – the knife, the tongue. The message sunk in. Though maybe not deeply enough.

Hod sighed, 'I don't see where you're going with this, Gus. Are you saying we just leave this to the filth? If that's your plan then you might as well kiss fuck off to finding out who done in your brother.'

His words sounded harsh, but that was his intention. They both felt as passionately about this as I did; I was lucky to have such support in my life.

'No, that's not my plan.' I picked up Radek's

address. 'We have to pay this cunt a visit. But on our terms.'

'Meaning?'

'Meaning leave that to me . . . Be ready to go when I say.'

A grin spread over Mac's face: he scented blood. 'Should we get tooled up?'

I thought it might not be a bad idea, but an image flashed of Arnie with that coffin full of shooters in *Terminator 3*, said, 'I'm not planning to knock the fuckers off here. I'm only trying to get Fitz to open his eyes. The filth are looking the other way. Fitz the Crime's got it into his head that he's going to nab the Undertaker and get himself some new stripes. There's more going on here . . . much more.'

'Like what?' said Hod.

'I don't know, I just can't get a handle on it yet. Davie Prentice is sweating now because he knows we're close to the truth and the Czechs are maybe sweating too if they topped Andy . . . I just need to draw them out into the open and hope that it comes good. If we get them rattled any more then something might fall out.'

Mac was in favour of more direct action. 'Why don't we just burst this Radek? All these hard nuts are pretty tinpot once you get the pliers on their pods.'

'And what if he holds out, or we go too far? He might just be the only one who knows who did off Michael. Trust me on this, Mac, I have to find my brother's killer, not just any killer. And when I do, there'll be plenty of opportunity to bust heads.'

Hod slapped the table. 'Count me in.'

I looked at Mac, said, 'Well?'

He nodded. 'Aye, fucking right I'm in.'

CHAPTER 24

I told Mac and Hod to keep their mobiles on and be ready to nash when I called. I didn't know when the opportunity I needed would present itself, but if it didn't, I'd have to make it happen. And soon.

As I crossed the road I caught sight of a newsagent's bill. It screamed at me: CITY BUSINESSMAN MURDERED.

Rasher had got his headline.

I went into the shop and picked up the *Hootsman*, read the byline first – old habits die hard. It was one of the new batch of college interns, I didn't know her. I thanked Christ I was no longer a hack: her intro read like shit. A worn clichéd comma-splice. If I was still holding down a desk, I'd be chucking up in one of its drawers about now.

The paper had obviously very little to go on. They'd run a few inches on the murder in the Meadows earlier but now the police had released Michael's name and the fact that he was a prominent local businessman. The wannabe reporter speculated wildly about the investigation, great swathes of editorialising that made me wince. But the thrust of the tale was factual. Fitz had given them a bland statement that read: 'Police are following a definite line of inquiry.'

Thought: Boilerplate. Is there a file they cut and paste this pish from?

No one had bought the mugging-gone-wrong cover story; it had backfired on the force for sure. Fitz knew by now he was going to be taking pelters from the *Hootsman* if he didn't have a suspect soon, someone in custody, charges laid.

I read on, shaking my head, said, 'Fucking hell.'

The bloke on the counter looked up, went, 'You buying that? If you're no' then the library's down the road.'

I folded it up, whacked it down, said, 'How much is it?'

'Seventy-five pence.'

I frowned: the cover price went up as the standard of reporting nosedived. Another casualty of our tragic times.

I handed over a quid, got my change thrown at me with a sarcastic 'Have a nice day.'

The mid-Atlantic drawl was beginning to get on my tits, big time. Someone was going to get slapped in the puss giving me those imported tropes. I turned quickly, headed for the door.

'Wait a minute,' the shopkeeper said. I looked around – the place was empty. He called me back.

I turned, said, 'What you want?'

He bent under the counter and took out a

shoebox, removed the lid. 'Want to buy some cheap razors?' He held up a pack, obviously knock-off, Gillette Mach 3.

'How much?'

'Fiver for ten.'

These things went for three times that. I took a box, passed over the cash, said, 'Where'd you get them?'

He touched the side of his nose. 'Ask no questions.'

It seemed policy.

As I got my razors in a brown paper bag, the shopkeeper said, 'Hang about.' He dipped under the counter again, produced another shoebox. Inside sat pairs of ladies' stockings. 'Want some tights?'

I looked at him. 'You wha'?'

'Nylons . . .'

I shook my head. 'Has the Luftwaffe been back?'

He looked scoobied. 'Eh?'

I said, 'Have we reversed all the way to 1944?'

He put the lid on the box, curled his mouth at me.

I left the shop with my newspaper tucked under my arm and my razors shoved to the bottom of my pocket.

Outside a glimmer of sunshine winked through the clouds. It threw me. I felt more comfortable with the grey skies and the freezing-cold winds battering. The hint of warmth made me anxious, as though there was a trick being played. The snow on the roofs had started to melt and every so often it came crashing in great lumps to the street. Drainpipes overflowed and flooded the pavements. I knew if the temperature dropped again it would bring a freeze, folk saying, *It's like an ice rink out there.*

As I crossed the road to the car, a maroon bus sprayed black slush at me. It splashed on my coat and trousers. I shot a finger at the driver but he missed it, or pretended to. The wetness was seeping through to my legs already.

At the car I expected Usual to be jumping up and down, barking at me. But he was nowhere to be seen. I thought he must be sleeping so I crept up to try and surprise him. He never stirred. As I looked in the window I couldn't see him at all. My heart rate ramped up, thought: Christ, he's been taken.

I looked in the back and saw no sign of him, then I went to the driver's window – it was smeared with blood all along the edge where I had left it open an inch. The blood had dripped down in thick streaks and dried on the glass. I couldn't get my head around what might have happened. *Fuck*, where was he? I suddenly caught sight of Usual's back legs sticking out from under the front passenger seat. He lay flat on his belly, a position I'd never seen him in before.

I rooted in my pocket for the keys, my hands trembling as I sprung the lock, opened up.

'Usual . . . Usual . . . come here, boy.'

He didn't move.

I wondered if he'd been wounded.

'Fucking hell, have you been hurt, boy?'

I crouched down, tried to pull him out from under the seat as gently as possible. My mind raced with all kinds of thoughts.

Had he been knifed?

Had he been shot?

Holy shit, someone had got to him.

As I eased the animal off the floor his head fell limply over my arm. He had blood all round the edges of his mouth.

'Usual, what's happened to you, boy?'

I tried to rouse him, but he was cold.

CHAPTER 25

I slapped the dog on the back, but got nothing. I put my ear to his nose and felt sure he was breathing, but only just. My mind whirred with dark thoughts. I lifted Usual onto the passenger seat and his mouth dropped open, his tongue flopped over the edge. As I panicked, tried to get my head working, I caught sight of something sticking to the carpet by the door. I reached for it. It was a piece of raw steak, half chewed.

'You fuckers.'

Someone had fed the poor animal a piece of dodgy meat. I knew at once I had to get him to a vet. The nearest one was a mile away.

'Hang in, boy . . . we'll get you help.'

I slammed the door and over-revved the engine so much that a cloud of smoke came flooding from the back of the car. The tyres spun on the slippery road as I gunned the gas pedal hard. I saw people pointing at me as I clipped the kerb with my back wheel but I didn't care. I had the car up to sixty on Easter Road and took the junction in a handbrake turn. The Punto skidded into London Road, near taking out the traffic lights.

An old giffer on the pedestrian crossing raised his shopping bag and mouthed abuse.

I took the bus lane and flashed my lights at anyone else who got the same idea. I had one hand on the steering wheel and the other on Usual's back. 'Hang in, boy. Hang in.'

My mind filled with all I had been through with this dog: I had rescued him from a shower of yobs who'd been torturing him on Corstorphine Hill. They had tied him to a tree, were firing air-rifle pellets at him when I stepped in. A frenzied dash to the vet had been called for then. He'd survived his ordeal; I hoped he would be as lucky again. There had never been a more devoted dog than Usual. He had grown into our little household and he worshipped Debs. She would be devastated if anything happened to him. *Fuck*, she would never forgive me.

I was sweating now, my brows collecting beads of moisture. I had my mouth set in a grimace as I raced through the gears, getting to the box junction at the Carphone Warehouse. The lights turned red but I ran them. A Volvo came out from the stadium road and I was inches from its massive front bumper. The driver braked suddenly, brought the Volv' to a halt. I flew past him; as I did, he regained some composure and pummelled the horn.

The dog didn't look as if he was travelling well. His tongue had changed colour, seemed to have drained of blood. I patted his back, but he didn't so much as murmur. I was losing hope, I sensed the dog slipping away from me.

'Come on, boyo. Don't you be leaving me. Come on, come on.'

I spun the wheel through my hands, it burned my palms. I hit a traffic island and the back end fishtailed out of control. I had to countermand the steering to get the car to right itself. The front end lurched at a parked car and there was a millisecond of impending damage before I got the bastard under control. I ramped up the revs again and the car lurched to the other side of the road. An oncoming motorist pulled out of the way, but we clipped wing mirrors.

'Fuck it.'

The Punto's mirror was hanging off. Banged on the side of the door.

In my rear-view I saw the driver of the other car stop. He opened his door and stood in the road, roaring at me. Like I gave a shit.

I had two streets to go. I took the car over the edge of the dropped kerb at the corner shop and rolled in neutral, then I had to slam on the anchors.

'Bollocks!'

There were roadworks.

Two fat builders in high-visibility coats directed a reversing dumper truck. The other side of the street was filled with a pile of stone chippings. The road was blocked. I gripped at the wheel. Smacked my fists off the dash. What the fuck was I to do?

I punched the steering wheel and the horn belted out.

The builders looked at me, mouthed something between themselves, then got back to work.

I looked at the dog: he lay lifeless. His body had slid towards the door when I hit the brakes, his face shoved up against the armrest. I put a hand on him – he felt cold, his nose dry.

'Oh Christ, Usual!'

I jerked my hand from him and reached for the door. I ran round to the passenger side and yanked it open. Usual's head flopped as the door's support was taken from him. I leaned over, put my arms under his still body and picked him up. As I held him close, I reached for the raw steak that sat on the floor, shoved it in my coat pocket and ran.

I tanked it down the slush-filled streets.

I felt my steps give way on the slippery surface but I kept up a good pace. As I rounded the corner I fell, landed on one knee but held on to the dog. As I looked down his head lolled like a rag doll's. I put my hand under the base of his skull, supported him. The vet's surgery was in sight.

Normally, parked cars were lined up out front, and all the way down the street, but today there were none to be seen.

'Oh, fucking hell . . . Don't be closed on me.'

I chanked it as fast as I could for the last fifty yards. I thought my heart might let out. My lungs shrieked; I cursed myself for smoking so much.

'Come on, be open. Be fucking open!'

There were no signs of life at the vet's. It was nearly holiday time – had they shut up early?

'Oh, Jesus . . .'

As I got closer to the door, sliding and cursing as I went, I suddenly saw a sight that fired hope in me – lights burning on a Christmas tree.

I rounded the path, grabbed the door handle. It opened – I gasped in relief.

Inside I got hit with the smell of disinfectant and dog food. I brushed past a man with a cat carrier in the foyer and took a noticeboard down with me. A woman on the reception desk looked as though I'd cracked it over her head.

'Hey, hey, what you playing at?' she yelped at me.

I shouldered customers out of the way; there was more yelping.

'Sorry, sorry,' I gasped, short of breath.

Some tutting was added to the cacophony.

As I reached the desk, I panted, completely out of breath. My heart was bursting. I was dizzy with exertion and fear. 'My dog . . . My dog . . .'

The receptionist was indignant. 'You've just pushed through the queue!'

I was ready to lamp her, but she caught sight of Usual in my arms and her tone changed immediately.

'Oh my God, is this a road accident? . . . Has he been hit by a car?'

I shook my head, rummaged in my pocket. 'It's this . . . *this*.'

She looked scoobied, had no idea what I was giving her.

I shook the steak – blood dripped from it. 'It's meat, someone's fed him this.'

Her brain clicked to *on*. She pushed back her chair. The wheels cut into the floorboards as she called out to the vet, 'Bob, Bob . . . There's a dog here been poisoned.'

The vet came running through, tucking a thermometer in his shirt pocket. He didn't look at me; all I saw was the top of his bald and freckled head as he poked and prodded at Usual. He picked up the meat and sniffed it, shook his head, then lifted the dog. I watched him jog through to the surgery, calling out instructions to a girl who appeared wearing a green gown and gloves.

I was still gasping for air as the receptionist placed a hand on my arm, said, 'Are you okay there?'

She seemed absorbed by me. I patted the back of the hand she placed on my arm, muttered, 'I think so, yes . . . Do you reckon he'll be all right?'

She had dark eyes; they stared up at me as she spoke. 'You should go and get a seat.'

'But, but I-I . . .' I gripped on to her hand.

She pulled it away from me. 'He's in the best place now.'

It sounded like the kind of thing she'd said to a million people before. I wanted more than that, but I moved back, said, 'Thank you.'

When I sat down in one of the practice's plastic

chairs, I sensed everyone turning towards me. I tried not to make any eye contact; knew full well that would only be an invitation to have them talk to me, and I was in no mood for chat.

I stared at my boots, let my heart rate reach a normal level again. I felt my breath returning but the blood still pumped hard in me.

I knew who had done this to Usual.

I could see the face on that parka-wearing pug as he fed the meat through the open window. I had both fists gripped. I'd fucking well feed him through a window when I got my hands on him. I didn't care if he was one of the Undertaker's boys, I'd do him. And I'd do him proper.

I got out of my seat, paced the floor.

Everywhere, pictures of dogs beamed from the walls: adverts for wormers, breed charts, an anatomy poster. I couldn't look. Turned for the door, called to the woman on the desk, 'I'm going for a smoke.'

She smiled. 'I'll give you a shout if I hear anything.'

I thanked her again.

Outside I sparked up. I was running low on Marlboros; I'd been smoking the ones Ronnie McMilne had left for me with Hod. The bullet rattled about in the pack. I took it out, looked at it. It was the size of the one on the *Full Metal Jacket* poster. When I got my hands on that pug, I'd lodge it in his fucking head, with or without a gun.

I could imagine the bastard laughing, telling his mates that he'd offed my dog because it bit him. I chugged deep on my tab. I knew chances were he'd poisoned Usual on the Undertaker's instructions. It didn't matter. I was going after the fucker whether he was working on initiative or not. He might be looked after by every face in Edinburgh – it wouldn't stop me.

I reached the tab's filter, lit another from the tip.

The sunshine had left the sky, great grey clouds came racing in again. I wondered if Usual would pull through. What was going on inside? There had to be a hope, there was, surely. The vet wouldn't have taken him through to the surgery if he didn't think there was a chance. I found myself staring at the sky. I knew God was dead, but it didn't matter.

'Please, God, don't take that dog. Don't take him . . .'

I'd got down to the filter again when I heard the hinges screech on the door behind me. It was the vet. My jaw tensed.

He pushed his glasses up on his freckled head. 'Hello there.'

I nodded. 'Hello.'

I watched him take a deep breath, put his hands in his pockets. I waited for words but none seemed to come, then he exhaled slowly, spoke: 'Can you tell me what happened?'

I hadn't expected this as a gambit; I'd expected to hear how the dog was. I raised my hand; ash fell from my cigarette. I played dumb. 'I-I returned to my car and . . . someone had fed the steak through the window and . . .'

The vet took his hands from his pockets, folded his arms. 'Had you any trouble with the dog? Had he attacked someone . . . or, I don't know, been involved in an altercation?'

'No. No. Nothing at all like that.'

The vet shook his head. 'It's very worrying this type of thing. Seeing it more and more.'

'He was poisoned, then?'

'Oh yes, ethylene glycol . . . That's antifreeze to you and me.'

I stubbed out my tab. 'Is he going to be okay?'

The vet played it businesslike. 'I've done all I can, coated the bowel to prevent any further absorption . . . but he's not out the woods yet, his kidneys could still fail.' He turned back to the door. 'You'll have to leave him to rest up for a few hours yet. We'll give you a call if there's any change.'

He told me to give the receptionist my details. I went back inside. She said, 'It's the breed: people think they're dangerous because the papers go wild when a wee kiddie's attacked . . . They just want rid, think they're all the same.'

I didn't respond. I was torn between relief that the dog had survived and feeling the need to do some damage.

I jotted down my address and telephone number. 'You'll call if there's any change?'

She smiled. 'Of course.'

I thanked her and left.

When I got back to the car two young lads were sat in the front seats. One was turning the wheel like it was the *Whacky Races*. I picked up my pace when I saw them; they clocked me and made a dash for it. I was already in a run as they scampered up a close, got a kick out to one's arse as I chased them. 'You little prick!'

He yelped, shot hands on his backside, but kept running.

'If I see you again, I'll wipe your face across a wall!' I shouted.

They had the jump on me and reached the end of the close before I could nab them.

'You auld cunt!' the lad yelled from the end of the close. The pair of them stood giving me the fingers.

I lunged again, made to run after them and they pegged it.

'Little cockheads,' I muttered as I schlepped back to the motor.

The Punto had lost the wing mirror. I didn't remember it falling off after the collision. I looked about to see if it was in the street. There it was. The little bastards must have yanked it off. I picked it up and placed it on the front seat. As I sat and stared at the broken and scratched plastic, I thought it was a poor substitute for Usual. I firmed my grip on the wheel, locked down my emotions.

'Right, McMilne . . . Let's see what your boy's made of.'

I punched the accelerator. The car shot ahead in first. I was in second before the end of the street, taking the corner like a lunatic. If this fucker wanted a piece of me, he could have it.

CHAPTER 26

The Undertaker had a lap-dancing bar in the part of town known as the Pubic Triangle. I parked at the foot of Castle Terrace, walked round to Lothian Road. I felt my adrenaline spike with every step. I was balling fists and had the familiar metallic taste in my mouth. If a warning flag waved, I missed it. I was off the dial, ready to take down all comers.

There'd been some protests to the pubs round this way: sleazy doesn't work for the Morningside twinsets up the road. I was about to take a protest of my own to the principal purveyor, but I wouldn't be waving a placard. I had an image of my boot stamping that pug's face through the back of his head. Way I felt, I mightn't stop there.

As I reached McMilne's club, saw the neon cowgirl twirling her hooters and firing off her six-shooters, I had a pang of regret: I should have got chibbed up for this. Thought, Fuck it, too late now. I felt armed with enough aggression to demolish the joint anyway.

There shouldn't have been anyone on the door

at this time of day. But there was. As I got closer I recognised him – the man they called Dartboard. He had badly acne-scarred skin, accentuated by the greased-back hair that sat in wiry curls over his neck. He had once been known as a useful welterweight, but had piled on the beef a few years back. The next stop was a trip to Matalan for a cheapo black leather, then a brain-dead bouncer's gig.

I stopped at the door. Dartboard didn't recognise me at first but when he did his eyebrows made sharp angles above his head. 'Dury, bugger me.'

We went way back: my old man was connected to all the local sporting worthies. 'You giving away yer poop-chute now?'

He laughed; didn't know where I'd found a line in humour with all that was on my mind to do once I got through those doors, but it did the trick. Dartboard put a hand on my shoulder and pulled me in.

A red carpet covered the stairs, some soft-porn photographs on the walls. Dartboard spoke: 'Was sorry to hear about your brother.'

I didn't answer; would have been happy for the conversation to end there but he wasn't.

'It's not long since your auld fella went, was it?'

I didn't like to hear the two incidents being hooked up; my father's passing was not something I'd lost any sleep over. 'No. Not long.'

Dartboard was the typical moronic door lump

– he didn't know when to shut his trap. 'But, *you're* still here . . .' he laughed, pointed me through the mirror-backed door at the top of the stairs, 'for now anyway.'

I watched him hold the handle. He had small hands for a boxer. I thought this was something worth noting, until I remembered being told Marvin Hagler had small hands too.

The club was kitted out like every one of these places from here to the black stump. Red walls. PVC seating. Big mirrors. Chrome rails. And a job lot of glitter balls hanging from the ceiling. I'd arrived at the wrong hour for punters. The lights had been turned up, which revealed the true kip of the place: shabby wasn't in it.

Dartboard tapped me on the arm, pointed to a seating area up the back, just shy of a wooden stage. A girl of twenty had her baps out, straddled a ceiling-to-floor pole. Her silver hot pants got slapped by the pug I'd came to see. He hadn't noticed me come in. As I checked the room for obstacles I heard a clink of glasses and spotted the Undertaker and two more girls seated to the left of the stage.

My heart rate reached the point just shy of a cardiac arrest as I walked down towards the pug. He was absorbed in the pole dancer's antics, though, and hadn't seen me. Dartboard fed a stick of chewing gum into his gob as I broke free of him and bolted for the pug. I had a sledgehammer right in his puss before he knew I was in the room; the second was on the way as he staggered back and fell over the stage. I turned quickly but my Crombie tails got tugged by Dartboard. His mouth sat open, the chewing gum balanced on his tongue as I put my fist in it. His head jerked back, but it did no damage – he'd taken too many knocks in the past to even register it. My break came when he started to choke on the gum, bent over and clutched at his throat.

I turned back to the pug. He reeled from a good crack to the nose and blood ran over his lips. As he tried to get up, he put back his hands to right himself from the stage and I put a boot in his mouth. The pole dancer screamed, covered her tits with her arms. It seemed a bizarre time to develop modesty. The girls beside the Undertaker screamed too, stood up and capsized the table. A shower of glass landed at my feet. A heavy glass ashtray came my way too. I picked it up and set about the pug's head. I got in two good pelts, opened up his face some more, before the ashtray split in two and he curled up on the floor, kicking out with his feet.

Falling is the strangest thing in the world: one second you're upright and focused, the next your world view is completely different. He'd caught my feet with a lucky sweep and put me on my back. I stared at a sparkly glitter ball as Dartboard loomed over me, knocked me out with one punch.

* * *

I didn't know how long I'd been out but when the bucket of ice water woke me I was bleeding from the head and my bollocks had been booted. I toppled over onto my hands, collapsed to my elbows as I gasped for breath.

The Undertaker laughed, a rasping sandpaper wheeze that set my spine on edge. 'Who stole yer toffee, Dury?' he said.

I couldn't catch my breath. I was still biting the air, trying to force some of it into my lungs. I cupped my pods in my hand and thanked fuck they were still there.

'Somebody stole his toffee,' said the Undertaker. It was the type of thing people said a generation ago; it seemed out of place here. I looked at him: his knees and elbows made sharp angles as he crouched above me. 'Pick him up,' he said.

Dartboard dragged me to my feet, walked me over to the seating area at the side of the stage. Nobody bothered to raise the table or the glasses. I noticed the pug looming behind the Undertaker. His face had been wiped on the sleeve of his white Henri-Lloyd sweatshirt. I managed to point at him: 'I'm gonna fucking have you.'

He came for me again, but the Undertaker raised a bony hand and he halted mid-stride. 'You'll no' have anybody, laddie. You give me any more bother and I'll fucking open you up like a sponge cake.'

His words carried a kind of practised menace I'd heard a few times before, but never delivered so convincingly. I felt suddenly out of my depth, like I'd fallen asleep on a lilo and woken up a mile out to sea. A queasy sensation rose in my gut.

The Undertaker shuffled over to sit beside me. He patted me on the thigh and said, 'Sit up.'

Like I was going to argue.

As I looked at him I saw he was worse at close range. On the shoulders of his polo neck sat some heavy-duty dandruff, and you could have used the bags under his eyes for a fortnight in Benidorm. The single landing-strip of grey hair that ran down the middle of his head made his gaunt features seem even more severe. I'd like to think a doctor would prescribe feeding up, maybe a course on the sunbeds.

'I'm going tae forget about this wee . . . incident,' he said.

I felt there was a *but* coming.

'But' – there it was – 'only if you do right by me, Dury . . . Is that no' fair enough?'

He spoke like a remnant of another time, the seventies maybe. He turned my mind to rubbish on the streets, white dog turds and *Kojak* on the telly. Maybe it was the polo neck.

I found my breath. 'What you after?'

He didn't like that. I was too lippy; and he wanted respect.

'You're no' in any position tae haggle, laddie. Cunt me around and I'll put you in a hole.'

The pug rolled on the balls of his feet. Laughed.

'Look, I don't know what the fuck you think I can do for you.'

Dartboard brought the Undertaker a glass. It was whisky, Johnnie Walker if I wasn't mistaken, and I never was. He took a sip, winced. His skull looked shrink-wrapped in his skin. 'It's a very simple wee matter . . . I want you to have a word with your late brother's business associate.'

I knew Davie Prentice was at the heart of this; I'd rip his out.

'Go on.'

'See, that fat wee cunt owes me some poppy. I make it about a hunner grand.'

'A hundred Gs . . . How the fuck did he rack that up?'

He took another sip, less of a show this time. 'We had an arrangement and fat Davie pulled the plug on it. I've got a trailerload ay Polish vodka sitting in dock waiting on him getting those fucking trucks of his rolling again. Every week my shelves are doon, it's another fifty bastarding grand he owes me.'

This was a message he could have delivered himself, much more forcefully. The reason he hadn't was obvious: Davie was held up by the Czechs. McMilne owned half the pubs in Tollcross, nice visible targets for a bit of fire-bombing. He didn't want a war he couldn't win. I pushed him: 'Why don't you tell him yourself?'

The Undertaker emptied his glass; he held it up for Dartboard to take away. He sighed as he spoke to me. 'I'm being, what d'ye call it? . . . diplomatic. Look, laddie, that fat wee prick's had us all over. You should be doing this for yer brother.'

I didn't want to hear him talk of Michael – it sent blades into me thinking of my brother dealing with this lowlife, said, 'That's not the way Davie tells it. He says you were the last one to see him alive.'

McMilne jutted his jaw, little stray cactus spikes came for me. 'If that was true, he'd still be here. I had nae bother with Michael, sound as a pound, he was . . . And let me tell you this: he was pissy bloody sick ay Davie's antics as well.'

'What antics? . . . What was he sick of?'

He spoke fast, frothy spit coming at me: 'Broon-nosing they fucking foreigners and cunting me around. Michael knew where his bread was buttered. Nice wee drink he got for himself out ay me . . . Now, you tell Davie this is his last fucking chance tae get those trucks back on the road or there'll be bother.'

I saw I wouldn't get away with much more cheek before the Undertaker lost it, decided to put me in the ground, but I was cocky. 'What if I don't want to be your messenger?'

He laughed – a hacking, throaty birr rose in his windpipe. 'Dury, I'm no' giving you a fucking choice . . . See yon rolly bastard, you better get him told to see sense. And when you come back to me, laddie, you better say what I want to hear. Or you'll find out what I do tae messengers that bring me bad news.'

It felt as if a firework was burning in my head, heat flashing behind my eyes. I knew I was screwed; out of options, said, 'I'll see what I can do.'

CHAPTER 27

Usual pulled through. When I drove him home from the vet's he curled in my lap, seemed too timid to ride in the passenger seat alone. Debs made a fuss over him; I didn't want to tell her about the poison, but felt I had to.

'*Poisoned*?'

'He was lying on the floor of the car when I came back.'

Debs riled, 'Gus, what the hell's going on?'

I tried to make an excuse. 'The vet said, y'know, it's the breed, makes some people go a bit mental and try to off them.' A white lie was one thing but I was making it worse, compounding the sin. I hated bullshitting Debs but what else could I do? I was trying desperately to keep the relationship from falling apart, again.

She didn't buy it, sparked up: 'Just poisoned because someone didn't like the look of him? . . . Och, come off it, Gus.'

I dropped into the couch, sighed. 'Look, Debs, lay off me . . . I'm sorry, I feel dreadful.'

Something made her reach out to me; she knew I wouldn't cause the animal any pain. She knew I was in pain myself. She let it go, but she knew I was keeping something from her. I'd definitely got away with less than I was due – if she knew what had really happened, what I'd gotten myself into with the Undertaker, I'd be carrying her bags down the stairs; or maybe sleeping on them myself.

I left Debs to get ready for work. She had the ironing board up and it left no space in our tiny living room for both of us. The smoked-glass table was covered in hair-styling products and the kitchenette was a no-go when she propped up the mirror on the window ledge to do her make-up. I slunk off to the bathroom and ran the taps, then slid the cistern to get to my speed. I'd had some serious insomnia – not a wink of sleep, hours spent staring into the darkness. I knew what I was doing, and I knew how dangerous it was in my fragile state of mind. *If you gaze for long into an abyss, the abyss gazes also into you* was a line of Nietzsche's I understood entirely.

I took a wrap of speed and chased it with another two. My tolerance had increased dramatically and tackling three wraps at a go was nothing for me. I'd been getting headaches and stomach cramps but I put that down to my general deterioration. I'd lost all appetite and had more or less stopped eating; the thing that had shocked me most, though, was the bleeding from my gums. I felt like my body was shutting down. Knew my soul wasn't far behind it.

I slid the cistern back into place, was about to go and grab a smoke when my mobi rang.

'Yeah.'

It was Mac. 'What's happening? We've been waiting for the nod on this Radek cunt.'

My plans had changed, for now. 'Well, I ran into some difficulties.'

'Such as?'

Did he want to know? I had to keep Mac and Hod informed if they were going to risk their necks for me. 'I went to see Ronnie McMilne.'

'You off yer fucking scone?'

'I'd say so, yeah.'

'I'd fucking say so too. What prompted that?'

I lowered my voice, checked Debs wasn't on the other side the door, and told him about the poisoning. 'I had no choice, it was one of those things.'

'The red mist.'

He wasn't wrong. 'Aye, that's it.'

He asked what I'd got out of McMilne and I gave him a brief rundown. He made the same assessment as I had – we could see all the pieces at the end of the kaleidoscope, but none of them were moving into shape.

'This isn't a help, it's no' good news,' said Mac.

'I know, I know.'

'In fact, Gus, I'd say it's actually fucked things right up.'

He was keen to get moving, to act. I had to wrestle him to the ground on that: 'Look, just fucking well hang fire, eh. You'll get the chance to use your hammer, but I have to sort some shit out first.'

A pause.

Mac's breathing grew heavy; he was pumped, I could tell. 'Right, okay. I hear you. Just don't leave it too long, yeah? These things have a habit of slipping away from you if you don't seize the moment.'

I heard Debs move from the hall to the bedroom. I dropped my voice, said, 'I'll have to go.'

Hung up, opened the door.

Debs stood outside the bathroom with the hairdryer in her hand. She tested: 'Were you on the phone?'

'Yeah, yeah . . . It was Mac banging on about the footy transfers.'

She squinted at me, knew I was bullshitting her once more. I saw she had me sussed – I was up to no good, doing exactly what she'd begged me not to – she just hadn't made up her mind how to react. Once she got a handle on how she felt about my behaviour, I was in the shit. I could feel the pressure building in my skull.

I played for a distraction, said, 'That dryer bust again? It'll be the fuse, electrics in this place are . . . shocking.'

She tried to smile, mocked, 'Har-har.'

I felt a blast of speed-fired optimism – had I won her round? Said, 'I'll get a screwdriver.'

Debs followed me through to the living room.

I dropped in the chair and started to open up the plug, took out the burned fuse.

'Everything all right?' she said.

'Yeah, fine.'

'You sure?'

I looked up at her, tried to steer the talk off the rocks. 'Well, you'll need a new fuse.'

She poked me in the shoulder. 'I'm not talking about that.'

'*I know*,' I snapped. My temper ramped up: 'Debs, everything's fine.'

She started to twirl her wet hair in her fingers. 'You're not . . . y'know, thinking about . . .'

'Drinking? . . . *Fuck no*.'

'Okay. Okay.' She turned away from me and went to the kitchenette, retrieved a comb from the windowsill. As she parted her hair she spoke: 'Do you have another appointment with Dr Naughton soon?'

Shit, I'd forgotten about that. 'Yeah, today as it happens.'

Debs leaned over, let her hair fall over her face and combed from the nape of her neck; she looked left to right and repeated the motion. 'Will you call me, let me know how it goes?'

I closed up the plug, tried it in the wall. The hairdryer blew hot air. 'Is that really necessary?' I sounded tetchy. 'I mean, I'm going, isn't that enough? . . . Do you have to check up on me?'

The dog heard the sound of the hairdryer and stirred in his basket. Debs knelt down, patted him on the head, placed a kiss on his nose. 'I'm not checking up. I just thought you might want to talk it through.'

I shook my head, carved the air with my hand. My heart was quickening as the speed raced through me. 'I don't want to talk about it, Debs. I'm going to the shrink and that's enough as far as I'm concerned.'

She made a moue with her mouth, wondered where the outburst had come from, spat out, 'Okay, fine.'

My pulse raced. I knew I was barking at her because I resented giving over my time to a pretence when I should be hunting my brother's killer. I didn't want to be told I needed to change any more. I didn't want to be moulded any more, or have the worst of me cut out so Debs could find the confidence to stay with me. I knew I needed to change, but that didn't alter the fact that I wanted her to accept me as a whole person. I needed to let her see this, make her understand how tired I was, but I was losing control now. It seemed like just a matter of time until things exploded between us and I couldn't take the pressure that was building – I needed to release it.

'Don't give me the fucking cold shoulder, Debs. I've said I'm going, haven't I?'

She stood up. Usual watched her movement as she came over and snatched the hairdryer from my hand. 'I was only trying to help.'

I turned away from her, punched out at the open

door. The hinges shrieked, then dust rose from the door frame and along the skirting. As I looked at my knuckles Debs shook her head. She said nothing as she turned away from me and started to dry her hair. The tension in the small flat had become too much to take. I stormed into the hall and snatched down my coat.

'Fuck this for a life,' I yelled.

The quarter-bottle of Grouse in my pocket cracked off my hip as I threw the coat on.

CHAPTER 28

I hadn't landed in the street and ripped the knees out my trousers while sober since I was a boy. Since the day Michael was born. The sensation of dropping to the ground felt familiar enough, like the direction of my life speeded up to a few milliseconds, but the collapse stung my pride. I'd come down like a meteor. For some reason, an image of my father flashed. Was it the thought of my brother, going back to the past? I don't know, but I saw my father hacking the legs off a gangly winger when he was playing in the reserves. It must have been one of his final matches; he carried a bit of a paunch then, but had lost none of his ferocity. I remembered the tackle had got him sent off, effing and blinding at the ref as he went. The winger's ankle had broken. I could see his face torn by pain as I raised myself, brushed off the wet, black slush and the white snow from my trousers.

An old woman stood back from her tartan shopping trolley. 'Are you all right, son?'

I felt such a fool, heat rose on my cheeks. 'I am, yeah.'

'You took an awful clatter.' She had a woolly hat

pulled down over her brows, stray white curls escaping its edges as she pointed to my legs. 'You've cut the knees out your trousers!'

I tried to laugh it off. 'I've done worse to myself.'

'Wait there, son.' She went back to her trolley and reached in a hand. She removed a little paper bag – it had the name of the chemist shop down the road on it. She struggled in her gloves to open it, said, 'I've got some Germolene . . . It'll take the sting out.'

As I watched the old woman I felt like taking her up in my arms and blessing her kindness. It seemed surreal to me, in this world, that there were still people with any compassion for others. I said, 'There's no need, dear. It's very kind of you, but really, I'm fine.'

She seemed to freeze in the street. I watched her breath escape beneath her dentures, but she didn't say another word. I wondered if I'd offended her, if I'd broken some protocol that had been instilled in her long before I was born; the thought wounded me.

'Thank you,' I said. It seemed so trite. 'Mind how you go on those pavements.' I smiled at her as I went. She stood holding the little paper bag, unmoving.

At the end of the road I turned back and saw her shuffling up the street, trailing the trolley behind her like a child with a teddy bear. What I wanted to know, as I stared at her on the frozen path, was who would look after *her*?

As I walked, my father followed.

I couldn't shake the memory I'd dislodged.

The reserves drew a fair crowd then. Cannis Dury was still a big name, even though his World Cup outing had faded in Scotland's collective memory. I tried to recall if Michael had been at the game, but I couldn't. I'd blocked him out. I was used to memories of my father flooding back to me unbidden, but I didn't want these heartscalds to be confused with any recollections I had stored of my brother.

I clutched the quarter-bottle of Grouse in my pocket again, played with the seal. I had just about worried the label away; it no longer felt smooth, it was coarse on my fingertips. I tried to still my jittering hand – had this become some kind of obsessive compulsion? It was like a nervous tick, a disorder. I pulled my hand from the bottle. It sank to the bottom of my pocket and lay still. I schlepped all the way to the Mile. At Parliament Square a crowd of shivering Japanese tourists spat on the Heart of Midlothian: they'd obviously been told this was an existing tradition at the site of the old Tolbooth. I thought, these days, it was more likely to get them arrested.

I felt low as I walked. My thoughts lit on my father again, then, inevitably, my brother. I hoped I was getting closer to finding his murderer, but I was also getting deeper into the shit by the day. I'd pushed Debs away too, and I knew she couldn't take much more; the real question was how much more could I take?

Dr Naughton's receptionist greeted me with a cheery hello and directed me to a chair in the waiting area to the side of her desk. Two piles of *National Geographic* lay on the table but I still didn't have the urge to read anything. As I sat, I heard the door from my therapist's room open. She was ushering out a patient. The woman looked like a librarian or a schoolteacher; some of the teachers I'd had were walking wounded – I wondered if I'd fallen into this category now.

My palms began to sweat as the doctor called me in.

I kept my coat on, covered the bloody knees that showed beneath my torn trousers.

'Wouldn't you be more comfortable with your coat off?' said the doctor.

I shook my head. 'I'm fine.'

She stood up, adjusted the thermostat on the wall. 'And how are you today, Gus?'

'I said already, I'm fine.'

She let the sting of that settle. I turned away, didn't want to catch her reaction.

The child's tricycle still sat in the corner. She caught me staring at it again. 'I thought we might try to talk about something different today,' she said.

'Oh, yeah?' I snapped. I really wasn't in the mood for playing the patient any more. I wiped my palms on my coat sleeves.

'Would you like to tell me about your working life?'

I rolled my eyes. 'Oh, sweet Lord.' I knew I was being difficult for reasons of my own, it wasn't her problem. I checked myself. 'Look, my career is over. The trade's finished, and I'm what you might call on the scrapheap. So, not a good choice of subject really, doc.'

She sat forward in her chair, put out her elbows as she crossed her fingers together. 'We can talk about whatever you like.'

I didn't want to talk about anything, so that was going to be a short conversation. I stood up, sighed, 'Is there much more of this to come?'

Dr Naughton's voice softened. 'That's up to you . . . Do you feel you've made any progress with these visits?'

I shook my head. 'Not really. I don't much like going over the past.'

She motioned to my chair. There was nowhere to hide in the room so I sat down again. 'Surely there must be some moments of happiness you recall.'

I kept my hands in my pockets, manoeuvred my coat over my knees again. 'Some . . .' They all involved Debs; it touched a deep part of me, registered why I was there.

'Would you like to tell me about one?'

I dredged up a few images: expressions on her face, how she looked at one time or another. How happiness felt. My heart seemed to still inside me, and a warmth washed over my mind. A precious memory lit up; I almost smiled.

'We were at the birth of my niece, Alice . . .'

'Go on.'

'It was special. Debs had taken a real interest when Jayne got pregnant – my wife, we were married then, she'd lost a child and couldn't have another . . . I think she got something out of being around Jayne, do you understand?'

'I understand, yes.'

I fiddled with a hangnail as I spoke. 'It was all, y'know, baby talk and baby books and clothes and so on for months. Jayne and Michael were so young it was a bit of a shock to them both but I think it focused them, it was a real spark for Michael making something of himself . . . He was still trucking then, was halfway across Europe when we got a call to rush Jayne to the hospital. We were on standby, so to speak, we drove her in the back of the car.' Now I smiled at the recollection. 'She was so bloody big, like a house. We could hardly get her through the door of the car . . . Debs sat with her on the back seat, doing the breathing exercises.'

I stopped to savour the memory. My eyes misted.

A prompt: 'And you drove the car to the hospital?'

'Yeah, yeah, I did that . . .' I remembered pacing the corridor. A nurse had asked me if I was the father and I had had to explain that Michael wasn't coming. I remembered the way Debs had lowered her head when the nurse asked me; she was wounded. I stopped smiling.

'Was it a simple birth?'

'No, not at all . . . *Christ*, I must have emptied that coffee machine, we were there all night. They put off doing a Caesarean for hours but in the end Jayne was so weak that they had no choice.' The moment we were called into the ward still lived in me: Jayne was almost too drugged to hold baby Alice, her head was lolling from side to side and Debs had to put her hand underneath to support it. We couldn't believe the black hair on her, thick, thick black hair. When Debs took Alice in her arms they looked so similar that they could have been mother and child. We both had so much love for her that it felt as if she was ours. Jayne looked exhausted but she had enough energy to cry – we all knew why.

'How did you feel when you held your niece for the first time?' said Dr Naughton.

My throat seized, my eyes filled and I knew if I moved my head, even slightly, tears would fall. 'I felt joy . . .' I said, 'real joy . . . and the most incredible pain that my wife would never hold our own child.'

CHAPTER 29

Debs had left a note stating she'd gone to stay with her friend Susan.

'Just . . . great.'

Susan would not be talking me up – we shared a mutual antipathy. The note was brief, said she'd taken the dog because he needed looking after and 'You have enough to do mending yourself, Gus.'

Debs claimed she wanted to give me some space, that I needed to think.

'Fuck that!'

Thinking was the last thing I needed more of right now. I knew why Debs had left, couldn't fault her for it, but it still felled me. I just couldn't expect her to stick around while I delved into my brother's murder. Way things were shaping up, she was safer out if it.

I stormed to the bathroom and kicked off the cistern. It flew in the air, made a one-eighty then clattered off the sink, splitting in two. I fired into the speed wraps and took myself back to the living room. As my heart rate increased I immediately felt panic settle on me. The flat was silent and cold, empty. I paced to the bedroom. Debs had cleaned out her make-up and styling products. A small wheeled suitcase that usually sat on top of the wardrobe had been taken and her dressing gown no longer hung on the back of the door. The room seemed to have changed very little, but what had altered was seismic. I loped back to the living room in a daze, sat on the couch. I looked through to the space we'd cleared under the kitchenette counter for Usual's basket. It was gone.

A throbbing started in my temples. I put my fingers around my skull and squeezed.

'This isn't happening,' I told myself; but I knew it was.

I picked up Debs's note and read it through again. She'd left the number for Susan's house. It seemed such a strange thing to do when we all had mobiles nowadays. As I thought it through I sussed she was trying to say I could still contact her, she'd still speak to me. At least I hoped that's what she meant; maybe I was being optimistic.

I got up and made myself a coffee, tried to buy off my shrieking brain with caffeine. Didn't work. I found myself back on the couch looking through Debs's Cranberries CDs and wondering what the hell I should do next. Nothing I'd tried so far seemed the right move. I was sure the shrink had made me feel worse, raked up old hurts. I wondered if there would ever be a future for Debs and me. It just seemed like the world was against it. We'd tried so many times to make it work but it always ended the same way – with me hurting her. I felt ashamed at the realisation.

I held my head in my hands once again, then my phone rang. The noise broke through the desolation of the flat.

I dived up to grab it from the mantel.

'Hello . . .'

'Ah, Dury, 'tis yer bold self.'

'Fitz.'

'Ye sound disappointed . . . Who were ye expecting, Angelina Jolie?' He laughed at himself. I wondered if he had a drink in him.

'What do you want?'

A harrumph. 'I was, er, thinking we might have a little, whatsit they say these days? . . . A catch-up.'

I remembered our last one: 'Do I need a brief this time?'

He roared laughing. 'Ah, Dury . . . yer some joker.'

I was deadly serious. 'I'm not laughing.'

'Okay, so . . . Look, I'm after clearing my desk of one or two items relating to your late brother's unfortunate demise, and I was needing to return some of it. I thought I could let you have them, save disturbing others.'

I got the picture, said, 'Yeah, fine. You want to meet the same place?'

'Caff on the Mile . . . Can you be there in an hour?'

'I'll be there.'

Clicked off.

The auld wifey from number three was coming up the stairs as I walked out.

'Hello, there,' she said.

I nodded, had passed her with little recognition when she spoke up again. 'Your wife told me about the poor dog.'

I stopped still, turned. 'She's not my wife.' The words came out too harshly. 'I mean, we're not married.'

The wifey creased her mouth into a thin smile. 'Well, the pair of you look made for each other . . . I'm sure there'll be a big day soon.'

I didn't know what to say, stumbled on the step.

She went on, 'She'd make a beautiful bride. A bonnie-looking girl she is.'

I found my feet, managed, 'I don't deserve her.'

The truth, I knew, was that she didn't deserve me.

The street looked as if it had just been dusted with icing sugar; another light snowfall had settled over the city. Footprints had started to erode the white covering on the pavement but the wider view was so bright it burned my eyes. I schlepped over the road at the Arc building and turned under the railway bridge. I bent into a chill wind that cut into my face and froze my jaw. I longed for winter to be over, for the temperature to rise and the sun to make an appearance again. Even the weak Scottish one that shows too rarely, and when it does, not for long enough.

At the foot of the Mile a tartan shop had taken a break from blasting the street with teuchter music and had turned to Slade's 'Merry Christmas Everybody' instead. I took a sketch in the window: the jolly kilted mannequin that spent his days drinking pretend whisky from a plastic tumbler had been strangled with a tinsel noose. He didn't seem fazed – laughing it up same as ever – but he did stare out at the new parliament, which was a joke the year round.

In the caff some student bell-end in a Cossack's hat danced before me in the queue. If he stood on my toe one more time he'd get a taste of my own footwork in his coal-hole. I was in no mood to indulge some Tarquin who was slumming it with the proles because mammy and daddy had cut back on his gin money during the economic crisis.

I tapped him on the shoulder. 'Excuse me.'

He turned round, a dramatic flourish of the arms as he went all Bronski Beat on me. 'Yes?'

I pointed to my boot. 'Do you see that?'

He eyeballed me.

Bad idea.

'A foot, for standing, perhaps walking,' he said. Sniggers from his shitkicker friends.

I edged closer, went nose to nose with him. 'Would you like me to introduce you to another of its uses?'

He backed away. If he'd went any faster he'd have given himself whiplash.

A gap appeared in the queue.

Ordered, 'A coffee, please, and a pot of tea. Can you hold the tea till my friend arrives?'

'I'm here . . . I'm here.' Fitz appeared ruddy-faced, cheeks on him like the fire station doors. He carried a bag over his left shoulder – the look was way too metrosexual for him.

We took a table. Fitz loosened his collar.

'Did you run here?' I said.

'Feck off, man. 'Tis that hill: damn near has me buggered.'

The tea and coffee came, got placed down before us.

I thought to ask him how the case was going, but knew if he had anything that he was prepared to divulge it would be dished up soon enough. He leaned back on his chair, reached for the bag. He took out a padded envelope. 'This is, erm, well . . . It's your brother's possessions.'

I imagined what would be inside. Little see-through plastic bags containing Michael's watch and wedding ring. Whatever else there was, I didn't want to see it. I took the package – it seemed very light.

Fitz said, 'There's a computer and some stuff we took from his office; I gave that to uniform to drop off at the factory.'

'Have you been into the computer?' I knew I was being optimistic.

'Oh yes, the boffins have been all through it. Nothing for us, I'm afraid.'

I expected no more.

I held the envelope in my hands as though it was made of the most delicate porcelain. It seemed to take my attention from Fitz. My thoughts wandered all over the place; I was no more than emotional carrion now. I broke out of my daydream, placed the package on the table. Fitz started to stir his tea.

I said, 'Thank you.'

'I thought, y'know, you might be better taking the bits and pieces to his wife . . . Might come better from you.'

I was grateful for the compassion. 'It was a generous thought.'

He flicked up an eyebrow, pointed with his spoon. 'I wanted to say . . . after our last chat . . .'

'Yeah?'

'I wanted to reassure you that, all we can, we're doing for you.'

I tutted. I knew what *doing for me* meant to most of the force. I swung from gratitude to anger: I knew I was the only one moving this investigation forward. 'Is that so?' I said. I leaned in, placed my elbows on the table. 'I've been doing a bit more myself since I saw you last, Fitz, and let me tell you, I'm not convinced your lot are doing enough.'

He raised his cup, slurped. 'Is that so?'

'Yeah, yeah,' I slumped back in my seat, 'I don't see you all over the papers announcing you've made any progress, like you've found the gun or have a suspect for Michael's murder . . . or Andy's, or Ian Kerr's either.'

That got him fired up. 'Fucking papers.'

'You'd be happy enough to have the press splash any good news about.'

He slammed his cup on the saucer. The spoon jumped. 'There is progress, but I can't tell you everything.'

I lurched for him. 'Why the fuck not?'

'Look at you . . . because you're away with it, man! You'd go haring in like some mad heller and get yerself and Lord alone knows who else killed if I gave you a sniff of what I'm on to.'

I wasn't wearing that, lamped in: 'Why haven't you busted the Czechs?'

'For what? I can't go around throwing just anyone in jail, especially foreign nationals. You want me with an international incident on my hands?'

I got up. I'd heard enough. I knew Fitz hadn't moved the case on an inch since our last meeting: he was still sitting around waiting for the Undertaker to fuck up and get his next glamour collar. 'I'm sure it'll all fall in your lap.'

As I bent down to pick up the envelope he grabbed my arm. 'C'mon, sit back down, Gus.'

I didn't trust him when he called me by my first name. 'Why?'

He nodded to the package. 'That wasn't the only reason I called you out.'

'No?'

'No, it wasn't.'

I sat back down. 'Go on, then.'

Fitz put a fat finger above his tie, stretched the loop wider, 'I don't want you to take this the wrong way, but . . . We had your niece down the station the other night.'

'Alice?' I wondered what she'd been up to now. Did I want to hear?

'Nothing heavy: she'd had a jug of something with a group of the local young crew . . . The uniforms printed her, took her down the cells, but I drove her home.'

I panicked – how had Jayne taken it? 'Her mother?'

Fitz shook his head. 'No. No. I never told the mother, woman has enough on her plate, I'm sure . . . Very bad time of year for, y'know, this type of thing.'

I scratched the top of my head, let out a long sigh. 'Thanks again.'

'No bother. I'd keep an eye on the lass, though. She was a bit . . . emotional.'

'Emotional?'

Fitz drew a deep breath, exhaled. 'About her father . . . I'd say she's struggling to get to grips. It's a bad age for her; I know, I've got daughters myself.'

I thanked him again, nodded. Said, 'I'll have a word.'

'Mind your family, Gus. Leave the investigation to us.'

I stood up, said nothing. Anything I thought to mention would only make him flare up.

He grabbed my arm. His eyes burned into me. 'I mean it: think how they'd take another loss so close to home.'

CHAPTER 30

I couldn't bear to open the envelope from Fitz. I looked at it: a padded manila job, dog-eared corners; on the front a white label with my brother's name and a case number written in black marker pen. I couldn't stop my imagination picturing what was inside, but I didn't want to go there yet.

I remembered Michael lying in the mortuary, how pale he'd looked, so still. The small grey hole beneath his heart, barely a half-inch wide, where the bullet had entered, and taken his life.

I sat with the envelope on my lap, then brought it up to my chest.

'Och, Michael.'

The blood was coursing through my arms as I gripped tightly to the package. I felt ready to howl out my hurt. I was ready to tear down the world that had taken away my brother. 'I find who did this, Michael . . . I'll kill them. I promise you. I'll take a life for yours.'

I got up too quickly from the couch – black dots flashed at the edges of my field of vision. I needed another wrap. I took the envelope through to the bedroom and put it on top of the wardrobe. I played with the idea of taking it straight to Jayne, but I knew she wasn't ready for that kind of shock either.

I fired some more speed, felt twitchy. The backs of my eyes itched; felt like scooping them out with spoons. Knew I was ramping up, raring to go mental. I'd reached the point where I just didn't want to think any more about how things might play out; I didn't care, it was an irrelevance now. The loss I felt was all-consuming. I was ready to start with the scatter gun; if I took down some innocents along the way, so be it.

I picked up my mobi. One side of it was covered in slap. I looked at the window ledge where I'd sat it and saw a thin layer of Debs's face powder; there was an oblong imprint where the mirror usually lay. It looked like dust had settled, as though more time had passed than was possible; the image tripped me out. I dipped my fingertip in the powder and watched the sheen transfer itself. It felt like touching a ghost.

I turned away. Rubbed my fingertip on the couch as I sat down, then buffed my phone in the same way. The powder showed up on the couch like a shiny film of grease. I rubbed at it with my hand but it wouldn't go away. I put a cushion over it.

I went into my contacts. I had two calls to make; the first to Alice went straight to voicemail. Thought, *Fucking hell.* I hate talking to machines, said: 'Hi, kiddo, it's Gus . . . Can you give me a call? Just wanted to check how you were doing. Is everything okay? Jeez, I don't suppose you'd say, would you . . . Look, just go easy on the Scrumpy Jack, eh . . . I know what I'm talking about, here . . . Right, so give me a call, huh? Be good, Alice, I'll see you soon.'

I winced at the pathetic tone of my message; I was trying too hard and I knew she'd sense that right off. I dropped the phone, got up, cursed myself and sat back down. I vowed to do a better job with the next one.

Ringing.

'Hello, David Prentice speaking.' I was surprised fat Davie had answered his own line, but then again, wondered why I should be – way things were headed in that place.

'I've got a message to give to you, Davie.'

'Who is this?'

I laughed down the phone. 'Don't play the wide cunt with me.'

'Gus?'

'Got it in one. Now let's see if you can keep up that perfect score. I have a message for you from guess who.'

'Is this some kind of a joke?' He actually managed to press a note of indignation into his tone.

'Fucking smart up, Davie . . . Do you really think I'm messing about? If you do, then maybe I've got to come and take you for another birl up the Craigs.'

His breathing faltered. 'No. No. I'm sorry, I understand, I-I mean, who? Erm, Ronnie? Is your message from Ronnie McMilne?'

'He shoots, he scores. That's two out of two, bonnie lad.' I lit a tab, let him hear the burn of it down the line. 'Let's try for a hat-trick, eh?'

Silence. I could hear the clock ticking on the wall.

'Yes . . .' said Davie.

'Good, good. Now, your friend and mine, the happy, smiley Undertaker, has got it into his head to be fucked off about something . . . What do you think that might be, Davie?'

He paused; I could hear him scratch the stubble on his chin. 'I know what that might be.'

'Oh, you do? . . . Great, because if you get the hat-trick, Davie, you win a prize. Know what it is? It's, well, it's not much of a prize, it's your sorry arse. You get to keep your sorry arse above the ground.' I let the words settle, took another blast on my Marlboro. 'Tell me then, Davie, what the Undertaker told me to remind you?'

He stammered, spat words: 'The trucking . . .'

I jumped up, yelled, 'Un-fucking-believable! . . . Davie Prentice, you are a winner!' I threw myself back on the couch. 'Yes, Davie, the Undertaker wants you to keep on trucking. He wants you to tell your Czech friends to get tae fuck and he wants you to know that every week that goes by that he's short of some Polish vodka to punt in his pubs, that's another fifty Gs you owe him.

How does that grab you? And don't say by the balls.'

No answer.

I heard movement on the other end of the line. 'It's not for me to—'

'Oh, no, you're not going to blank our friend Ronnie, in favour of your new friends, are you?'

'I–I . . .'

'Come on now, Davie. Are you telling me you've got a better offer?'

'Gus, it's not as simple as that. You don't understand what kind of people we're dealing with. I–I . . . I mean, we're not dealing with rational people here.'

I adopted a sarky voice. 'Are you saying they're the kind of people that might do you some damage if you crossed them?'

Fat Davie's words trembled over the phone: 'I think that's understood.'

I sat up straight. Hammered nails into my pitch. 'What's understood, y'cunt, is that you're about to be thrown to the wolves, Davie . . . Just like you did to my brother.'

I hung up.

CHAPTER 31

Hod pushed the Hilux hard. I nearly ate my chips backwards as he tore through the gears. He amber-gambled on the lights and clipped a traffic cone at Waterloo Place. A ned in a Burberry cap, wankered on Buckie, held up the bottle in approval as we passed. I turned to Mac and laughed. There was no point slamming Hod's driving – it was an expression of his masculinity that went way beyond criticism as far as he was concerned.

'Look at that wee fannybaws in the hat,' said Hod.

'You look at the fucking road,' Mac told him, 'you're gonna tip this motor.'

'Bullshit. I'm rock . . . look at me!' Hod took his hands off the steering wheel and held them in front of him. 'Steady as the day is long.'

Mac lunged for the wheel. 'Get them back, y'arsehole.'

I had to laugh. It was like Bill Murray in *Stripes*, taking the pictures of the old cow in the fur. 'Mac, he's pulling yer chain,' I said. 'Don't play up to it.'

Mac leaned forward, took the bolt-cutters from the floor. 'I'll pull his fucking teeth!' He was only half joking – I could see him having a go at it.

Hod fell into a throaty laugh. 'You crack me up, Mac boy . . . This is gonna be fun, eh!'

Mac snapped the cutters at him, got so close he threatened to catch the tip of Hod's tache. I thought they seemed a wee bit too hyped for what we had planned, but I let it slide; I was pumped for the job myself. The Czechs weren't an outfit to mess with – I'd seen what they'd done to Andy Gregory and Ian Kerr – but if the filth weren't digging them out, then somebody had to.

We got through Leith Street before the buses left the stops but got snagged on the roundabout at Picardy Place. Hod tried to change lanes. 'Fucking tram works. Who wants shoogly cars anyway? . . . We'll never get down the Walk.' He pushed his way in front of a bloke in a white van, took pelters and a blast on the horn. I eyeballed the driver and he looked away. Thought: Wise back-down, fella. Testosterone shot about in the cab like electricity looking for an earth. First wido to cross us was likely to be fitted for a plaster-of-Paris jumpsuit.

On Broughton Street Hod cut a right and revved too high, sent the wheels spinning on the icy road. Mac had let up complaining, turned on the radio. Some talking head banged on about more casualties in the economy. So many retail chains were folding we'd soon have nothing but boarded-up shopfronts.

Hod sighed, 'I didn't see Woolies going under, that was a shocker.'

'What about the old MFI?' said Mac. 'That's gonna hit the doer-uppers.'

Hod scrunched his brows. 'What you on about, doer-uppers? There's no fucking housing market left. It's ground to a halt.'

Mac barked, 'That's maybe why they went bust then, eh.'

The pair still sparred as I leaned over and turned up the volume to drown them out. Another gobshite had come on the airwaves, said, 'It is time to end the workshy's reliance on the state.' I thought he was on about our government ministers until I sussed that he was one himself.

'Och, fucksake . . . they're slicing into the jammy roll now,' I said.

Mac's attention shifted: 'The dole's being cut?'

We listened to the political pigmy who had been fronted to deliver the news that, as the multi-billion packages to bail out banks had to be paid for somehow, there were going to be cutbacks in the dole.

'That's bad news,' I said.

Mac riled up: 'Says he wants a million folk off benefits whilst the country's losing jobs left and right.'

'This is going to end in anarchy . . . Watch this space: we'll be stringing them from lamp posts.'

Hod joined in: 'Put me down for some of that. I'll even bring my own fucking rope.'

The temperature in the Hilux rose. I wound down the window a couple of inches but the air outside was too cold, had to close it again. I read the thermostat in the dash – it was four-below. As we drove past the banana flats, down to the waterfront, I saw frosted windscreens on every car parked along the side of the road. Some of the roofs had an inch or two of hardened snow on them. In the gutter, the night before's beer tins lay trapped in the frozen puddles.

'Do you know where you're going?' I asked Hod.

'Aye, I did a wee dry run last night.'

'Any sign of life at the place?'

'I didn't stop, just drove by . . . Nice big hoose.'

Hod's detour to miss the tram works on the Walk meant we had to snake back through the side streets, but the entire port was in disarray: building materials dumped in the roads, cables stacked up against dumper trucks, machinery waiting to be carted to the site of the main track work.

As we reached the Links, I checked the road for a black Pajero. Plenty of cars were parked up along the kerb, but I didn't see a Pajero. Hod spied a space, pulled up. We sat opposite an old No Ball Games sign; a newer foreign-language one had gone up beside it.

'The fuck's that?' said Hod.

'Polish,' I told him. I'd read in the paper that the city's Polish community had been congregating on the Links in big numbers – there'd been some revelry. 'Apparently, the toon cooncil has had complaints about some big-time Polish piss-ups . . . It'll be a warning notice.'

'Pish-ups on the Links, eh,' said Mac, he started to snigger. 'Whatever next.'

'I know, it's not like the place isn't hoachin' with brassers and our own home-grown jakeys.' The double standards folk applied to migrants appalled me; the way our own country was going, we'd all be migrants ourselves soon enough.

Hod picked out the house for us. It was a large Georgian number, would have cost some poppy back in the boom but my guess was, current climate, no one would be able to shift it. The building sat over three storeys, with a basement level and, I'd guess, substantial extensions to the rear.

'Looks empty,' said Mac.

'Uh-uh, check it.' Hod pointed to the window in the second floor. A light was burning; a bloke in a white hoodie paced the floor.

I tried to get a deck at the fella. He was dark-haired and heavy, that was about all I could see. He passed the window another couple of times then disappeared. The light went out after him.

'Think that's our man?' said Mac.

'Our . . . Radek?' said Hod. 'Couldn't tell.'

'Well, let's give the cunt a pull anyway,' said Mac. He leaned forward in his seat, twisted. 'Come on, Gus . . . get the door open.'

I put a hand on his chest, shoved him back down. 'Just give it time.'

'What do you mean, give it time?' Mac scented blood: he was gantin' to burst some heads, any he could get his hands to.

'I want to see what the lie of the land is,' I said. 'Trust me, I have a game plan here.'

Mac sat back in his seat, mouthed off, 'I thought we came here to go in, no' just sit outside.' He picked up the bolt-cutters, started to snap them.

I spoke over him: 'Hod, tell me about this guy again.'

'Radek's a nut-job . . . seriously off his cake. I spoke to a few more boys off the sites – no one's got a different opinion. Although there's quite a bit of guesswork going on around town as to why he's over here.'

'Oh, aye . . .'

'Rumour has it he's a wanted man back home. You get that shite a lot on the sites when someone appears from elsewhere, but mostly it's talk, someone biggin' himself up. Nobody doubts it's true in Radek's case.'

Like this mattered now. But I was interested. 'What do they say he's wanted for?'

'That's the thing, nobody knows.' Hod shrugged. 'If it was just bullshit, folk would know all about it.'

Mac tapped on the dash. 'Aye, aye.' The door of the house eased open, our man in the white hoodie appeared. He spoke into a mobile phone as he locked the door. When he jumped down the steps we all saw that he fitted the description of Radek perfectly.

'Right, let's nash,' said Hod. He opened his door.

'Wait,' I yelled. A black Pajero pulled up in front of the house. The bloke tugged the hoodie over his head as he jumped in the front. The driver gave a quick glance into the road and spun wheels.

'Fucking hell, he's on the move,' said Mac.

Hod slammed his door, put the key back in the ignition, said, 'We going after him, then?'

CHAPTER 32

'Sit tight.'

'Gus, *Jesus*, the fucker's getting away,' said Mac.

We watched the Pajero speed up. The driver did a left-to-right at the end of the street, then burned it. We got close enough to see into Radek's eyes as he passed us.

'That's our man,' said Hod.

'That *was* our man,' said Mac.

I pulled the door handle, stepped out onto the street. The pair of them looked at me like I'd suggested colonic irrigation all round. 'Come on, then.' I held the door, waved them out, 'Are you coming or not? And you better get those bolt-cutters.'

My foot struck a Lech lager can as I walked to the house – they'd replaced the Omega cider ones round here. I kicked out, put the can in the air. Mac and Hod followed from the truck. I had a hand jemmy in the pocket of my Crombie, but I wondered if I might have been better getting hold of something with a little more firepower. I'd passed the point where I gave a shit for myself, but I worried about the pair behind me. If we ran into any grief, I knew they could handle themselves better than most, but I replayed those pictures of Andy's face. The sight of his tongue, cut out and attached to his chest with a knife, wasn't an image I was going to forget any time soon.

'What you thinking here, Gus?' said Hod.

'He locked the door behind him, so I'm guessing the joint's empty.'

Hod jogged up to my side. 'That's no' much fucking use to us.'

He was well wrong. I said, 'You don't know what might be in there, Hod . . . Might be the belly of the whale.'

He looked at me like I'd gone scripto, turned to Mac and raised a finger in a swirling motion at his ear. Mac firmed his jaw and focused on the front door of the house.

As we left the road and started up the driveway my guts tightened. I gripped the jemmy in my pocket and took a sketch down the street. The place was quiet; it was too cold to be venturing out of doors unless totally necessary.

The house looked like a doss, the paint peeling from the door and every window frame. There was only one set of curtains hanging: the rest of the windows were covered by taped-down newspaper and pinned-up, faded pieces of cloth. It was an end terrace. The house next door had been recently whitewashed, but this joint was painted grey and hadn't been touched up for a few years. A pallet of cement sat in the front garden, a tarpaulin stretched over it, and what looked like a rusty alternator had been left by the doorstep.

A dog barked ahead of us.

Mac spoke: 'That's not up the path, is it?'

I turned, saw the dog over the fence. 'It's in the next garden.'

'Thank fuck for that.'

I nodded towards the side of the house, the others followed. A jerry-built carport was attached to the gable end. I imagine it looked as ramshackle the day it went up. Hod put a hand on the supporting block, shook it. 'Nobody sneeze,' he said. 'That's bloody rough work.'

At the edge of the path a gate rattled in the wind. It had a hasp-lock secured with a wooden peg; I slid out the peg and opened the gate, its hinges screaming out for oil. 'Anyone bring the 3-in-1?' I said.

Mac shoved me through. Hod followed and closed the gate behind us.

More building supplies cluttered the back yard. A cement mixer and a trailer filled with pickaxes that didn't look as though they'd been used in months. Several layers of frost had settled on them; I'd take bets they'd remain stuck together for the rest of the winter.

Hod peered into the basement window. The

steps leading down there lay covered in ice. 'Looks empty.'

'You not going to check?' said Mac.

'See the state of those stairs? Fuck that . . . I'd be on my arse.'

Mac eased up to the extension, looked as if it might be a kitchen. He checked in the window, said, 'What a fucking kip house.'

Hod and I joined him. Inside sat a row of bunks; they were made of bare, untreated wood and looked as if they'd been put together with nail guns. On the bunks lay empty sleeping bags, in between them sat a large blue Calor gas bottle. A rubber hose came from the bottle, but it didn't seem to be connected to anything.

'Not exactly the Balmoral, is it?'

Hod tried the handle on the back door, then looked at us and shook his head. 'It's double-locked.'

I leaned over, tested it. 'You're right.' I put the jemmy in the jamb and prised away. It eased a couple of inches and we heard the first lock give. I pressed the jemmy in again, higher up the frame; I didn't need to apply any force before the second lock sprung open. I pushed the door in.

The air came thick with a confusion of smells, predominantly paraffin. Beside the back door a wheelie bin had been brought in. It overflowed with takeaway cartons and crushed-up lager cans;

someone had tried to flatten them into the bin, succeeded only in spilling them on the floor.

'It's Abe Lincoln in here,' said Hod.

'Somebody needs to get about with the Shake 'n' Vac, eh.' The soles of my Docs stuck to the carpet as I walked. More bunks sat out behind the door, greasy sleeping bags lying on top of them. In the hallway was a spare 4x4 tyre and another two bunks, head to toe.

As we looked about the place we kept our voices down. In every room as many bunks as possible had been crammed in. Odd signs of habitation showed here and there, like a can of deodorant or a pair of socks drying on a radiator, but the bareness of the place was startling.

'I've stayed in better workie huts than this,' said Hod.

'I bet you have,' I said, 'it's worse than fucking *Auf Wiedersehen, Pet*.'

On the second floor the carpet ran out. We got down to bare boards. The rooms had more bunks, more greasy, filthy sleeping bags. Stacks of rubbish sat about everywhere – pizza boxes and KFC buckets, empty two-litre bottles of Sprite and Coke. Hod opened a cupboard, wheeled out a vacuum cleaner. 'Bet this gets used a lot.' He wheeled it back, saw the plug had been removed, laughed. 'Explains it . . .' He closed the cupboard door, said, 'Surprised they never squeezed another bunk in there. Must've seen fifty already.'

At the foot of the stairs to the top floor, Mac grew restless. 'There's fuck all here, Gus. Is there any need to go further?'

I took his point: it didn't look like there'd been much left behind. Wondered why Radek had even bothered to lock the door. 'Well, we're here now. Might as well check the lot.'

We took the stairs, Mac sighing as we went. There was less headroom on the top floor, but they'd still managed to cram in the bunks. At the end of the hallway lay a pair of rolled-up carpets, that had been flattened – a sleeping bag sat on top of each one.

'There's your carpets,' said Hod. 'Lifted them for a kip.'

'This is mental. I can't believe anyone lives like this in Scotland.'

'Believe it, mate . . . Believe it.'

Mac had strolled off round the bend in the hallway and started to test the handle on a locked door. When we joined him he had the bolt-cutters on a heavy padlock that had been attached beneath the keyhole.

'Aye, aye . . . What you found?' I said.

'Dunno, let's see.'

The bolt-cutters went through the padlock as though it was made of plasticine. It clattered onto the floorboards. The door was still locked but Mac put his boot up – it caved in.

We entered the room.

A double bed sat at one end, a *Playboy* duvet cover on top. 'Klarse!' said Hod.

At the other end of the room a PC and a phone sat on a desk. A television and DVD player perched on top of a solid-metal filing cabinet.

'Think we got the executive suite?' I said.

'Bang on,' said Mac.

Hod turned out the wardrobe, dropped clothes on the floor. He looked to be enjoying it, even let himself tear the odd shirt pocket off. As Mac took the bolt-cutters to a padlock on the filing cabinet I rifled through the drawers running down the left-hand side of the desk and tipped them out on the floor. On the other side of the desk the drawers were locked. I took out the jemmy and bust them open. As they sprung out Mac called me over.

'Any use to you?' He held up a bunch of Czech passports.

I took a look at one of them. 'What else you got in there?' I walked over to Hod at the wardrobe and picked up a bag, dumped in the passports.

'Dole books,' said Mac, 'some more passports . . . Giros too.'

I took the lot, stuck them in the bag. 'Gives Fitz something to go on,' I said.

Mac emptied the files, tipped over the cabinet. I watched Hod tear into a suit jacket as I went back to the drawers I'd just sprung open. They held more documentation, wage slips and written contracts, some stuff in Czech I couldn't figure. I bagged it all, but I wanted something stronger, something to nail Radek with. As I tipped out the final drawer I found it. Mac and Hod turned with the heavy thud as it landed on the floor. I bent my knees and carefully peered over it.

'Is that what I think it is?' said Hod.

I leaned in, cleared away the mess of papers to get a better look. 'What we have here is . . . a gun.'

CHAPTER 33

The shooter was inside a sealed polythene bag. I grabbed hold of the corner and raised it. Mac and Hod came in closer.

'Looks like an old Webley,' said Mac.

I turned it round: it was a revolver, a well-used one. 'Looks fucking ancient.'

'It will be, aye. Lot of old guns like that get knocked off. You wouldn't believe how many are still kicking about from the war.'

Hod spoke: 'Why's he got it in a bag?'

I wondered that myself. I edged the seal open, brought the contents up to my nose. 'It's been fired . . . I can still smell the burned powder – the bag's sealed it in.'

'Doesn't tell us why it's in the bag,' said Hod.

I sealed it up again, my mind sparking, 'There's only one reason why you'd put it in a bag – to preserve it.'

'Maybe wanted to keep it dry,' said Mac.

'In a fucking drawer . . .' I was sticking to my hunch: 'Somebody's dabs are on this, maybe the person I'm looking for.' I placed the shooter in the bag with the passports and paperwork. 'I need to get this lot to Fitz, soon as . . .'

I felt an adrenaline rush as I headed for the door. I knew I had, potentially, the weapon used to murder my brother in my hands. My thoughts mashed. Did this mean Radek wasn't the killer? There was no way he would hold on to the gun if he'd offed my brother, so what the fuck was he doing with it? There had to be an angle, but I couldn't see it.

'Gus,' Hod called me as I reached the door. 'You better check this.'

'What is it?'

He pointed to the window. I walked back to the desk, looked out into the street – the black Pajero had pulled up. Behind it was a minibus disgorging a stream of hefty blokes; they headed straight for the house.

'*Shit.*'

'And you're the one holding a shooter,' said Mac.

'Are you off your fucking nut? We can't use that, it's evidence.'

Hod stepped forward, nodded. 'He's right.' He put a fist on Mac's shoulder. 'Have to be old school, mate.'

'I knew we should have got fucking well tooled up,' said Mac.

I tied a knot in the carrier, said, 'Just stay calm . . .'

The front door opened, the sound of voices came rattling in. Heavy boots shook the floor beneath us. 'Come on,' I whispered, 'follow me.'

I retraced the way we'd come in, watching over the banister to the blokes below. Their voices grew louder, blasting my ears with a language I didn't understand. They seemed to be filling up the rooms at the front of the house, but I couldn't be sure. I heard the bus's engine ticking over outside and then the driver engaged the clutch and put it into gear. The diesel engine purred loudly then took off. A few seconds later the front door slammed.

'They're all in,' said Hod. His voice was too loud; I flagged him quiet.

Mac nudged him with his elbow. 'Shut up, man . . . You want to get us killed?'

I peered out the window. 'Think we can jump.'

Hod shook his head. 'We're too high up . . . and I've got these fucking bruised ribs.'

Mac leaned over, whispered, 'Don't be fucking silly – *jump*.' He patted his space-hopper guttage. 'This doesn't mean I bounce, y'know.'

I checked out the window again. The ground below looked frozen solid. I knew they were right: we'd break our legs. I felt my chest constrict; the most intense need for nicotine seized me. I couldn't think. Mac and Hod stared at me. As I turned from them, I caught sight of a white hoodie moving on the stairs below.

'Fuck, it's Radek.'

Mac and Hod shifted over the banister, jerked back. They looked at each other briefly then returned their gaze to me. I felt my jaws clench.

My mouth dried over. The image of Andy, the tongue cut out of him, came back to me once more. Fucking hell, this nut-job didn't mess about. Something sparked: 'Right, come on. Back this way.'

'Gus, Gus . . .' said Hod. He pointed to the stairs. 'That's the way down.'

'I fucking know,' I grabbed him by the arm, 'but we're going this way.'

I ran through to the large room at the back of the house. An old sash window looked out over the roof of the extension. I edged my fingernails under the ledge, tried to open it.

'It's stuck.'

'Fuck off,' said Mac. He came over, made to raise it. It still wouldn't move.

Hod stayed at the door, watching through the gap. 'He's coming . . . Hurry up.'

We struggled with the window. 'It's painted down,' I said.

Mac nodded, his cheeks inflating as he went to pull the sash ropes. I brought out the jemmy and slid it under the frame. Mac shook his head: it would be too noisy.

Hod rushed into the middle of the room, brought a finger to his mouth. '*Sh-h-h-h . . .*' He pointed to the door.

Mac and I stood still. All three of us followed the sound of Radek's footsteps outside the door.

I held the jemmy in my hand but my palm was sweating now. It slipped through my fingers before

I could get a grip. The sound of its clatter as it fell halted Radek in the hall.

I looked at Mac, then to Hod.

Both their eyes opened wide.

My heart seemed to stop beating.

The silence stretched; we all looked to the door. I expected it to fly open and Radek to burst in with a sawn-off, blast us through the walls. A floorboard creaked outside on the landing. The muscles in my stomach clenched, then released as Radek's footsteps continued up the stairs.

Hod nodded, moved towards us. I knew we had only a few seconds before Radek discovered we'd been in his room. I slid the jemmy under the window. The wood was rotten and the metal bit away at it.

'Fucking hell,' said Mac.

'This isn't happening,' said Hod.

I dug deeper with the jemmy; the metal tip ate more and more wood. I thought I'd be on the other side of the window before long.

'Are you fucking digging through it?' said Mac.

'Shut the fuck up!'

I kept on and the jemmy found a grip. I leaped onto the handle and the window sprung open.

'*Get out*!'

Mac threw out the bolt-cutters, clambered over the edge and lowered himself onto the extension. Hod and I followed. It was a felt roof and it started to give beneath us. There was little run-off and the surface had iced over. My worn-out Docs struggled to find purchase. I saw Mac start to slip, keel over.

Hod grabbed him. The pair staggered onto the roof's edge like a pair of pissheads. We stood over the guttering as Radek let out a howl. He roared out to the house. As I looked back I saw him through the window: he was leaning over the banister, his face flushed red, his arms slicing the air.

'Fucking move it,' I yelled.

Mac knelt down, lowered himself onto his gut and swung round his legs. I stood over him watching. His feet were a couple of yards from the ground and as he let himself go his jacket and T-shirt rolled up against the wall. He landed with a thud and fell backwards. He'd hurt his ankle, grabbed his foot up in his hands.

'Shit, you all right?' I said.

He nodded, waved me away. 'Aye, aye . . . Come on, get doon.'

Hod lowered himself onto his backside, his ribs still too sore to touch the edge. He made a more athletic leap and landed squarely on his feet. Little more than a wince crossed his face.

As I readied myself to jump, I grabbed a last look at Radek. He was racing down the stairs. He hadn't seen me. I stood on the edge of the building, about to leap, when the neighbour's dog started to bark and throw itself at the fence. It didn't bother me until I saw the Czech bring his run to a halt and dive to the window. He clocked me face on, started to scream in my direction.

'*Shit . . .*' I said.

I dropped myself over the edge. My knees buckled but I stayed up, shouted, 'We're rumbled . . . Run like fuck!'

CHAPTER 34

Because we'd jemmied the back door, there was nothing to hold the droves of Czechs from pouring through it, and onto our heads. The neighbour's dog went madhouse, saw something was up. Mac pushed me in the back and got me headed for the gate. Hod was already there. By the time I reached it he'd pegged it all the way down the drive to the street. My legs moved quicker than they'd done in years, but I didn't seem to be getting anywhere fast – sure as shit, not as fast as I'd like.

'Come on, Mac,' I yelled. He lagged behind me as we reached the street, limping on his injured ankle.

'Gimme the shooter, Gus.'

'Fuck off – *run*.'

He held out his hand. I saw the first of the Czechs break through the gate. 'Gimme the fucking gun, Gus.'

I grabbed his arm and dragged him. I pulled too hard and he fell in the street. The Czechs shouted, yelled at us. I couldn't see Radek anywhere but

I wasn't taking too close a look. 'Get up, Mac . . . Get the fuck up.'

I raised him, but he couldn't put weight on his ankle. 'We're fucked, Gus. Gimme the shooter.' He wrestled me for the bag. I saw one of the Czechs make a break from the rest; he was well ahead of them. I stepped back from Mac and yanked the bag away. As I did so Hod rounded the bend in the Hilux, horn blaring.

He screeched to a halt. 'Get in! Get in!'

I lifted Mac into the cab. He struggled with the pain of putting weight on his ankle and I had to push him. As I made to climb in behind him I felt a fist in the kidney. I fell back, got grabbed by the neck. The big Czech put me in a stranglehold. I couldn't breathe. I dropped the bag with the gun on the street. I saw more of the Czechs coming towards me. They yelled, faces red with rage. I saw Radek's white hoodie too.

Hod kept the revs high. Mac roared at him, 'Get out and fucking help him!'

I knew if Hod left the truck we were all fucked.

As the Czech squeezed my throat I widened my stance so he was forced to lean over with me. He held on to me but when I lifted him off the ground he lost his grip, snapped upright. I went over with him and caught his nose with the back of my nut. He keeled sideways, a limp fountain of blood from his nose trailing his fall. I spun round, had a kick timed and ready but the crowd was too close.

I leaned down for the bag, snatched it up, then grabbed the door of the truck. Had one foot in the cab when Hod spun the wheels, filled the street with smoke and the smell of burning rubber.

'Fucking floor it!' I yelled.

The Hilux's bonnet rose as we tanked it down the road. I turned back to see the Czechs running after us. The engine churned through the gears as Hod worked the wheel, spinning left and right as we rounded parked cars. I saw Radek running to the Pajero but it was parked facing the wrong way. He didn't have enough room to turn in the street and headed off in the opposite direction. As we turned the corner, the last glimpse I took of the scene was of Radek mounting the kerb to avoid a head-on with a slow-moving Micra.

'We're in the clear,' I said.

'You sure?' said Hod.

'Old biddy in a Micra just ran him into the railings.'

Mac started to laugh; he set us all off. I slapped the dash and near chucked my guts in convulsions.

'Holy shit . . . What a fucking run-in,' said Mac.

I laughed so hard the muscles of my face got sore. 'Fucking right.'

'Thought you were toast there with yon big fella,' said Hod.

I felt a shiver pass down my spinal column. 'So did I.' I patted the bag. 'Mission accomplished, though . . . wouldn't you say?'

'Oh aye.'

Hod booted it along Salamander Street, headed out Porty way before doubling back towards the city. I began to feel light-headed as I stared out the window, watching the blur of the street. The Meadowbank tenements were decked out in for-sale signs, every other window had an estate agent's name and number on display. I wanted another blast of fast powder, but had to get the haul from Radek's kip straight to Fitz.

'Chuck a right here,' I said.

'Where to?' said Hod. 'Not going to the swan pond, are you?'

'Fettes.'

Mac jumped in, 'You going to just walk into the nick with that?'

'If I give Fitz the choice he'll only sit on this, play silly buggers . . . I'm putting it in his hand.'

'He's right,' said Hod. 'Better not hang on to it.'

I looked into the bag – it was all there. Did I have the necessary to drop my brother's killer? I knew this was going to bring some action on that front, said, 'There's no knowing where things'll go from here, but Radek's not going to sit about waiting for a knock from plod. I need to get Fitz moving right away.'

Hod floored it past the Palace of Holyroodhouse, gave his usual one-digit salute to Her Majesty: it was policy. He looked hyped after our result, feeding the wheel quickly, pumping the pedal, and singing, 'My moustache brings all the girls to the yard, *damn right*!'

Mac laughed it up. I tried to, but I was still focused on the events ahead. My head was so full of how this might play it felt as if a blow-torch was burning behind my eyes. A siren roared up ahead of us and my jaw firmed. I scanned the road but it was only a paramedic van, racing off to some half-jaked reveller, no doubt.

When we reached Fettes Hod slowed down, stayed within the speed limits. We pulled off Carrington Road onto Fettes Avenue. Outside the nick my hands began to tremble. My mouth was dry and I tasted blood where I'd been worrying my inflamed gums with the tip of my tongue. I needed the police to take this over now, I knew I couldn't play the Undertaker off the Czechs and stay above the ground for much longer. If Fitz didn't go for this right away, I didn't want to think about what came next.

'You all right?' said Hod.

'Aye, aye,' I snapped back, '. . . fine.'

I got out the truck, closed the door. Mac rolled down the window. 'Good luck, mate.'

'Cheers,' I said. I waved him away. 'Stay off that ankle.'

I watched them pull out and drive up the road. Hod gave two quick blasts on the horn as they went. I turned to face the station. I held the bag with the gun in one hand and my quarter-bottle of Grouse in the other. I felt the remains of the worn label flaking off under my nails as I went. I was sorely tempted to take a pelt on the scoosh, just one to settle my nerves – I fought it off. I needed to keep it together, more than ever.

At the door I shook myself, took a deep breath and went in.

It was the same dour eyesore of a receptionist. 'Yes?' she said.

'I'd like to see Fitzsimmons.'

She sighed, picked up the phone and directed a chipped red fingernail towards the buttons. She seemed to know who I was. 'Yes, he's at the front desk.' She raised a biro, tapped it on the counter. 'Okay, I'll tell him.'

As she replaced the receiver I waited for her response. None came.

'*Well*?' I said.

She gazed up at me, put a lazy eye to work. 'He's on the way down.' She looked through me, indicated the row of plastic chairs beneath the crime awareness posters.

I said, 'Thank you.'

When Fitz appeared he was eating a sausage roll from a Greggs paper bag; as he shook my hand his fingers felt greasy. He nodded to the room behind the reception desk, lifted the counter and I squeezed past him. As I went, I noticed he had ketchup on his top lip.

We sat down and Fitz scrunched the Greggs bag, took out a white handkerchief and wiped his mouth. 'So, to what do I owe the pleasure?' He looked at the sauce on the hankie and cursed.

I handed over the carrier. The gun made a thud on the desk. Fitz glared at me over the bag; for a moment he didn't move. Slowly, he reached over and looked inside. When he saw the gun he spoke: 'What the feck is this?'

I played it low-key. 'I think it's a murder weapon.'

He closed the bag, ran the back of his fingers over his mouth. He said nothing more for a few seconds, returned to the carrier, peered in and hooked the gun on the end of a pencil. 'All bagged up?'

'That's right.'

He placed the gun on the table. His eyes seemed to have trouble leaving it there. 'And what's the rest?'

'Passports . . . paperwork.'

I explained as briefly as possible, told him where they came from and that he needed to get Radek hoicked in quickly. Fitz hunched his shoulders and shook his head. He was having difficulty with this turn of events; I'd thought he might.

'And what do ye expect me to do with this lot?' he said. 'Eh, tell me that, Dury . . . There's no court in the land would look at it now, the way ye came by it.'

'What, you haven't bent the rules before, Fitz?'

He leaned forward, then back again. He seemed to be unsure of his next play. 'Okay, so . . . I'll run it through the boffins.' He tapped the desk with his forefinger. 'But I won't be able to act on it, Dury.'

I stood up. There was ice in my veins. 'I will. Just tell me who fired the gun, Fitz . . . And leave the justice to me.'

CHAPTER 35

It was Christmas Eve. It didn't feel like it. I woke in a cold, empty flat. The space where Debs had lain beside me for months was empty. I reached out, touched the other side of the bed; it was as if no one had ever been there. The night before I had tried to fill the gap she'd left by putting her pillow at my back, but I'd removed it – didn't want to wake up and think she was still there, face yet more disappointment.

I stared at the ceiling, heard movement upstairs. They had a kid that was running around, laughing. She would be excited at the thought of Santa coming later on; it made me think of Michael at that age. I remembered bawling him out then, telling him to shut up as he went on and on about *Star Wars* figures and whether he'd be getting a Boba Fett or a Gamorrean Guard in his stocking.

The memory was too painful; I tried to replay it the way I would like to have remembered it. I spoke kindly to my younger brother, said there might even be a *Millennium Falcon* coming his way, but it didn't work. Any thoughts I held of him, real or otherwise, were now too raw to confront.

I dragged myself up, went through to the bathroom. The flat seemed desolate without the dog running around, wagging his tail, barking at any movement coming from the stairwell. I turned on the taps and the pipes rattled, a thin trickle of water made its way into the sink. I put my hands under and jerked them away – it felt frozen.

I tried to shave with the knock-off razors I'd bought from the dodgy newsagent – they cut my face to bits. I didn't think I'd used a worse blade; they were obviously not the brand they claimed. I scraped the remainder of my coupon and collected more nicks and abrasions. The sink grew smeared with blood. I dropped the razor in the bin and dabbed my wounds with tissue paper.

As I looked in the mirror I was stunned at how low I'd fallen. My eyes were sunken in my head. It seemed as if they'd been planted in the ground, stamped down. My cheeks were hollow and I had crow's feet that had crept a further half-inch down my face since the last time I'd looked. I hardly recognised myself any more. I drew further to the mirror and took full stock of the damage: more broken blood vessels had appeared in my eyes and my forehead had fixed itself in a frown. Lines spread left to right across my brow and when I stretched my neck they lengthened. I looked beyond rough.

'The fuck happened to you, boy?' I said.

I didn't know myself.

What had I become?

I remembered hearing someone say that ageing brought with it a surrender of dreams, but an understanding and maturity that compensated for it. If I had held any dreams, I had lost them for sure. But where was my compensation? I was more confused by life than I'd ever been. As I looked at the man I'd become I wanted my understanding. I dipped my head. 'I want my peace.'

I fired up the shower, got it as hot as possible without removing skin and stood below the battering jets. The steam rose and filled the small bathroom and after a few minutes I felt its worth as my aching head began to ease.

Debs had removed all her shampoos and products and I had to make do with only a dried-out old sliver of soap but I persevered, scrubbed myself and hoped I would clean away more than the grime. I let the water soothe me some more, must have been under it for all of twenty minutes before I hauled myself back to the bedroom.

I dressed in a white T-shirt and a clean pair of Diesel jeans that had been bought for me by Debs. As I combed back my hair I spied the padded envelope from Fitz that I'd placed on top of the wardrobe. I took it down and went through to the living room.

I laid the little package on the smoked-glass coffee table and went into the kitchenette. As I boiled the kettle, I sparked up a Marlboro.

The envelope stared back at me; I knew what was inside and I needed to face it. The kettle pinged.

I took my mug of Red Mountain and sat down. As I dowped my tab in the ashtray, I heard a key turning in the front-door lock.

'*Debs*?' I called out, stunned.

She came through to the living room with her Bagpuss keyring out in front of her. 'Hi,' she said. There was no sign of the suitcase.

'You're back . . .'

She shook her head. 'No, not quite . . .' She pointed to the dog's cupboard. 'Usual's not settled at Susan's, I thought I'd pick up some of his toys.'

It seemed a lame excuse; she was checking on me. It was a spot-raid to see if I was back on the sauce.

'I see.'

She flinched, squeezed at the keyring, then shoved it in her pocket. Her eyes settled on the padded envelope. 'What's that?'

I told her, 'I'm just building up the courage to open it.'

'Oh, Gus . . . I'm . . .'

I didn't want her sympathy. I didn't want her to come back because she felt sorry for me. I ripped open the envelope. It was as I'd thought. Little plastic bags containing watch, wedding ring, car keys, a few pounds in coin, an empty wallet and a Nokia mobile with the screen smashed.

'Not much, is it?' I said.

Debs came over and put her arm around me. 'I'm sorry, Gus. I really am.'

'For what?'

She sighed, removed her arm, scratched at the palm of her hand. 'I went to see Jayne, she's all over the place . . . Dusting and scrubbing.'

'I know. It's her way of coping, I suppose.'

Debs raised her head. Her finger traced the line of her eyebrow. 'She's worried about Alice . . .'

I wondered what my niece had been up to now. I told Debs about the drinking and the message from Fitz.

'Bloody hell,' she said. 'Did you talk to her?'

'I tried, yeah, her phone keeps going to voicemail.'

Debs shook her head. 'Phones are, like, so last century for teenagers . . . You need to leave a message on her Bebo.'

I was scoobied. 'Her what?'

'Bebo page . . . Social-networking site. It's like Facebook for kids.'

I didn't go anywhere near those sites, but I'd need to be a resident of Jupiter not to have heard of them, way the media obsessed over them. 'Right, okay . . . I'll do that.'

Debs eased back the corners of her mouth. It was a weak smile that I didn't want to try to decipher. She stood up, walked over to the dog's cupboard and took out Usual's favourite plastic hotdog toy. I watched her fill a bag. As I peered over she tucked her hair behind her ear; the movement was all hers, so Debs – the familiarity of it stung me.

I stood up, walked over to her and placed my

hand on the bag. 'This is stupid, Debs . . . Why don't you come home?'

She looked into me, sucked in her lips, and turned away. I thought she might cry.

'Debs?'

A hand went up to my mouth. 'Don't, Gus . . . Don't ask me that. It's not fair.'

I didn't know what she meant. 'What? . . . I mean, why?'

She stepped back from me. She tied a knot in the top of the carrier bag, tugged it tight, spoke firmly: 'I know you won't stop, I know you'll go on and on until you get an answer and I know I've no right to get in the way of that, but I can't watch you do this to yourself any more . . . I just can't.'

I put my hand out, touched her fingers. 'Debs, come home.'

She jerked away from me. 'No, Gus . . . Do you know what it's like for me? I sit here and I wonder if there's going to be a call or a knock at the door telling me you've went the same way as Michael . . .' I put my arms round her, she pushed me away. 'No. I won't do it . . . I won't wait for you to be killed, Gus.'

Debs elbowed her way past me, made for the door.

I called after her, 'Debs . . . Debs . . .' I darted into the hall; she was opening the door. I slammed the heel of my hand on it.

'Gus, let me go.'

'Debs, please . . .'

She pulled at the handle. 'Let me go.'

'Debs . . .'

The door edged open an inch. 'Let me go!'

'I'm sorry, Debs . . .'

She struggled with the handle, hauled back. Tears fell from her eyes.

'I'm sorry, Debs . . . *I'm sorry*.'

I stepped away.

As the door slammed, I pressed my back to it. The wood was cold against my T-shirt. I slumped all the way to the floor. A chill draught blew just above the carpet as I curled over and held my head in my hands.

CHAPTER 36

I lay hunched up on the floor until the draught from the stair started to freeze my spine. I knew I had to go on, hauled myself to my feet; but I knew also Debs wouldn't be coming back. I'd hurt her again, perhaps more than I ever had. Her face had tensed at the thought of my grief and I knew she felt deeply for me, but she couldn't help me. That was her revelation – Debs had sensed there was nothing she could do for me, because there was nothing I could do for myself. I had brought my demons to the relationship once more, and they had defeated us both.

I took the quarter-bottle of Grouse from my Crombie and walked through to the living room. I sat down and unscrewed the cap, placed the bottle in front of me. I smelled the whisky working its way to my nostrils; the mere scent of it triggered a sensation in my brain. I felt the wonder of it putting my thoughts to sleep already. I smiled, laughed. One sip and I'd have a legion of help to beat back those demons.

'Dury, you piece of shit . . .'

After all Debs had done, after all her efforts, here I was.

I picked up the bottle.

My hands trembled as I brought the rim to my lips.

'You fucking loser,' I laughed out. The glass edge touched a tooth, I felt the whisky vapour rising into my throat. And I froze. My mind seemed to hurtle down another path.

'No.'

I put down the bottle, stared at it and screwed the cap back on. I knew that one sip would have thrown me on the flames. One sip would have undone all Debs had put herself through for me. One sip would have let my brother's killer off.

I straightened myself. Got up and grabbed my mobi from the mantel.

Dialled.

'Fitz, what the fuck's happening?'

He latched on to my tone. 'Calm down, Dury, there's a limit to what I can do.'

'Limit . . . I gave you the gun, what have you done with it?'

He cleared his throat. 'Would ye feckin' watch what you're saying, Dury . . .' Fitz dropped to a whisper, 'The boffins say the shooter's a match . . . but.'

I clenched my teeth, felt my pulse racing. 'But what? . . . I need a name, Fitz. Just give me a fucking name.'

A pause, his voice rose again: 'We don't have the prints tied up yet.'

He was bullshitting me, I smelled it. 'I want the name, Fitz.'

He locked me down: 'Dury, I want you to listen to me very carefully. There are things about this case you have no idea of, no idea!'

I went back at him, 'That's why I've come to you. Don't brush me off, Fitz.'

He paused again. I heard him shuffle forward in his seat. 'Look, we've busted the house in Leith . . . We've got Radek in the cells. There's a warrant for murder out on him in the Czech Republic . . . He won't be going anywhere.'

If he was telling me this, he knew Radek wasn't our man as well as I did. Fitz wouldn't be slow in slapping a murder charge down. 'What about Davie Prentice? . . . What about the Undertaker?'

'Dury, would ye ever feckin' listen to me? . . . We are on top of it. Let us do our work.'

'And let me do mine. I'll call back soon, I want to know whose dabs are on that Webley, Fitz, and I'm not fucking around.'

I threw my phone at the couch. Cursed Fitz.

He was holding out on me and I knew it. I needed to get moving before he dragged someone in; if he got to them before I did, chances were I'd be watching my brother's killer grinning at the cameras on the *Six O'clock News*, after receiving a slap on the wrist. I had proper justice in mind for the fucker.

I paced the flat, sparked up a Marlboro. The place seemed so empty again without Debs. Her words kept singing in my ears. I heard every one of them like they were being replayed to me on a tape recorder. I knew what she meant; I was out of control. Nothing could stop this rig smashing into the wall. I wouldn't let up until I'd squeezed the life out of Michael's killer.

I thought of my mother's struggles to raise Michael, how she had taken the news of his savage beating by my father all those years ago. I thought of Catherine and of Jayne and of Alice. Little Alice, whom Debs and I had held in our arms the night she was born. My niece had been robbed of her father. Michael had tried so hard to be the kind of father we never had, and it had all been for nothing.

I couldn't focus any more. My thoughts sprang one way then the other. I remembered what Debs had said about minding out for Alice and I booted up the computer. The internet connection was slow, almost dial-up speed; I cursed the service provider and slapped the monitor in frustration.

'Fucking piece of shit!'

My Yahoo homepage was full of doom-laden news about business collapses, house prices nose-diving, car lots full of unsold motors and the Prime Minister, as ever, proclaiming he was doing everything in his power to stabilise the fallout. I wanted to spit, but I clicked away from his smug coupon instead.

I had no idea of the web address so I Googled Alice Dury and Bebo together. The search threw up a page of responses, but Alice's name and page sat top of the list.

I double-clicked.

The page took a while to load – seemed to be a lot of photographs – but then Alice's photo appeared, a yellow smiley face and a few lines of biog beside it.

I grinned, said, 'Hello, Alice . . . found you.'

The site had a stack of puerile comments from schoolfriends, all accompanied by thumbnail pictures of them taken on mobile phones. To a one they looked half-cut. Teenagers know how to party these days; in my time, I was always the most pished in the room.

I read and scrolled, and then I stopped.

I didn't expect this.

A photograph of the Czech lodger that my brother had installed in his home had been put up. Vilem was standing in the garden, seemingly unaware his image had been captured. In the comment box beside the photo Alice had keyed: 'Welcome to my Boy Zone!! . . . More to follow!!'

I didn't know how to interpret this – was it just a teenage girl being a silly wee lassie? She'd posted the picture a week before my brother's death. A few of Alice's friends had posted comments in their hybrid language of text-speak and slang, but Alice hadn't updated the site again. It seemed pointless to leave a message for her there if she wasn't using it right now.

I logged off the web.

Shut down.

I felt guilty for not giving Alice more attention. I knew she was taking the loss of her father hard. I should have intervened earlier, maybe come down on her harder about the drinking. Decided I would try her mobi again. I had the contacts book open, finger hovering on the call button when I heard a knock at the door.

I jumped up to the spyhole. The back of a head covered it. I opened up, immediately regretted the move.

A shoulder forced the door into my face. I went back, tumbled downwards and felt my palms get scorched on the carpet. Next thing I felt was a backhander knocking me into the wall.

'All right, Gus boy.' It was Dartboard; the pug with the parka stood behind him. '. . . You and me are going on a wee visit to a friend of ours.'

He grabbed my hair and hauled me up.

'Get his coat, Sammy.'

CHAPTER 37

The Undertaker was dressed in a double-breasted grey suit. The last time I saw lapels that wide it was in an Edward G. Robinson movie. He had on a black shirt and it was open at the collar, an eyeful of bling played for attention beneath a heavy white chest rug. His eyes followed me as Dartboard prodded my back all the way across the bar floor. My head throbbed from the spank he'd given me in the flat, and I was sorely tempted to land a fly jab in his puss. Only thing that held me back was I knew this boy had some moves; maybe I was learning.

The Undertaker nodded to Dartboard and he pointed me to a velour-backed seat. 'I'll stand, thanks.'

I didn't see the fist coming for my gut, but I felt it, compressed me like an accordion; I made as much noise too. Fell onto my knees, panting and wheezing. I looked up at Dartboard, tried to figure how he'd packed so much power into a blow that had come straight from his pocket.

'You're gonna . . .' I coughed my guts onto the

floor, tried again, 'you're gonna have to show me how to do that.'

He smiled, impressed with himself.

The Undertaker stood up. 'Get the cunt in the chair.' He looked even closer to death than the last time. Under the full glare of the lights his skin was almost transparent. He was like a waxwork of himself, before they'd applied the paint.

Dartboard dragged me into the chair, sat me down. I watched as he retreated to the other end of the room with the parka prick they called Sammy. Neither spoke, just stood with their hands at their sides, clenched fists.

The Undertaker walked the floor. His legs were so thin beneath his baggy trousers that his kneecaps poked out like shards with his every step. He was like a cadaverous Peter Crouch. There's a phrase, *all arms and legs*.

'What did I fucking ask you, laddie?' he said. His tone had changed too: the sandpaper rasp was still there but now a belt-grinder was working it. He was keenly pissed at me, proper furious. 'Eh, [illegible]*t* . . . What did I ask ye?'

I held in my entrails. I felt that if I took my hand from my stomach it'd spill on the floor. 'Do you mind standing still?' I said. 'It might come back to me then.'

He stopped dead. I saw the false teeth in his head as his mouth widened. The Undertaker looked as if he'd been poked in the arsehole with a sharp pencil.

Sammy seized the initiative and dived forward, clapped a mitt on my jaw. I fell off the chair. He had a way to go before he was in Dartboard's league. I shook it out and clambered back onto the seat. 'You've stopped pacing, good. The answer you're after is . . . Davie Prentice. You gave me a message, and I passed it on. So why the fuck am I here?'

The pug with the skinhead got nodded away, the Undertaker approached me. As he leaned in I saw the grease on the back of his collar. His breath smelled as though a rat had been living in his mouth for a year and there was dandruff falling on me from his shoulders as he spoke. 'Aye, that's right, laddie, I gave you a wee fucking simple message to pass on to that fat cunt . . .' He turned to Dartboard and Sammy. 'Should've been *simple*, eh no?'

The shit-lickers nodded. Dartboard tucked his hands behind his back. He looked as if he was trying out for a job at Slater Menswear.

The Undertaker started on again: 'Well . . . you fucked it right up!' He grabbed me by the ear and hollered, 'Davie's fucking scarpered . . . He's had it away on his toes, and I'm oot my poppy!' He let go of my ear, stepped back. It was like watching a stork wading into a river for fish.

I said, 'He's what?'

'Fucked off . . .'

It was news to me. 'When was this?'

'The factory's been closed doon. His fucking

Czech fancy man's been hauled doon the polis station and I'm no' best pleased, Dury.'

It made sense to me: the Czechs were Davie's shield; without their protection, what choice did he have but to go rabbit? The prospect of getting any cash out of him seemed distant now. I wondered where all of this left me, and Michael's killer.

I said, 'I'm sorry to hear that.'

'Don't play wide with me, Dury,' he said. 'Remember what I told you last time I had you in here?'

I replayed the speech: 'You didn't like bad news.'

'And remember what I said I'd do to you if you fucked up, Dury?'

I nodded.

'Aye, well, I had a wee think aboot that and came round to the conclusion that since you clearly don't give two fucks for yerself, I'd have to take it out on someone else.'

I sat up in the seat. I thought of Debs leaving the flat shortly before me: fucking hell, had they grabbed her? I rose to my feet. Dartboard came behind me and grabbed my arms.

'If you've . . .'

The Undertaker leaned over me. He looked like a suited-up Albert Steptoe as he spat at me, 'If I've what? . . . Hauled in yer wee niece and her Czech boyfriend, tied them up ready for going the same road as your brother?'

I struggled to get to him. Dartboard twisted my

arms up my back. The pain sent nails into my joints. 'You fucking dirty bastard . . .'

He started to chuckle, frothy spit gathered in the corners of his mouth. His whole frame shook and then he fell into a hacking cough that rattled off his ribs. 'Come on, Dury . . . deal's a deal after all. That's what I told yer brother before he got his.'

I stopped struggling. Played him hard: 'You're shitting me . . . You don't have my niece.'

'That right, eh . . .' He called the pug over. 'Sammy, get that fucking fancy phone ay yours over here.'

The screen of the phone got shoved in my face. A video played. I saw Alice on her knees in a field. She was gagged and tied. Vilem was tied behind her; he had tape over his mouth, a badly bruised face, and blood on his shirt. They'd both been tethered to a rusting tractor axle; Alice struggled to try and free herself, tugging at the rope on her hands. I wanted to reach out to her, and then the scene shifted, a flash of sky as the camera moved on an excavator in motion. The driver leaned out the cab – it was Dartboard – then he lowered the digger into the frost-hardened ground. As the screen's angle shifted again I saw he had already dug one hole in the ground. Dartboard was working on the second as the screen changed again, homed in on a Transit van. An arm came before the camera and opened the back doors. Inside was stacked with pine-box coffins.

I'd seen enough, looked away.

The Undertaker took the phone up. 'That niece ay yours has got a tidy wee arse on her . . . No wonder the Czech was poking her.'

I didn't want to listen. I saw the pug start to laugh.

The Undertaker pointed to the phone. 'See this Czech boyo here? Your brother told me they put that cunt in his hoose to keep an eye on him, make sure he didn't do anything stupid like break their wee arrangement.'

I looked up, saw the Undertaker twisting his mouth at Vilem. I said, 'What are you saying?'

He shrugged. 'See me, I don't waste time thinking, Dury . . . I act. When those cunts cut me oot I told Michael, get those wagons running again or there'll be bother. Your brother was a smart laddie, he knew I didn't waste time on threats. No like these Czech bastards . . . That's why he went home to tell that fucker to get out his hoose, and get his nose out our fucking business.'

'He killed my brother?'

'Oh, I'd say so . . . Wouldn't you?'

I strained to free myself again. 'I'll kill him.'

The Undertaker stepped back. 'You might no' get the fucking chance.' I looked up at him. He continued, 'You'll do something for me if you want your wee niece back . . . And your hands on her boyfriend.'

My head burned up. I couldn't think fast enough to take it all in. 'What do you want?'

'Simple, Dury. That fat cunt's no' going anywhere owing me the poppy he does. Bring him back here and I'll do you a wee favour – since it's Christmas – I won't put her in the ground till she's dead.' He paused. 'Way the weather's going, though, that won't be long.'

He started to wheeze with the exertion of baiting me, rasped into a cough. He broke away, nodded to Dartboard.

I felt my arms released. I landed on the floor.

'Get the fuck up, Dury,' said the Undertaker. 'Time's ticking away, laddie.'

CHAPTER 38

I stood in the snow facing Tollcross in the dark of night. The Christmas lights draped over the road glowed down on the traffic, danced on the car roofs. I heard screams and wails carry from the showground in Princes Street Gardens. The sounds sliced me as a double-decker bus passed by, wet spray flying from the gutter. A man with gift-wrapped parcels in his arms tried to squeeze past me, grunted when I didn't move. He dropped a glove, failed to notice; I didn't tell him.

I stood staring. Watching the traffic lights change, the taxis turn in the road. I started to get wet. The snow fell heavily. I'd never seen snow like it. It settled where it lay, inches of it already on parked cars. My hair flattened to my head, stuck to my brow. An old woman approached me and held up the fallen glove. She asked if it was mine but I didn't answer. She waved it at me but I ignored her. The woman's mouth kept moving and moving and moving but I didn't hear the words. Eventually she walked away, placed the glove on railings and continued up the street.

I felt cold. My lips grew numb and my hands

froze in my pockets. I stood and I stared ahead and I felt the tears forming in my eyes, but they wouldn't fall. They held there like I held myself to the exact same spot on the pavement and then I felt a dig in my shoulder as a late shopper pushed past me, and the tears were dislodged. I turned to hear the shopper apologise, wiped my face with the back of my hand. I didn't know what to say. I was beyond words. Words could be formed into thought and I didn't want to think. I didn't want to think and I didn't want to feel. I wanted to trade places with my brother. I didn't want any part in this misery called life any more. I knew I couldn't go on if anything happened to Alice.

'Gus, Gus . . . fucking hell, Gus.' Mac called me from the street.

I looked up. He had Hod's truck stopped in the road; a trail of angry drivers blasted horns behind him. I found myself moving towards the vehicle, automatically opened up the door and got in. Tyres spun on the wet road as he took off.

'Jesus, you were away with the pixies there, mate,' he said. 'What's up?'

The heater blew in front of me. I started to thaw.

'I know who killed my brother.'

'*Wha'*?' Mac turned his head. 'Who?'

I saw my fingernails turning pink. 'It was the Czechs . . . They put one of their own in Michael's house, as a frightener.'

Mac pulled over the truck – we drew in beside the Meadows. 'How do you know?'

I told him what the Undertaker had said. 'It all stacks up. On the night he died Michael went to see McMilne; he says he was going to cut out the Czechs.' I looked out to the Meadows, where they had found my brother's body. 'Michael must have went home and had it out with Vilem.' I saw nothing in the park but blackness. 'We have to find fat Davie: he's legged it since Radek got lifted . . . McMilne has my niece.'

Mac spoke: 'Your niece?'

'He'll put her in a hole if we don't bring him Davie . . . We have to get that piece of shit right now.'

Mac started the engine. 'Let's go.'

I jerked my head away from the blackness. The Undertaker's lumps had been searching the city and got not a sniff of him. 'Where to fucking start?'

Mac pulled right across the road; a blast of car horns went up. He engaged reverse and went for a three-point turn. 'I've got a fair idea where he might be.'

We headed back towards Tollcross. I said, 'Where are we going?'

'Remember when I was tailing him, I told you he had a wee scrubber stashed away in a flat in Restalrig? . . . I bet you a pound to a pail of shite the fat wee gimp's up there.'

Mac bombed it down Lothian Road, ran lights on Princes Street, but the traffic ground to a standstill on George Street. The middle classes in their uniform Barbour jackets trotted back and forth between the glitter and the tinsel and the bright lights. A crowd of excited schoolgirls giggled and shivered at the crossing; I thought of Alice.

'Come on, Mac . . . punch it.'

'It's chocka. Christmas Eve, mate.'

I didn't want to be reminded. Alice should have been like those girls, having fun, laughing and joking. Preparing for a school party, Jesus, getting tipsy. How could I have been angry with her for that? I wanted to say sorry to her and hug her and promise to look after her. She'd lost her father, we'd all lost Michael; we couldn't lose anyone else. I saw Debs's face as I thought of Alice tied in that field. Debs would never be able to take any hurt befalling Alice, it would be the end of her too.

Jayne.

My mother.

My sister.

The list grew in my mind.

'Come on, come on.' I slapped at the dash. The cars sat still, going nowhere. I opened the door, got out and shouted, 'Get moving, come on, fucking move it!' The New Town shoppers stared at me. A woman flicked her scarf over her shoulder and muttered something to the concourse. I pounded the bonnet of the Hilux with my fists.

Mac called me, 'Get in, Gus, you're not fucking helping.'

That was my problem; I wasn't helping anyone. I hadn't been there for Michael, and now I'd let down his daughter, my niece. Knew I was transferring my own self-loathing to the surrounds. Anger and hurt burned in me.

I got back in the truck and Mac eased it through a gap in the bottleneck. He tore through York Place until we hit the roundabout. We rolled into a quiet stretch, and topped sixty most of the way to Jock's Lodge. At Restalrig we roared through the streets, flashing anyone who got in our way with the headlights on full beam.

Mac dropped gears, threw two wheels on the pavement and hit the anchors. 'Right, follow me.' He opened the door and eased out of the truck. He hopped on his sore ankle but there was a steel in his gut that told me he'd tear down walls to get to fat Davie. The flat was in a street of ex-council maisonettes. There'd been no maintenance done here since before the Thatcher years, save the odd lick of paint by late-boom developers looking to turn a quick profit.

'It's up there,' said Mac. He pointed to a skanky door, banging on its hinges. I went in behind him. The stair was in almost complete darkness – one dim light flickered beside the front door. A pram with a bent wheel sat in the hallway alongside a giant yellow Tonka truck that had been trashed and spray-painted. The young crew's graffiti artists had also tagged the stairs and there was the familiar stench of Special Brew and pish everywhere.

At the top of the steps Mac pointed to another door. I didn't need any more information, put my boot to the lock and it shed a few strips of peeling emulsion. The second kick put the whole frame in; the top hinge collapsed, spat out some screws.

As I walked in I heard the theme tune from *Only Fools and Horses* starting, another Christmas special rerun with Del and Rodney. I stormed through to the living room and a bleach-blonde stick insect with a nose piercing and an Embassy in her grid screamed at me. I put my hand over her mouth and pushed her back into the chair she'd leaped from. She screamed again, 'Fucking cunts come into my fucking house!' Her face lit up like a lantern as she spat.

Mac stepped from behind me and cracked a knuckle on her brow. She flopped like a deflating sex doll.

Fat Davie sat in his chewing-gum-coloured Y-fronts and a stringy semmit, toasting his stockinged toes in front of a three-bar electric heater. One of his brown socks had a hole in it; his big toe had worked its way out. He had a tinfoil Chinese carry-out box balanced on his belly and a forkful of egg noodles poised before his open mouth.

'Hello, Davie,' I said. The noodles dropped into the box. Some chow mein sauce splashed on his chest and he jumped with a start. Mac leaned over and smacked the carry-out from his hands. It splashed on the wall and the electric fire sizzled as the beanshoots and chicken strips bounced off its red-hot bars.

'Gus, ehm, I was thinking about what you told me . . .' said Davie.

I leaned forward and grabbed a bunch of his semmit, yanked him up. 'No, you fucking fat waste of space, you *weren't* thinking.' I threw him to the door. 'Folk like you never fucking think, Davie.'

He stumbled and put his hands out to break his fall. Mac pulled a pair of beige Farah slacks from the back of a chair, threw them at fat Davie. 'Get dressed, y'cunt.'

As Mac kicked shoes towards Davie, I looked about the room. There was a travel bag and a leather briefcase sitting by the fireplace. I opened up the bag first: it was full of clothes. 'Going somewhere, Davie?'

He jerked his head towards me, nearly lost balance as he tried to put a foot in his trousers.

'I was just . . .' he said.

'Shut the fuck up,' said Mac. He slapped him across the face. A trickle of blood fell from Davie's nose and caught in his pale moustache.

I opened up the briefcase: stacks of paperwork, bankbooks, chequebooks, and a few hefty rolls tucked away underneath. I held up some twenties. Mac gave Davie another belt. The sack of shit whimpered.

'Don't see your tickets, Davie,' I said, 'for Disneyland.'

He wiped the blood from his nose. 'What? *What*? . . . *Disneyland*?'

'Maybe not . . .' I shook my head. 'I think your Donald Duck just ran out.'

Mac picked up a blazer and shoved it at Davie. 'Come on, get your arse out that door.'

The fat fuck turned back to me, whimpered again. 'Gus, Gus . . .'

'Get through the door, Davie . . . If you speak nicely to him, the Undertaker might let you say a prayer before he puts you in the ground.' I walked over and pushed him in the back. 'But if he's hurt my Alice, I'll fucking dig you up and finish the job with my bare hands.'

CHAPTER 39

Mac put the Hilux into gear and released the clutch. We shot out of Restalrig like the four-minute warning had just sounded. Fat Davie pleaded at my side like a spoilt child: 'Gus, I only did what was best for Michael, I promise.'

'Don't use his name again.'

He whined, 'I wouldn't do anything to harm Michael . . . or his family.'

I lost it, put a fist in him. It was like punching a mattress; I felt my knuckles sink as I pummelled Davie's gut. 'I told you, don't use his fucking name. Didn't I tell you?'

I'd disturbed the balance of the truck – it started to slide on the road.

'Whoa, whoa . . . Cool the beans there,' said Mac.

I locked it down, sat back in my seat. Davie toppled over. His knees hit the ground, his legs buckled under his weight. I grabbed him by the collar, hauled him up. He winced in pain, shrieked, 'I haven't done anything wrong . . .'

'Shut it.' He sounded pathetic. I couldn't believe

the way he was still yabbering, after all he'd done. After all the grief that Davie's antics had brought to me and Debs, to Jayne . . . the death of Michael, and Andy, and Ian Kerr. And now there was Alice. Oh Christ, *Alice*. The snow was falling heavily now: she couldn't survive much longer.

'Davie, let me say this only once.' I tried to keep my voice steady, but it quivered, betraying my emotion. 'The Undertaker has my niece bound and gagged in a field, there is a hole in the ground dug for her. The only hope for that girl is you. Do you understand?'

Davie's face froze, turned white. His lips tightened into a knot and refused to let out any words. He nodded.

'When I hand you over, Davie, I don't care what he does to you. I don't care whether he demands money or puts you in the ground . . . All I care about now is Alice.'

The words seemed to register with him; he turned away. Davie stared out of the window like a man who was watching his final moments in slow-mo. I hoped he was thinking about what he had done. About how his actions, his greed, had hurt so many others, and was hurting them yet. I wanted Davie to feel the pain I felt. I knew he hadn't murdered my brother but he had played his part, and I wanted revenge.

The roads grew busy but Mac pushed on and flashed the oncoming traffic as we powered through the town. The snow pelted down, and the sky darkened with cloud covering; if there were night stars out, they weren't shining over us.

Christmas Eve revellers started to appear, groups of lads tanked up on designer lager and barely dressed young girls staggering from bar to bar. In an hour the blokes would be singing 'Danny Boy' and the girls walking barefoot, their heels in their hands. There would be barf swimming in the gutters and aggro in the kebab shops. Just another Christmas Eve in Edinburgh, but it stung me to think of anyone enjoying themselves while Alice faced a grim death.

I looked at the thermometer in the dash: it was eight-below.

'Can't you go any fucking faster?' I yelled.

'Trying . . . trying.' Mac rounded the bend onto the Grassmarket. A tart in reindeer antlers was touching up a guy in a Santa hat; they stood bang middle of the road, going for it. Mac slammed on the anchors, yelled out, 'Get up a close!'

The wee hingoot twisted her face and Santa hat pulled in his belt, headed for the car. Mac yanked on the handbrake, opened the door. The guy strutted as he walked towards the truck. He put back his shoulders, gave Mac a come-ahead flick of the fingers. Mac managed three or four paces on his sore ankle, let the guy get closer on his own. When he drew up to the bumper Mac put him down with one sledgehammer right. It was clinical. He dragged him to the side of the road and got back in the cab, gunned the engine. The tart took off her antlers as we passed.

The end of the road looked like a Hieronymus Bosch painting, bodies seething everywhere. Queues from the pubs spilled onto the road. Mac blasted the horn and swerved. The Hilux mounted the kerb as we drove onto West Port; we hit fifty before Tollcross. The truck skidded to a halt outside a busy pub, folk queuing to get in already.

I leaned over and opened Davie's door, said, 'Out!'

He was silent now, accepting.

Mac hobbled behind me on his one good ankle, jangling the car keys. 'Right, let's fucking nash.'

The snowfall was heavier than I'd seen it all year, and it was the harshest winter I could remember. I thought again of Alice, out in that field, tied to a rusting tractor axle. She was so thin, so frail. I couldn't believe she wouldn't perish. I tried to focus, to get moving. I knew I was her only hope – but I just couldn't shake the sight of her, the image that the Undertaker had shown me on that phone haunted me.

I pushed Davie in the back. 'I'm telling you now, Davie, anything's happened to my niece . . . you're fucking well done for.'

He slipped in the street, fell. The knees of his beige Farah trousers turned black. I put a grip on his belt and hauled him to his feet. His soft shoes slid about all over the pavement as he walked, glancing back at us.

'Just fucking get going,' said Mac.

At the Undertaker's lap-dancing bar in the Pubic Triangle a flannel-shirted Scouser was arguing the toss after being refused entry. I didn't recognise the doorman, but I recognised the type. I fronted up, said, 'We're expected.'

'By who?' He put in some attitude.

We didn't have time for games and Mac knew it. His chest went out. 'Ronnie fucking McMilne . . . Don't play wide, y'arsehole, or I'll hand you yer eyes.'

The lump did a mental calculation, nodded us inside. We got pointed up the stairs and told to turn left at the mirrored door. 'Ronnie's in the office, down the end of the hall.'

I pushed Davie up the stairs. He was dripping wet now as the snow melted on him. He stumbled and dropped into a crawl for a few steps. I put a hand under his arm and yanked him up. He gasped for air as we reached the landing.

'Down here,' said Mac. He led the way to the end of the corridor, pushed open the Undertaker's door. He was the first to be greeted as we walked in.

'It's yer bold self,' said McMilne, 'Mac the Knife, indeed.' He sat on a leather chair, his feet up on the desk as *Only Fools* spat canned laughter from a wee portable. Dartboard and Sammy picked over the remains of a pizza box that Sammy held in his hands like a chav laptop. They laughed at the telly as Del Boy and Rodney appeared in Batman and Robin costumes.

'Ron,' said Mac.

'Haven't seen you for a while, you still . . .?' He made a slicing motion in front of him, as though he was carving someone with a Stanley blade.

Mac shook his head, turned to me.

'Can we get down to fucking business?' I said. 'I thought it was this cunt you wanted to see.' I dragged fat Davie to the middle of the room.

The Undertaker sat up in his chair; he put those falsers of his on display. 'Ah, you found him.' He seemed unimpressed, turned back to the telly. Dartboard and Sammy picked anchovies off the pizza, dropped them in the box. They got in the way of the telly and the Undertaker kicked off. 'Get oot the fucking road!'

I looked away. A black-and-white monitor showed pictures from the floor of girls with their baps out, dancing round poles. I tried again. 'Yeah, so . . . I've done my bit,' I said.

The Undertaker looked irritated, turned and sized me up. 'So fucking what?'

A bolt of adrenaline hit me, the flash of heat going to my head. I stormed over to the desk and slapped down my palms. As I moved I felt Mac pull me back but I shrugged him off, roared, 'I want my fucking niece and I want my brother's fucking killer!'

The Undertaker lifted a thin leg, then another, lowered his feet to the floor. He sat forward in the leather chair and made a steeple of his long fingers. 'And just what're you gonna do if I say no, laddie?'

Dartboard and Sammy threw down their pizza slices. I stepped away from the desk and looked at Mac. He squared his shoulders. Fat Davie trembled so much beside me that I could hear the change rattling in his pockets. The television blared on; *Only Fools* had finished – they started singing about Hookey Street being *magnifique*.

The Undertaker stood up. He was the tallest in the room by a head, but his frame was stooped as his neck jutted forward. He looked like a lamp post that had been struck by a car. 'I've missed the end now,' he said. 'I fucking like that show as well.'

I tried to think of something to say but my heart was pumping too hard, the adrenaline spiking through me, making me jumpy.

Dartboard wiped the back of his hand over his mouth and Sammy picked a paper napkin from the pizza box. I tried to watch every movement, but my eyes followed the Undertaker as he went into a drawer at the side of the desk. I felt sure a shooter was coming out. I saw Davie collapse at my side. Mac grabbed him, held him up. As the drawer closed the Undertaker slowly raised his hand from below the line of the desk, and then he stopped. 'You know the trouble with folk like you, Dury?'

It was a prompt. I shook my head. 'What's that?' I kept watching him closely.

'Nae sense of humour.' He lifted up his hand. 'I'm only having ye on, laddie, y'need to lighten up a wee bit.' He threw an Ordnance Survey map at me. Dartboard and Sammy started to laugh.

I picked up the map: it was folded over at a section of Midlothian. 'This where they are?' Biro markings indicated a line from the bypass at Straiton to a circle around a smallholding.

Mac peered over my shoulder then took the map from my hand. 'Come on, I know where this is.' He let go of Davie and the fat prick fell on the floor. Dartboard and Sammy laughed once again; the Undertaker joined them.

On the stairs I grabbed Mac. 'Gimme the keys.'

'*Wha'*?'

'Gimme the fucking keys.' I tore the map from his hand. 'You're not coming.'

Mac looked me in the eye; he knew what I had planned. 'No way, man. You're hypo, you'll get in some right fucking lumber if—'

I pushed my forearm against his neck, forced him up against the wall, hollered, 'Gimme the fucking keys, Mac, I'm not messing about.' He froze. I pressed my arm deeper. 'I mean it, Mac . . . gimme them.' I felt his arm move at his side. His hand went into his pocket and brought out the keys.

I let him go. Ran down the stairs.

As I went, Mac shouted, 'Gus, don't fucking do it . . . They'll put you away, man.'

I didn't listen.

In the street I tanked it; my Docs slipped all over the pavement. At the truck my hands shook so much I struggled to get the key in the door. When I got it started I put the steering to full-lock and spun the tyres. It was a tight spot and I clipped the tail of a jeep; its alarm sounded. Pissheads pointed as I reversed and smacked the car behind but I didn't care. I got out of there and pelted it.

I couldn't find the wipers, kept hitting the indicators as the snow fell harder. Christmas lights shone from the shopfronts and jakeys rolled into the road but I got out of the city and made for the bypass.

It was a white-out on the main road. Got trapped behind a gritter. The snow came heavier, stacked itself on the road. It was a blizzard now. I drove faster and then slowed in a panic at the thought of coming off the road, but edged the needle up higher and higher until I had to brake.

The back end slipped away. I thought it would fishtail but the truck righted itself. I felt the wheels lurch and then I headed for a ditch at the edge of the road. I pumped the brake again as the truck skidded and saw the front end dip suddenly – I thought I was in the ditch – but the truck had stopped on the last inches of tarmac. I put it into reverse and rejoined the road.

I raced on for a mile, driving into the blizzard.

There was very little traffic and I was thankful for that. A couple of night buses had pulled into lay-bys; I saw people inside shivering, waiting for a break in the blizzard, or perhaps the snowplough.

I found it hard to follow the map and keep eyes on the road. It was made worse by the countryside being completely blanketed in snow – the signs were all blocked out, the markings indistinct.

The map indicated a turn-off and a smallholding with outbuildings but I couldn't find the turn-off. I backtracked, got out and wiped the snow from the front of a signpost. I got rolling again, followed the instructions, but there didn't seem to be any smallholding.

I banged the wheel, thumped fists into the dash. I stopped the truck and got out again. The whole area was in darkness, there were no street lights. I climbed up the side of a fence, slipping on the icy, frozen slats. All I thought was: Alice, Alice, Alice. 'Hang on, Alice . . . please hang on.'

I leaped a gate and ran through the blizzard.

She had to be close by. This was the smallholding, I was on it now.

It was too dark to make anything out. I went back to the truck and turned in the road, revved and headed straight through the gate. I drove a circle in the field. Saw nothing. I drove further. The tyres had little traction on the icy surface – it was like skating.

The land undulated and I bounced in the cab; my head kept hitting off the roof. The temperature gauge hit the max, I felt sure the truck would cough any minute, and then I saw I was heading straight for a drystone dyke. I slammed on the brakes and skidded out of control, the truck spun and the headlights danced on the side of an outbuilding. I glimpsed it only for a second before it fell out of view. On the second pass, I caught a better sight of it. As the truck stopped, my heart stilled.

It was Alice.

She was slumped on her side, still tied to the rusting tractor axle.

I put the truck into first and rolled over the field.

'Alice, Alice . . .' As I ran from the truck she lay still. The headlights burned over her; she was covered in snow, almost completely white.

I saw Vilem tied behind her – he had freed his legs and kicked out to let me know he was there.

'Alice . . . Alice . . .' I said.

I grabbed hold of her: she was cold. Her eyes were closed.

Vilem tried to speak, kicked out again with his legs.

I put a hand on Alice's head, wiped away the snow. She was almost as pale beneath it all. I removed the gag and her mouth flopped open. I put my face to hers to see if she was breathing. I couldn't tell.

Vilem kicked out again.

I tried to untie Alice's hands but I couldn't. My fingers turned blue in the cold, I lost feeling in them. I tugged at the ropes but I couldn't get them off. I ran to the truck, grabbed the little tool case from the glovebox. There was no knife, only a screwdriver. I poked it in the knot to ease it open. Alice's arms fell at her sides as I untied her. I did the same to the knot on her legs and dragged her feet free.

There was no movement, no life in her, as I lifted her from the ground and took her to the truck.

I placed Alice on her back, across the seats. I got the heater blasting, high as it would go. I took off my coat and put it over her. I expected to see some colour return to her face, but none came. She didn't even shiver. I held her hand, tried to find a pulse but I couldn't.

'Alice, come on . . . fucking *live*.'

I slapped at her wrist.

Nothing.

I didn't know what to do next.

There was no sign of life.

CHAPTER 40

I lowered my head; the heater was going full blast. I felt my heart thumping, the blood pumping in my veins. My thoughts mashed: a million grim and grimmer scenarios played out on the screen of my mind. Oh God . . . Michael, and now Alice. I gulped down my hurt, cuffed away the emotion. Was time to man up – put brass-knuckles on my feelings. Someone had to pay.

Vilem kicked out again as I returned to him. His legs flailed wildly, he was panicked; he'd no idea. He shouted from behind the tape that covered his mouth. The sounds came muffled – I sensed the desperation in his voice, but whatever it was he said, it didn't matter. This fucker was going to learn about loss.

I picked up the screwdriver and went for him.

His legs shot up, swept the air in grand arcs, I knocked them down. He jerked his shoulders violently, tugging to release his hands. He was too well tied. His eyes widened; I could see the fear spreading in him. It fed some need in me, I knew what it was: revenge. I smacked his head with the butt of the screwdriver. He blared out in pain.

For a moment Vilem seemed to gather more strength, flared nostrils at me. I hit him again and then a dark finger of blood ran from his hairline to the bridge of his nose. I watched his chest rise and fall, his chin sink into his neck and then his eyes rolled up in his head and he fell to the side.

I stepped back.

Blood splattered snow as I struck him across the face with my boot again and again. The red on white was stark. The warm blood seeping and sinking into the cold of the snow until the two became one amorphous pink mass. I watched Vilem as he tried to focus his eyes but he was stunned, his lids falling and closing involuntarily. He made a lame effort to raise a leg, to knock the screwdriver out of my hand, but he had no co-ordination, the tank was empty; he was beat.

I thought of Michael. I thought how he had faced the same terror as his killer did now. My brother, who lay on that mortuary slab, a small hole beneath his heart. Grey, drained of life. He wasn't coming back to us. My breathing stilled as I loomed over Vilem.

'Did you think I would let you get away with it?' I yelled. I heard the words but they didn't sound like mine. The voice was mine, yeah, but I'd long since ceased to be the man I thought I was; this was new territory, beyond any previous misdemeanours. I knew what I was about to do, I knew the consequences, but I didn't care. Nothing mattered now – I'd lost everything, there was nothing left; what did it matter if I lost myself too? 'Did you think I would let you kill my brother and live yourself?' I roared.

Vilem groaned, moved his head to the side, smeared more blood on the snow. I lifted my boot and stamped on his face, crushed in my heel. His nose split. Blood came in a flood; he gasped for breath, choked it back. I watched him struggle for air as I drank in his pain.

'My brother was a good man, but what kind of cunt are you?'

He convulsed before me, rocked to and fro as the blood went down his throat. I watched him suffer, wanted to feel his anguish. I was revelling in his misery; was I sick? Fucking A.

'And now Alice too . . . my niece.'

I grabbed his collars, heaved him to me as I pressed the screwdriver against his jugular. He rasped, spat blood. I wanted to be close enough to hear his death rattle; I wanted to see the lights go out for good. 'You're going to fucking die just like them.'

I gripped the handle; my palm was sweating, I held it tighter – so tight my fingers ached. I hesitated. My heart was racing, I felt the blood ping in my temples – what was this, conscience? Never. A fucking eye for an eye; I drew back my arm.

'No!' A yell came from the front of the truck. 'No . . . Leave him!'

I turned. 'Alice . . .'

I watched her stood shivering in the snow. Her

thin arms were held out to me. Her delicate shoulders trembled. She looked so frail, so weak, and white enough to meld into the landscape. 'He hasn't done anything, Gus.'

I didn't understand. I was gone, off some place where words seemed meaningless – action was all I knew now. I turned back to Vilem, put the point of the screwdriver to his throat again.

I heard Alice stumble through the snow. She yelled, 'It wasn't him!'

I looked back; I didn't want her to see this. I wanted to run to her. I wanted to pick her up in my arms and carry her away from this, but I had come too far to stop now. How did I tell her? How could I explain what I had to do? I couldn't, she was just a kid. She didn't understand a fucking thing about this world of hurt and misery – she was just a kid, wasn't that the way it should be?

'Alice, stay out of this!' I yelled.

She came stumbling through the drifts towards me, grabbed at my arm, shrieked: 'No, Gus, don't – he didn't do anything . . . It wasn't him.'

I felt the nerves in my fingers twitch as I held tightly to the hilt of the screwdriver. I looked down at Vilem: he was still choking on his own blood. The air seemed to have been squeezed from my lungs; I couldn't breathe. Hot bursts exploded behind my eyes; I couldn't think. All I could do was stare at Alice, shaking before me. 'What are you fucking saying?' I hollered.

She held tighter to me, grabbed with all her

strength. 'Dad came home and he saw us, he went crazy, he was shouting and hitting Vilem . . .'

Words. All words. I felt like my head was being pushed under water every time she spoke. I wanted to listen, wanted to come up for air, but I couldn't.

'What? . . . *What*?'

She spluttered, tears rolling from her eyes. Her mouth twitched and twisted as her speech came fast: 'He had a gun . . . Dad had a gun and I ran . . . I ran to the Meadows.'

I felt my grip on Vilem slip; he fell. I went to Alice. 'You ran?'

'They came after me, and there was a fight . . . Another fight, and the gun fell . . .'

I watched the snow landing on her as she spoke. Her whole body was shaking now. She looked like a weak sapling thrown about in a gale. So fragile, so utterly at the mercy of a cruel world; what had happened to her? What had happened to our little Alice? I walked closer to her. I saw my brother in her eyes. I spoke: 'The gun . . . Who took the gun?'

She was coughing and wheezing; tears came faster, her voice was barely a whisper, the words already broken and cracked before she could get them out. 'I did . . . I picked up the gun.'

I saw the whole image race before me. It felt like my heart was ablaze, like my chest had been cut open and a petrol-bomb chucked inside. I knew no pain like it – it engulfed me. I saw everything clearly now: the struggle, the confusion, the trigger being pulled, the muzzle flash.

'You . . . shot him.'

She nodded.

Alice's hands fell to her side, then she dropped to her knees. Her head lolled for a few seconds and then she fell over onto her shoulder and curled up before me. 'I did it,' she said, her voice strangled by emotion. I hardly took in the words, then she closed arms round herself and shook. 'I killed him.'

I must have let a minute pass before I spoke. 'Why? . . . Why, Alice?'

She raised her voice, sobbing, heart-hurts to a tear. 'I–I thought he was going to kill Vilem. I didn't mean to, I–I just wanted it to stop . . . I didn't mean to . . . I didn't . . .'

The screwdriver slipped from my hand, landed softly in the snow. As I looked ahead, into the night, I felt as though I had been dropped into another world. Nothing seemed real. The falling snow. The dark sky. A niece I no longer recognised, offering another bale of grief to add to my heavily burdened back. How? Why? Did any of these questions matter now? My world had ended. I wanted no more part in this life of men. I felt my knees give; my calves twitched in anticipation of a fall . . . and then, sirens wailed. I looked out to the road and saw the blue lights flashing. Police cars roared over the flattened gate into the field.

I looked at Alice curled on the ground and

something sparked in me. 'Get up!' I ran over to her, yanked her to her feet. She felt so light – there was no weight in her – as I bundled her into the truck.

She cried, 'What's going to happen?'

'Nothing . . . Nothing's going to happen.'

I tried to turn the ignition but the truck wouldn't start.

Alice screamed, 'They're coming, they're coming for me!'

The engine suddenly purred to life and I floored it. The wheels spun wildly as the truck jumped into gear. 'They're not fucking having you.' I made it to the edge of the field. The police cars flashed in front of the truck but I swerved round them. 'Get out the fucking way!' I yelled. I lined up the gate, but a Range Rover skidded in, blocked the way. I braked heavily and the truck fired into the side of the dyke.

Uniforms swarmed on us. Where did they come from? Who tipped them off? They were mob-handed for sure. Not messing about. I got out, balled fists. I still had a barrel of adrenaline racing through me, was ready to go. As I swung out, I felt a good crack connect, went again. 'Fucking leave her . . . *Leave her.*'

I took down another flatfoot but got grabbed this time, held back, as they piled onto me. Four, five burly filth. My arms were pinned behind me as I was forced face-first into the cold snow. I saw Alice hauled from the truck; my thoughts stilled.

I knew it was over but managed a lame 'No . . . don't take her.'

Plod reversed the Range Rover and took Alice to a police car. Her eyes darted left to right in quick time. I followed her every anguished movement, desperate for her to be left alone, left in peace. She'd been through enough. But then I could watch no more. It was all too painful. I knew how this ended now, and it crushed me. As I turned away another car arrived, a burgundy Lexus. The doors slowly opened and Fitz emerged. Mac hobbled behind him.

'Let him go, for fucksake,' said Fitz.

My heart still pumped wildly as the uniforms released me. I'd been held so tightly my arms were numb, but I was ready to go again. I jumped up, spat out a mouthful of snow. I looked at Mac. 'You told them where I was?'

Fitz spoke for him: 'I pulled him in, Gus . . . Didn't give him a choice.'

Mac shrugged; his brows creased, his eyes were pleading with me. 'They know it was her,' he sighed out slowly. His hand came up to his mouth as he spoke – it looked as if he didn't want to utter the words. 'They took her dabs off the gun.'

Fitz rolled on the balls of his feet, put up his collar. He frowned as he spoke – he sounded harsher than Mac – 'Radek spilled his guts: he was blackmailing Davie with the gun.'

My despair blackened. I felt my mouth widen.

I tried for speech but it was beyond me. I didn't feel human any more.

Fitz spoke again: 'Davie was holding out to protect Alice, thought he was doing best by her.'

The feeling started to return to my hands, but the numbness seemed to have moved to my mind. I wanted to batter fists on my head, try to get some thoughts flowing. 'Davie Prentice . . .'

Mac came round to my side, sighed. He placed a hand on my back. 'Gus, they hauled in the Undertaker . . . fat Davie too.'

I felt as though I'd been hollowed out with a pickaxe; I didn't want to hear any more. I lost balance and leaned on the side of the truck. I saw the uniforms untying Vilem, said, 'What'll you do with Alice?' Soon as I said it the question seemed stupid; I knew the answer already.

Fitz frowned, tried to steady me with a hand on my arm. I jerked it away. 'Gus, let me get you home.'

I turned to the road. Alice sat in the back of a police car now. Her hands had been cuffed behind her back. She looked so young it struck my heart. I felt my throat tighten as she stared at me, pleading for help. She widened her eyes and for a second we shared a locked glance of utter terror. As the police car took her away I stared into the blackness of the empty street and remembered holding an infant in a hospital ward many years ago.

'Gus . . . Gus . . . Let me take you home to Debs,' said Fitz.

I put eyes on him. 'She won't be there.'

I took my coat from the truck, started to walk towards the black road. I felt the quarter-bottle of Grouse in my pocket, took it out and unscrewed the cap. The first burn of it reached like a flame down my throat. The next hit went straight to my gut and made room for more. I turned up the bottle's neck and drained the lot in one smooth belt.

An old song sung in my head; I had a taste for more.

Fitz yelled as I went, 'Come on, Gus, you're in the middle of nowhere.'

I walked on, said, 'Don't I know it.'